Roxanna ran her fingers over the jade green muslin. 'Are you not afraid of what people will say when they see me so attired?' she asked. 'Apart from the obvious conjectures, they might begin asking where and how you acquired such a piece of merchandise. Everyone knows such goods have not been brought into this country since the beginning of the war.'

'Why, little cat, are you concerned for me? Rest assured, their questions cannot harm me. Most people know that anything can be acquired at the right price. Everything—and everyone—has a price. Even you. It seems I have yet to find out what it is.'

Roxanna gasped at the insult. Without thinking, she grabbed up the parcel and flung it at him. It came open, and the muslin fell in a tiny huddle at his feet.

'I don't want your gift. I cannot be bought. Not by your money or your favours. I will never be your wife. Never!'

Valentina Luellen has been a successful and popular author for some years, and until quite recently she lived in the English countryside with her husband and their son Jamie. However, her husband became seriously ill and she packed everything—including the car, two dogs and five cats—and went to live on a small farm in the Algarve, Portugal. There her husband's health improved, and she now divides her time between the kitchen and the study of her newly-renovated farmhouse.

The Devil of Talland is Valentina Luellen's eighteenth Masquerade Historical Romance; others include *The Silver Salamander*, *Elusive Flame of Love*, *Mistress of Tanglewood*, *Black Ravenswood* and *Lord of Darkness*, which was published earlier this year as a special longer historical romance.

THE DEVIL
OF TALLAND

VALENTINA LUELLEN

MILLS & BOON LIMITED
15–16 BROOK'S MEWS
LONDON W1A 1DR

First published in Great Britain 1985
by Mills & Boon Limited

© Valentina Luellen 1985

Australian copyright 1985
Philippine copyright 1985
This edition 1985

ISBN 0 263 75242 9

Set in 10 on 10½ pt Linotron Times
04–1185–71,600

Photoset by Rowland Phototypesetting Limited
Bury St Edmunds, Suffolk
Made and printed in Great Britain by
Cox & Wyman Limited, Reading

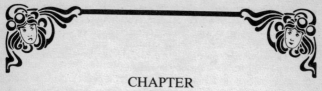

CHAPTER
ONE

'How is he?'

Roxanna dragged her eyes from the blood-soaked shirt of the injured man at whose side she sat, desperately trying to stem the flow of life-blood which seemed to be ebbing from him at an alarming rate, and lifted them to the grey features of the man pacing to and fro across the room, his impatient manner betraying the agitation raging inside him. They had been anxiously awaiting the arrival of a doctor for the past hour. Sixty long minutes since the landlord of the wayside inn, where the hired transport was to stay overnight, had sent one of his servants riding in all haste to the nearest village. As the minutes ticked by, she felt as if she held the life of the man in her hands!

She looked past the man's shoulder, out of the window. Rain lashed the window-panes. The day was bleak and unfriendly and it had been raining continuously since first light, but she was too excited at the prospect of seeing her new home to mind the bad weather. The countryside after leaving Plymouth had begun to grow exceedingly desolate as the journey progressed; so different from London, where the houses were crammed close together and the streets were dark and littered with stinking refuse—the home of footpads and ruffians.

The air was so different here, clean and fresh. She could scarcely contain her excitement until the morrow and her first glimpse of the sea. She hoped someone would still be at Liskeard to meet her, or she would be forced to make her own arrangements to reach Talland, the home of the Countess Elizabeth de Villon, who had lived in Cornwall since her flight from France during the Reign of Terror in 1792. She had engaged Roxanna to be companion to her young granddaughter, Lisette, whose father was an exiled Bourbon sympathiser. The Countess had made all the arrangements for Roxanna's journey and was to provide a carriage to meet her at Liskeard—but she was almost a day late in arriving! Perhaps it had not waited.

'Well?' the man demanded, unable to contain himself no longer.

With a sigh, she shook her head, and a single curl broke loose from the ribbon confining the tawny gold tresses at the nape of her neck, to tumble across a cheek still ashen from the shock of the violence she had witnessed in the gardens earlier.

'The bleeding has eased a little, I think, but if he does not receive attention soon . . .' She faltered, and her words hung in the air between them. For a moment, only the laboured breathing of the man on the bed interrupted the tense silence in the room.

'He'll die! Damnation! Where is that doctor?' her companion ejaculated.

'He will come soon, I am sure,' she said, trying to reassure him.

'Not soon enough, I'm thinking, and then . . . My God! If only I had got here ten minutes earlier,' the man groaned in despair.

'He—He is a close friend?' Roxanna ventured to ask. She was not sure if she liked this man or not. His manner was brusque and rude. He was certainly concerned for his friend, but despite all her attempts to help, he still spoke to her as if she was a servant. Yet he was dressed little better than a seaman!

A servant, in truth, she was! Did it show that much? She wondered sadly, returning her attention to her patient.

He came to stand beside her, looking down at the figure on the bed. 'The best friend any man in this world could have,' he muttered fiercely.

'Then you are indeed lucky to have known him,

whatever happens now,' she returned quietly. 'Few men ever share such friendships.'

He gave her a piercing look as if surprised by the insight in one of such tender years, and she lowered her gaze before his searching eyes.

How deceptive appearances could be, she thought, returning her gaze to the man beside her. She had been travelling alone in the coach until this man—ashen, breathing shallowly, eyes tightly closed, had flagged it down just outside Plymouth. She had heard him tersely explain to the driver how his horse had gone lame and been left at the last village. He was in a hurry, and accepted most begrudgingly the fact that he would have to journey to Liskeard and hire another horse there. She had thought him rather an abrupt and arrogant person as he climbed into the coach, cursing the weather under his breath and splashing spots of water on to her dress from his saturated cloak. Without so much as the courtesy of an apology, he had flung himself into a corner and remained silent from that moment on.

The handsome features which had then worn an impatient, half-angry expression were now twisted with pain. The lean mouth clamped tightly together as she placed another wad of cloth over his wound. He looked strong, but if the pistol-ball was still lodged in his side, as she suspected it might be, all her ministering would be to no avail.

She had never before seen a man so close to death, nor been witness to such violence as had taken place before her eyes. Two men quarrelling was not an unusual occurrence. It had embarrassed her to come upon them, however, and she had turned to retrace her steps when the sound of an alarmed shout brought her wheeling about. Before her horrified eyes she saw the man who had been her companion for many long, silent hours deliberately shot by the other man who had come out of the inn to engage him in heated conversation. It was plain that they knew each other, and that neither was pleased at the encounter. The latter had then run to his tethered horse and ridden off.

Deliberately? Cold-bloodedly? Perhaps not. The young man with the pistol had been very angry indeed. Overwrought, she would have said, by his expression. Driven to an act of recklessness that might well result in murder, by the man before him, smiling—she still could not understand how anyone could smile so calmly in the face of death—at the weapon pointed at his chest, whose narrowed gaze, bleak expression and curt, low tones seemed determined to provoke his companion. Had she misread the scene? It had all been very confused and frightening.

There was blood on her skirts where she had tried to help him until the landlord had run up, together with a new arrival, the same burly man who now paced the floor like a caged animal—who had ridden up on a lathered horse and dismounted to help—and between them they carried the injured man into the inn. Her best dress ruined! What would the Countess say when she arrived at Talland looking like a beggar-girl? Roxanna wondered in dismay. She would be sent back to London in disgrace. No, she must not even consider the possibility. Without this position, she had no means to provide for her father or herself. No one wanted to engage them after the scandal which had surrounded them these past twelve months.

It had been a blessing that the Countess had taken a chance on her. But she had, and Roxanna was determined at all costs not to let anyone down. No matter what it cost her, she was going to keep this position.

'An hour, dammit!' She looked up as the man beside the window took out a gold watch on a heavy chain and stared at it. He did not look wealthy enough to possess such a valuable item, she found herself thinking. He looked like a seafaring man. Like most townspeople, she had heard stories of Cornwall and the coastline where wreckers went about their heinous business almost unhampered by the soldiers. Ships guided to their doom on jagged reefs. Passengers floundering in the water . . .

screaming for help . . . being beaten to death as they reached the shore and supposed safety.

'What are you staring at, girl?' he demanded, and she flushed, realising that her thoughts were mirrored in her green eyes. 'Overcome with curiosity, are you?'

'Surely you must expect a little, sir. I am unaccustomed to seeing men shot down before my eyes,' she returned sharply, and the rugged face before her grew wary. As if questions would bother him, she thought. 'Is your friend a seagoing man too?'

'Why do you think I am? Speak, girl? Do you know me?' A lean hand snaked out and fastened over her wrist so tightly that she cried out in pain. 'Answer me!'

'No, I mean . . . I thought you looked rather like a seaman. My brother was at sea for four years before the fever took him. His manner—his speech, I find similar to yours. Forgive me, I did not mean to pry.'

'Women are always inquisitive creatures, damn them,' the man retorted, releasing her with a scowl. 'Trouble-makers, the lot of you!'

'Nicholas, have I not told you many times that a velvet glove will get you further than this brusqueness you possess? Have you not heeded me at all?' The faint—yet mocking—voice came from the bed, and they both turned in astonishment to find the man there was conscious and watching them with eyes clouded with pain. Yet for all of the discomfort Roxanna knew he must be feeling, she felt as if he was very much in control of himself—and the present situation.

'Be still, please,' she pleaded as he attempted to sit up, and firm hands on his shoulders restrained him gently but firmly. 'You have lost much blood.'

'And you have not thrown a fainting fit? You are to be congratulated, young lady.' The mockery stung her, brought fierce colour to her pale cheeks. She was not a society débutante, given to swooning at the least little thing, fluttering her eyelashes behind a feather fan at the admirers she kept at a discreet distance. Roxanna had always thought how fragile—and useless—they were.

Destined for only one thing—marriage, and probably a loveless one at that. Groomed from the cradle to the altar for nothing else but to please the man they married. Silly little coquettes, with not a single, sensible idea in their heads. She did not like her life, but she would never change places with one of them! One day she would have earned enough money for a little house where she and her father could live in comfort for the rest of their days. It would take many years, but she was determined to work hard to achieve her dream—and, in doing so, she would have more than they did. She would have gained her independence.

'If I had, sir, you would have surely bled to death before anyone arrived,' she said stiffly, and a pair of dark eyes, so dark they appeared almost black in the shadowy room, raked her from head to toe. They lingered on her soiled skirts and she felt something hitherto unknown stir inside her.

'Then you shall be repaid for your—ministerings. See to it, Nicholas. A new dress, I think for . . .'

'Roxanna Dane. Thank you, but that will not be necessary. I have many more. This is but an old thing I put on to travel in. The weather was so atrocious that I did not want to spoil one of my better gowns.'

Why was she lying so blatantly? Of course she needed another dress—but, as many times before, Roxanna's pride rose up to bring a sharpness to her tongue, a frostiness to the pale green eyes which dwelt on the man's face.

'A pity! I was about to suggest a gown of jade green silk, to match those beautiful eyes. Then you could have bewitched all the men you meet.'

'For heaven's sake, Ross. The girl is no more than a . . . servant. I'll give her a few coins, and she'll be on her way in the morning,' the man called Nicholas intervened.

Bristling, Roxanna drew back from the bed and then became still, finding her wrist coupled by lean, brown fingers.

'Forgive my friend? He has yet to learn that politeness costs nothing,' Ross murmured, and a fleeting smile touched the grey features. 'I thank you for your help. I shall repay it . . .' He broke off, a spasm of coughing rendering speech impossible. Roxanna was released as his hand went to his injured side, and her eyes widened in alarm as she saw that the bandages she had placed there were spotted with fresh blood. If the doctor did not come soon, she thought anxiously . . .

'Be still, Ross,' Nicholas entreated. 'There is a doctor on his way.'

'Where is he?'

'Gone. He didn't even stop to see if he had made a good job of it or not.' Roxanna realised that they were discussing his assailant. So they *both* knew him!

'He never did like the sight of blood,' Ross's face contorted in pain. 'God, man! I can't lie here. Get me to a horse.'

'You'll be dead before you get half-way home.'

'And what am I supposed to do? Lie here until the damned doctor comes? I'm weak, Nicholas. I can feel it. God in heaven! If I die now, he will inherit everything, he will know everything . . . I have to stop him, you know that. Thank God you were riding close behind the coach. I thought him home by now, licking his wounds . . .'

Roxanna drew back from the bed, feeling more than a little afraid at the conversation going on about her. Such depths of passion coming from the man Ross. Fear, almost, that if he died someone quite unsuitable would inherit . . . something . . . but what? He did not look a man of substance. His clothes were well cut, but not in the latest fashion. He wore little jewellery and very old leather boots. She did not like the one called Nicholas, and was beginning to wonder about his companion, too.

'I always said you should have married,' Nicholas snapped. 'At least a wife can be controlled.'

'Find me a woman, then, and I'll marry here and now,' Ross returned with a chuckle that made his lips tighten once again in pain. And then Roxanna felt his gaze alight on her. She caught her breath at the intentness of his scrutiny. 'An angel from heaven, Nicholas. Need we look any further?'

'Are you out of your mind?'

'Probably. I don't have much choice, do I? Give her anything she asks, do you hear me? Anything . . . but make her agree.'

The heavy lids closed over his eyes, and he lay so still that Roxanna thrust a hand against his heart, but relaxed again as she felt the slow but steady throb of life beneath her fingers. She had often ministered to her father, who had been in bad health for many years, but never before had she been so bold with another man. His skin was warm beneath her fingers . . . the chest dark with hair. Quickly she drew the blanket up round his shoulders.

'Well, girl? Will you marry him?' Nicholas demanded, and her eyes widened with the shock of his words. Surely the suggestion had been made in jest? A dying man regretting he had never taken a wife? No—she could see it had not!

'Marry—him?' she gasped. 'The man is a complete stranger to me and could die at any moment from his wound. Are you mad, sir, to ask such a ludicrous thing of me?'

'It is because he is going to die that desperate measures have to be taken. He might not look a man of substance, but believe me he is. This is a very important man, and a gentleman! You will be well paid for a few minutes of your time. In return for what will be a substantial amount of money—more than you have ever clapped eyes on in your life, I'll warrant—all you have to do is say two simple words . . . I will! After that, you can go away and forget today ever happened,' she was told.

'Are you so accustomed to acts of violence that you can walk away and forget what has taken place?' she snapped. 'I cannot. Nor will I be a party to—to such an outrageous suggestion.'

'Name your price. It will be paid . . .'

Roxanna had opened her mouth to fling the offer back in his face in no uncertain terms, when she suddenly found herself considering what was being offered. There was no commitment on her part—she would never have given it a second thought had there been any—and she would be paid handsomely for her services. Money to buy medicines for her father . . . to pay the rent of his room for another few months. Perhaps enough to take her back to London to see him soon, or to find a trustworthy woman to care for him. The landlord had promised to look after him, but she suspected it would be only so long as she paid him extra. No! It was too preposterous. Marriage! Yet she would in a way be aiding the injured man.

As if sensing the tumult taking place inside her, Nicholas bent over her, his mouth close to her face. 'His estates and his money must not fall into the wrong hands. Those of his brother.'

She looked up at him in puzzlement and asked quietly, 'If anyone should handle them, should it not be his own brother?'

'The man who shot him? Who hates him?' came the curt retort. 'After the ceremony, you will be given papers which you will sign, relinquishing any claim on Ross and his estates, and an undertaking to say nothing of this day. They will be taken care of by a family friend who can be trusted. You must do it, girl. I can't tell you how much depends on this! His brother must not inherit, do you hear me. Agree! Here . . .' He fumbled in his pocket and produced a small pouch. 'An advance payment for your services. There is more in my packs—and in his. You shall have every gold coin we possess between us if you will help us now.'

'I—I cannot,' Roxanna whispered, hovering on the brink of acceptance.

'Are you saying you don't need the money?' came the cruel question, and the man's eyes centred on her ruined dress.

She bit her lip in vexation. To agree would mean she

could do so much for her ailing father . . . But what of the man called Ross? She looked down at the still figure and felt hot tears prick her eyes. She would have more money than she had ever had in her life—and he would be dead! It was unfair! Unjust! She should do it just to ensure that his wicked brother did not profit from his crime, and although she wanted to do more for him, she knew that was beyond her power.

Mutely she nodded. Nicholas sprang away from her with a low oath, flung open the door and bellowed for the landlord. The man on the bed stirred as the loud voice reached into his subconscious. A minister was being summoned . . . It was all so unbelievable, but in a short while she would be a married woman—and a widow—almost simultaneously. She shuddered at the knowledge, and found the dark eyes were wide open and looking up at her questioningly . . .

'Don't be afraid. I won't forget this—ever! I swear it. One day I shall repay you.'

Such sweet words meant to console her, when Ross well knew that he would most likely be dead within the next few hours. His friend Nicholas had been quite explicit that unless the bullet was removed, he would die.

'Don't talk. Save your strength,' she said firmly. She would have left his side, but his fingers closed round her wrist and held her fast.

'Stay. How I can I die with an angel watching over me?'

'You, sir, have a smooth tongue,' Roxanna replied, blushing furiously, but nevertheless she remained at his side, watching him drift into a restless doze. From across the room his companion watched with eagle eyes, as if afraid something might pass between them which was not to his liking.

As it grew dark outside the windows, a maid brought a lamp and drew the heavy curtains. Roxanna was grateful when some hot lemon tea arrived and she managed to free herself carefully from the grasp of the sleeping man.

She drank two cups straight off and ate several of the ham slices, accompanied by thick wedges of buttered bread. She had eaten nothing since a sparse lunch earlier in the day—on her limited budget for the journey, the most frugal of meals were called for—and she found the snack most welcome. It was a relief, too, to stretch her cramped limbs and move away from the bed for a while. Her every movement was watched by the man called Nicholas, who was still breaking the silence of the room from time to time with his curses on the doctor, not yet arrived.

It was another hour before he came, soaking wet from the teeming rain and already tired from a long journey to another village to attend a pregnant woman. He was in no mood for Nicholas's impatience, and told him so in no uncertain terms as he shed his sodden outer clothes and went to examine his patient.

'Where do you think you are going?' Nicholas demanded ungraciously as Roxanna turned to the door, unable to bear the sick-room a moment longer.

'To my room. I would like to wash and do something about my dress.' Once again his rudeness made her bristle with indignation, and it was an effort to keep a tight rein on her temper. She was also tired. They all were. Tired and concerned for the injured man—but was that an excuse for him to treat her so unfairly?

'Tomorrow you can buy a new one. You'll have enough money for a dozen. Ross is not an ungenerous man. You'll not try to run out on me—on our agreement?'

'The road to Liskeard is strange to me, sir, and, on a night like this, I should think extremely hazardous. I have no intention of walking it,' she retorted. 'I shall be in my room when you require me again.'

She was in fact sprawled out across the bed, fast asleep, when Nicholas came to fetch her. She had changed into a simple grey dress which buttoned high under her chin. The severity of the colour was broken only by the touches of white lace about the collar and the

long tight-fitting sleeves. It was her Sunday-*cum*-special
occasions dress and was all of three years old, but it was
still as good as new, for she had had little occasion to
wear it over the years.

She had spent an hour, near to tears, as she tried to
erase the mud and blood from the one she had removed.
Perhaps when it was dry . . . she thought, as she hung it
over a chair before the fire. If not, she would wear the
grey to meet the Countess in the morning and hope that
no one would notice how out of date she was with her
clothes. First impressions were the most important, her
father had always told her. Those first few moments
when you are under the scrutiny of a prospective employer will decide whether or not the position becomes
yours. The Countess had seemed satisfied with her at the
interview in London, and she did not want to give her a
chance to have second thoughts.

'How—How is he?' she asked, as she hastily ran a
brush through her tangled tresses and secured them at
the nape of her neck with a ribbon.

'Failing fast, which is why we must hurry. The minister
is waiting, and also a lawyer to ensure this whole sordid
business is completed legally. We want no loose ends, do
we, Miss Dane?' His eyes fastened on her accusingly.
Did he think she would try to extort more from him
when it was over, in return for her silence? What an
unpleasant world he must move in!

'Your friend must be a most important man for you to
labour so painstakingly on his behalf,' she replied cuttingly as she swept out of the room ahead of him.

Was she mad? Roxanna thought, as the brief ceremony
was performed in the small, dimly lighted room. Why
did she not turn and run from the side of the sick man to
whom she was being married? Away from the pain-filled
dark eyes which never left her face from the moment she
came into his view. From beneath the frightening gaze of
his friend, and the searching glances of the minister,
who, although she suspected was seething with questions,

was also being well paid not to ask them. As she was. Who were these two men? Why was this man who held her hand so important?

'Ross James, wilt thou have this woman . . .?' A weak affirmation from the figure on the bed, now so weak he could scarcely lift his head. She knew that the pistol-ball had been removed and he had lost more precious blood in the process. He had no strength left, surely, to fight the angel of death perched on his shoulder. Roxanna was suddenly seized with an over-whelming desire to make him somehow live. Her fingers tightened round his, and she sensed an awareness of her touch growing in his eyes. A slight pressure was returned, and a smile touched her pale cheeks.

'Wilt thou, Roxanna, have this man . . .?'

Her own answer in return, quiet but clear. She was surprised at her calmness. Here she was, married to a total stranger! Ross James . . . Instinctively she knew that was not his full name. She would never know it. She would never know whose ring she wore . . .

Ring! There was no ring. The minister paused and looked about him . . . Ross released her to fumble with the heavy gold ring he wore on the little finger of his left hand.

'Use this—would you have the poor girl possess nothing to remember me by?' he chided, searching once again for the reassuring comfort of Roxanna's hand.

'She is being well paid.' This remark from Nicholas, of course. She did not even look his way.

'Old friend, you see only on the surface. Look into these lovely green eyes. She is not what you think . . . Would I had more time . . . Some day some man will buy emeralds to match those eyes, mark my words.' He broke off in a fit of coughing, and Roxanna went down on her knees beside him, holding fast to his shoulders until the moment passed. She felt hot tears scald her cheeks, and could no longer contain them. Gently Ross wiped them away and slipped the ring on to her finger . . . And the last words binding them together were delivered. It was done! She felt weak-kneed, and a little heady.

The doctor ordered her away from the bed. Nicholas took her arm and led her to a table, where several papers were already being made ready for her signature by a bald-headed man who showed a total lack of interest in the proceedings. How much was he being paid, she wondered?

'You can write, girl?' he enquired sarcastically.

She ignored him and signed her name in the places he indicated. Before she had a chance even to glance over them, they had been snatched from her view.

'What are they?' she demanded. 'For all I know, you are not his friend at all. Perhaps you hatched this whole plot to get your hands on his money . . . or whatever it is that's so important to you! How do I know otherwise?'

'You don't.' For a moment she thought he would strike her, and recoiled from the fury on the sea-beaten features. 'You've done your part—here's the rest of your payment.' The pouch he flung down on the table was heavy, she could see that. More money than she had ever dreamed of possessing in her life. 'Now you can go back to your room and forget what has happened here. Forget you ever saw either of us. It will be in your interests to do so, believe me,' he added, and a soft expletive came from the man on the bed.

'For God's sake, man, have you forgotten the papers? Get them to London this instant. And I want the girl here with me.'

'Do you know what you are doing . . .?'

'Not very well, but if I'm going to die, I shall do so in my own fashion. What better company can I have than that of my bride? Besides, I want to hold her hand some more. You are not afraid, are you, Roxanna? To stay with me? I'm hardly in a position to take advantage of the situation.'

'Indeed you are not, and you are being extremely foolish wasting your strength in speaking to me like this,' Roxanna declared, seating herself on the edge of the bed, despite Nicholas's warning glare. 'Please try to sleep. I'll stay, I promise.'

'Then I rest easy . . .' The mockery gleaming up at her from his dark eyes faded and died as he drifted away from her into a semi-conscious state that was to last the whole night. The lean fingers painfully tight round hers, as if contact with her was, somehow, to him, contact with life—the life he was fighting to sustain . . .

The doctor left, promising to return in the morning. From the way he took his leave of her, Roxanna knew he did not expect to find his patient alive. The minister also went, after offering words of consolation. He, too, was sure the worst was to happen. She would not let it!

'There is nothing you can do here, so why don't you go downstairs and have something to eat? You look exhausted.' Nicholas stood beside the bed, frowning down at her. Not so much concerned for her welfare as for getting rid of her, Roxanna thought, as she shook her head.

'Please do not let me keep you,' she said, and looked up into the suspicious face. 'I shall not steal his purse while he lies here.'

'You already have, girl—and mine,' he muttered, indicating the pouch on the table. 'That's every coin we possess between us—as I promised. He wanted to give you more . . .' He turned away from her, and it came to Roxanna that despite all his curtness and ill manners towards her, he was genuinely concerned for his injured friend. She watched heavy hands bunch into fists as he fought to regain his composure.

'I shall be here when you return. I know that is not to your liking, but I shall. See how he clings to my hand? Perhaps it is the thread of life to him. Would you have me withdraw it? Perhaps if you would be good enough to bring me back a little coffee . . .'

She looked away from Nicholas as Ross stirred uneasily; large beads of perspiration were gathering on his brow. Snatching up the cloth in a bowl of cold water on the table close by, she bathed them away, still without freeing her one hand from his. Every movement she made tightened his hold. He knew she was beside him! Praying for him—praying for the stranger who was her husband. Not once did she ever consider what would be her position if he did indeed recover. How she would react to having a husband . . . and he a wife, who, although useful in a moment of crisis, was unwanted . . . and, according to his friend Nicholas, far beneath his station. And a gentleman did not marry a companion. He might flirt with one, even seduce one, if the fancy took him, but never, never commit himself to marriage.

Some time later, when he grew calmer, she looked around and saw that Nicholas had left the room, taking the pouch from the table with him. His way of ensuring she was there when he returned, she thought angrily. At that moment, the money meant nothing to her.

'I'm thirsty.' Ross's voice was hardly audible. 'Who's there? Nicholas? Give me some wine, man, I'm parched.'

'He—He is not here. It is I—Roxanna. Let me go a moment, and I shall fetch you some water,' she said quietly. He did not seem to know any longer where he was, she thought, as she watched his eyes rove around the room, trying to focus on shadowy objects as if looking for something, or someone. And then they came back to her face.

He ordered, 'Bring the candle closer. I can't see you clearly.'

She reached to the table and held it between them so that he could see her features more clearly. The soft, muted light fell across high cheekbones and wide eyes, as green and depthless as the sea. A small soft mouth, stubborn little chin. Arched brows beneath a mass of tawny gold hair. He reached up and caught a lock of it between his fingers, feeling the silkiness of texture. Roxanna found she was holding her breath, and quickly she replaced the candle.

'Like the mane of a wildcat,' he whispered, tugging gently so that she was forced to bend her face closer to his. On doing so, she found that his eyes, which she had at first thought black, now had flecks of blue darting in them. The intentness of his gaze made her inwardly tremble. 'Kiss me, little cat.'

Roxanna gasped at the audacity of the suggestion and tried to draw back again, only to find her hair wound firmly round his fingers.

'I will not!' she protested. 'Let me go—please.'

Even as she spoke, she found herself wondering what it would be like to be held in those strong arms, subjected to the kisses of such a man. She had never encountered the like of him before.

'Am I not entitled to one? A small one, at least? After all, I am your husband . . . perhaps only for a few hours more.'

'Don't think those things,' she reproved sharply. How could he speak of death so lightly? Did he not fear it? 'If only you would rest . . .'

'I promise I shall—as soon as you have kissed me,' came the insistent answer, and she felt the colour rise hotly in her cheeks. What kind of girl did he think she was?

'I—I have never kissed a man before,' she confessed, lowering her gaze. 'At least, not anyone important. I mean cousins and my brother and father, but never anyone . . .' She had no wish to remember that other, horrible, man.

'What a waste!' Ross groaned, the devil's lights in his eyes mocking her lack of experience. 'Let me show you how pleasant it can be.'

She allowed him to draw her face down to his. What else could she do? His lips touched first her glowing cheeks and then the corners of her mouth before they sought and found hers, trembling and uncertain. Roxanna felt as if time suddenly stood still—nothing existed for her in the moments which followed but this little room and this man who awakened the strangest fluttering feeling in the pit of her stomach. Like the touch of a butterfly's wings . . .

His kiss was gentle as he explored her mouth. She felt his fingers loosen their hold on her hair and plunge into the thick curls, was aware of his free hand moving along her arm, caressing her shoulder, cupping the firm breast pressed against his chest. She caught her breath at his boldness and knew she should pull back from him, but she found she was no longer in control of herself. She, who was so critical of the way women conducted themselves in the presence of men, ridiculing their idiotic attempts to get themselves noticed by the décolleté of their flimsy gowns, or their simpering, helpless attitudes, now found herself reduced to a trembling nonentity by a single kiss! She was shameful!

As salt tears touched his mouth, Ross tilted back her head and stared at her in astonishment. His eyes narrowing sharply, he demanded, 'For yourself? Or me?'

'For you, of course,' she faltered. How could he think otherwise? Yet were some not also for herself? For the cruel stroke of fate that had brought this mysterious man into her unhappy, troubled life and given her a moment she would never know again, only to take him from her in death!

'Don't cry for me. Believe me, I am not worth any woman's tears, and those eyes should always be full of laughter, not sadness.'

'It—It isn't fair,' Roxanna sobbed, wishing his hand would not wander so freely over her body. Even through the material of her dress, his touch burned like fire and excited her in a way she had never imagined. He would have known many women. With his good looks and money, he could have anyone he wanted, she thought. 'About—About what happened . . .'

'Life often isn't. We have to make the best of what comes along. Thanks to you, my affairs will be taken care of, if the worst occurs. Has Nicholas—paid you?'

'Yes.' She tossed the golden hair indignantly, anger gleaming in the green depths of her eyes. 'What does that matter? It's you . . . Please stop being so foolish and go back to sleep. Do you want to die?'

'Not in the least . . . Especially now.' He gave her a wicked grin, his eyes shadowed with mounting pain again. 'Kiss me then, my cat—something to remember you by when I am strumming my harp up above.'

'Oh! You are—a devil!' she cried, shocked by such blasphemous words.

'It must be true, for you are not the first person to call me that.'

She knew he would not let go of her until she did as he bid and slowly bent over him. As she hesitated, his fingers fastened in the nape of her neck, bringing her mouth down to his. A hand against her back held her fast against him as he subjected her not to a gentle, sweet kiss as before, but soul-searching, searing, demanding kisses which drained her of all thought, save one. To answer him! It was madness, but what did it matter?

She lost herself in the ecstasy of his touch, aware of every nerve in her body pulsating with excitement. Her fingers touched his face, a sunburnt cheek, where a faint scar lingered against one dark eyebrow and lost themselves in the mass of black hair which curled at the nape of his neck. Her lips flared to life beneath his, her unawakened body resisted momentarily the knowledge-able hands caressing it before surrendering to the exquisite pleasure they aroused in her. A pleasure too wonderful to deny, for she sensed she would never know the like of him again.

Ross gave a groan. His hands fell away from her, breaking the spell. She drew back, and was alarmed to see fresh perspiration on his forehead. His breathing was laboured. Instantly she was contrite . . . and angry, too.

'Oh, you fool!' she cried in exasperation. 'Now look what you have done—and for what? A silly kiss.'

He gave her a strange look. His strength was ebbing fast, and they both knew it, yet the hint of a smile touched the mouth, where lines of pain lingered and momentarily they were wiped away.

'Think of me sometimes, little cat—not unkindly. I owe you more than you will ever know . . . I wish . . .'

'Hush.' She laid her fingers across his lips, bathed his wet face, and pulled the bedcovers securely about him once more. She was aware of him fighting desperately to remain in control of his faculties, but within minutes he had drifted into another restless slumber—and she found that her fingers were once again tightly clasped in his.

She felt shocked to the very depths of her soul. What had he done to her in a few short minutes? She felt different. Alive! He had been trying to show his gratitude for what she had done, Roxanna told herself, seeking to reason away his actions, and she had not resisted because to have done so would have caused him more pain. He was grateful, nothing more, and she must not attempt to place any other explanation on what had happened. Simple gratitude. Doubtless he had kissed a hundred women in the same way . . .

'Little cat', he had called her. Unconsciously her fingers strayed to the dishevelled hair about her shoulders. She had been thinking how nice it would be to have it cut and arranged in one of the new fashions which went so well with the simplicity of dress these days; but now, she decided, it would never be touched. She would always think of it as a tawny mane . . . the mane of a wildcat!

How the hours dragged. Her arms and back were cramped from sitting in one position for such a long time, but whenever she stirred, Ross would start and his fingers curl painfully round hers until she was still again. He had alternate bouts of fever when he tossed and turned, muttering incoherently.

During these attacks, as she sought to calm him, sponging his face with cold water and pleading with him to be still and quiet, Roxanna was only too aware of his friend in the corner, head tilted back against his chair, eyes closed, as though asleep. She knew differently. He was watching, listening, aware of every movement, every sound, every whispered word from the direction of the bed. The pouch was back on the table. She had made no comment when it reappeared. His attitude was beneath contempt—beneath her anger.

During Ross's quieter periods, she managed to close her eyes and rest a little, but never did she allow herself to fall asleep. Consequently, as the first light appeared through a chink in the curtains, she was barely able to keep awake. Dark shadows ringed her dull eyes. Her hair was loose, tousled about her shoulders, the skirts of her gown creased. Her head drooped tiredly . . . She jerked herself back into wakefulness, realising that the tight grip on her fingers was no longer there. Ross's hand lay limply on the coverlet. He was pale and so still . . .

'Come quickly!' Nicholas's chair crashed to the floor as he leapt towards the bed, pushing her roughly back. Roxanna held her breath as he laid a hand against one pallid cheek, and thrust it inside the covers against Ross's heart. She heard an oath explode beneath his breath, and stepped back, eyes widening in alarm.

'No . . . surely not!'

'There is nothing you can do for him now. Take your money and go.' He strode to the table, plucked up the pouch and pushed it towards her. 'The carriage will be leaving for Liskeard in an hour. Be on it. I never want to set eyes on you again. Don't touch him!' he snapped, as Roxanna stepped towards the bed, her eyes riveted on Ross's features. How peaceful he looked, as if he was only sleeping. 'He is nothing to do with you any more. Remember that.'

Hours of angry frustration, of suffering his humiliating taunts and rudeness rose up to snap the thin thread of her self-control. Without thinking, she lashed out at the leather pouch and sent it flying across the room to crash into a far wall. Coins rebounded everywhere as they came to earth, but she did not notice as she wheeled about and ran from the room.

The consequences of her foolish action came home to her as she sat in the carriage on its way to Liskeard some two hours later. She was as penniless as when she started out from London. It had all been for nothing—the farce of a marriage . . . enduring all those hours of suspicion

and scorn . . . and yet it had not! In her heart, she knew
that the man called Ross had realised she wanted only to
help him, and even though he was now dead, she had
done just that. The brother who had shot him would
never inherit his wealth, which was what he had wanted.
A small thing for her to have done for a man about to
die. The money was nothing; she would work to earn
more. Besides, some of it had belonged to the odious
Nicholas, and she wanted nothing belonging to him.

Forget ever having seen them—or else, he had
threatened. She would never do that. Him, yes—but not
Ross. In those strange hours as she sat beside him, she
had felt so close to him, even though she knew he was at
times unaware of her presence as the fever descended on
him again. She could not define the feeling in her as she
held his hand—or rather as he held hers and she ministered to him . . . She had never known it before. A
warm, very personal feeling, stirring something deep
inside her. For all his unpleasant manner, Nicholas
could never take that from her.

She unfastened the top buttons of the grey dress which
it had been necessary to wear after all—the other was
still stained about the skirts, and would need special
attention when she had more time—and took out the
gold ring suspended on the chain about her neck. On
closer inspection she had found it to have some kind of
crest engraved on it, but it was so worn that she could
hardly make it out. The only clear thing was part of a
ship with towering castles fore and aft . . . rather like a
Spanish galleon, she had thought, remembering pictures
of Armada ships she had seen in her father's history-
books. It seemed to confirm her suspicions that he had
been a smuggler or even a pirate, and that this ring was
perhaps part of the booty taken from an unfortunate
Spanish ship at sea.

Her eyes closed. She could no longer fight off the
exhaustion which came upon her. Ross and his unpleasant companion were forgotten for the duration of
the journey as she slept, untroubled by the bumpiness of

the roads or her hard, uncomfortable seat. She came back to reality to find herself being firmly shaken by the driver. They had arrived in Liskeard—and there, across the street as she alighted, waited a small private carriage. She almost wept with relief. She knew it at once by the blue and red livery of the driver and the lackey who stood beside the door. Within a few minutes she was settling herself into the corner of a plush velvet seat, arranging across her knees the blanket presented to her. The events of the past few hours were pushed firmly to the back of her mind, where they belonged, she told herself, as the last stage of her long journey began and she sat forward to stare out of the window, eager for her first sight of her new house. She found that, once Liskeard had been left behind, the countryside was sparsely populated and became even more desolate as they grew closer to the coast. But there was a wildness about it which she found both exciting, and a little frightening. They travelled a narrow, uneven track for hours, prolonging her suspense, and then—at last—she heard it! The sound of the sea was in her ears. She glimpsed vast stretches of blue grey water and miles of sand. Huge white-topped breakers pounding over craggy rocks, the sight of which made her shiver as she contemplated some unfortunate ship sailing to its doom on them, lured to a terrible fate by a light somewhere on the headland before it.

The rain had eased, but there was still heavy cloud. And a mist, too, hovering at the edge of the seashore. She watched, fascinated, as it seemed to climb the rugged cliff face ahead of the carriage and creep like a white swirling blanket towards a gaunt stone house which stood out like a lonely sentinel on the headland.

The carriage began to slow down. Now it was turning off the track on to another, barely wide enough for it to pass over in safety. They were heading towards the same house where the mists now clung about the bottom storey, almost obscuring it from her view. This was it, then! This was Talland!

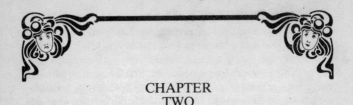

CHAPTER
TWO

ROXANNA'S FIRST impression of Talland was of strength.
The walls of the house, built completely of grey stone
probably quarried locally, looked thick and impreg-
nable. Whoever had built it had intended to keep people
out—or in! The carriage approached along a wide drive
after passing through massive iron gates, which were at
least fifteen feet in height. Visitors were not welcome
here, she suspected, and wondered what manner of
place she had come to? It looked positively sinister with
the eerie atmosphere created by the clinging mists about
it. More mist was rolling in from the ocean, which, to her
surprise, she could no longer see. There was nothing but
the white blanket rolling ever closer, obliterating everything in its path.

She stepped down on to the drive, adjusted her
bonnet, which had been set at rather a pert angle
by the jolting ride, and of which, she was sure, the
Countess would not approve, smoothed down the
skirts of her dress beneath the plain woollen cloak she
wore and turned towards the impressive front door.

It looked as if it was made of oak a foot thick. It had
brass hinges and was adorned with many large brass
studs. The door-handle was looped, like a twisted rope.
The knocker, brass again, was a ship. A galleon, she
realised, as she drew closer. Not unlike the one on the
ring she carried with her. A coincidence, she told herself, Cornishmen had always been seamen. She would
no doubt see many such emblems in the months to come.
But where were the men of Talland? Not out fishing on a
day like this? The village she had passed through, little

more than a cluster of a dozen houses set well apart from one another, had looked deserted. She had seen only three people, who had shown no interest in the carriage. There seemed to be no signs of activity, no work being done. No produce being sold, no sound of the smithy plying his trade at a busy forge. There were always horses to be shod, she reasoned. How did the people live, if no one worked?

Again her mind returned to Nicholas and the unpleasant suspicion that he might somehow be connected with the sea—and all that entailed. Smuggling? It was not uncommon in these parts, and this sparsely-inhabited part of the coastline would be a paradise for such men. She shivered, knowing that the coldness she felt was not from the mist clinging to her clothes, but from fear. The carriage moved off. She found her well-worn trunk—it had belonged to her father in his teaching days—on the gravel behind her. As she looked around her in bewilderment and growing confusion, the massive door of the house opened and a liveried footman came down the five steps to where she stood, and smiled into her reticent features.

'Miss Dane? The Countess de Villon will receive you in the Blue Room. Follow me please, miss.'

Clutching her reticule close to her, Roxanna mounted the steps after him and entered a large hall, which, to her amazement, she found was panelled on all sides by full-length mirrors. Because the day was so dull candles were already burning in the magnificent chandeliers hung above her head by long chains. She felt as if she had stepped over the threshold into another world. The outside of the house, sombre, brooding almost, had not prepared her for such grandeur—such beauty—as her eyes now beheld.

In front of her, a marble staircase led the way to the floors above. As her cloak was taken from her, together with her bonnet—so engrossed was she in her appraisal of her surroundings that she hardly noticed—she glimpsed oak doors leading to the upstairs rooms, all

brilliantly polished and gleaming in the candlelight.
Candles were everywhere. In wrought-iron holders on
the walls alongside gilt framed paintings. In tall, floor-
standing holders, as many as a dozen at a time. Furniture
reflected the soft glow which fell upon the mahogany and
oak surfaces.

A door was opened, on the first floor, and she was
ushered through. As it closed behind her, she clutched
her reticule a little tighter. This was the moment she had
dreaded. Was her hair in disarray? Her skirts creased
from the journey? If only she could have been allowed a
few minutes to make herself look more presentable . . .

'Come into the light, Miss Dane. My eyes are not what
they were, and I cannot see you clearly from here.' The
command came from a high-backed chair placed before
a chasm of a fireplace which dominated the large room in
which she stood. Everything was blue, she saw, as she
approached. Curtains, carpet, chair-covers, cushions. A
tall dresser, at least five feet long, stood against one wall
containing Willow Pattern china and Dresden figurines,
enough to serve fifty people at least! Another dresser
held cut glass decanters and glasses which sparkled in the
firelight playing upon them and caused them to give off a
multitude of colours. Only the best for the inhabitants of
Talland, Roxanna thought, quite overawed by the splen-
dour of her surroundings. None of the houses she had
worked in while in London had displayed such wealth—
or comfort. The room *was* comfortable. A combination
of the subtle varying shades of blue, coupled with a
tasteful selection of furniture, made it a very pleasant
room indeed. And after the hideous mist outside, the
fire was a heavenly sight. Suddenly she no longer felt
awkward.

She found herself face to face with the autocratic
Frenchwoman who had engaged her as companion to
her granddaughter, Lisette. It was difficult to assess the
age of Elizabeth de Villon. Her dress sense was impeccable. She wore a black silk gown in the latest fashion;
her grey hair was secured on the top of her head in curls

by a bandeau of shimmering diamonds; the same jewel
graced a slender throat, where no lines yet marred its
gracefulness although Roxanna was sure she was well
into her sixties. Rings glittered on the thin fingers of the
hand which indicated that she could seat herself in a
chair close by. She perched herself on the edge of a
tapestry seat.

'You are late, Miss Dane. You were expected to
arrive yesterday. Another few hours, and the carriage
would have returned without you. It had been waiting in
Liskeard for two days!'

'The delay was due to a flooded road just outside
Exeter, madame. The rain had caused a river to over-
flow its banks. All the passengers were forced to wait in
the coach until the road was passable—about five hours,'
Roxanna explained in as calm a voice as she could
muster. Five long hours during which she had been
frozen to the bone.

'I see. No wonder you look blue. A wretched journey,
was it?' The Countess's voice softened slightly, and
Roxanna warmed immediately to the change.

'Terrible. And then . . .' She broke off, not wanting to
divulge what had taken place at the inn, but was quietly
prompted to continue. 'There was—an—accident . . . A
man was hurt. The doctor was out on another call, and
. . . I helped as best I could, but, apart from the time I
have cared for my father, I have little nursing experience. I am afraid the man . . . died early this morning
. . .' She was horrified to find tears on her cheeks.
Hurriedly she found a handkerchief and wiped them
away, aware of the woman's eyes on her. Would she
never be able to forget how peaceful Ross had looked?
She had thought him to be sleeping . . . Wildcat . . .
Wildcat with the tawny mane. Even now, just remembering how he had looked, she could again feel the
touch of his hands on her, the urgency of his mouth on
hers, as if he knew life would soon be over for him.
'Forgive me—madame. I did not realise how shocked I
still must be.'

'Sleep will erase all the unpleasantness you must have experienced.' Elizabeth de Villon rang a silver bell on the table at her fingertips, and almost immediately the door opened and a servant stood waiting for her instructions. 'My granddaughter has gone out for the day with friends and will not be returning until quite late. Under the circumstances, I think it best that we should delay the introductions until later. She will have danced her shoes into holes, and you look exhausted, Miss Dane. I suggest you catch up on the sleep you did not have last night. Frederick, show the young lady to her room. Instruct Rosie to help her with her unpacking, and then she is to have a spiced toddy and go to bed.'

Roxanna was led up to the second floor, and along a long corridor. Her feet sank into the deep carpet. Again candles lighted her way past shuttered windows with burgundy velvet curtains. Even so, she could hear the sound of the sea—and the wind.

'There's be a gale tonight, miss. The best place for you, if I might suggest it, is in your bed,' the footman said cheerfully as he showed her to her room. It was far larger than she had ever dreamed of, and she stood in the doorway with a feeling of excitement mounting inside her. Talland was so different from what she had imagined. This time, she would tell her father when she saw him again, first impressions were deceptive. 'If it gets blowy, you'll probably hear all manner of strange noises, but don't worry. This house was built to last. Rosie, here she is. Make her welcome, but don't linger too long, girl. There's work to be done below.'

Roxanna went straight to the fire blazing in the hearth and stretched out her cold hands to the inviting flames. The young girl by the bed smiled, and studied the newcomer with a directness that Roxanna found refreshing. Instantly she knew she would have no trouble settling in with the other servants if they were at all like the two she had met so far.

'So you're the new one—the governess, I mean.'

'Companion,' Roxanna corrected, also smiling. 'I think Miss de Villon is a little old for a governess. She is eighteen, isn't she?'

'Sometimes she acts twenty-five—you know, all grown up and knowing everything. Sometimes she's a little girl, throwing tantrums because she can't have her own way. Lonely, that's what she is. What with her mother being murdered by those Frenchies and then her father never coming to see her . . .' Rosie broke off, the look on her chubby face proclaiming that she had said too much. 'You can't be much older than she is.'

'I'm nineteen.'

'The young master will like the look of you. He's bored for a new face. Miss Lisette leads him a merry dance.' At Roxanna's puzzled expression, the girl gave a giggle. 'You don't know much about the people you are working for, do you?'

'As a matter of fact, very little. The Countess engaged me in London. I was told only that I was to be companion to her granddaughter. I haven't even met her. I hope she likes me.'

'You are going to have a long wait, aren't you? She won't be back from London for at least a week. What a rush there was to get her packed and away this morning—in the master's personal carriage, if you please! There, that's most of your clothes unpacked. I'll do the rest in the morning for you, if you like. And there's a warming-pan coming up any minute, along with your toddy. I must say the old lady, anyway, seems to have taken a liking to you.'

'Don't worry about the rest of the unpacking. I can manage. Thank you for your help. Did you say London?' Roxanna echoed, a frown wrinkling her brows. 'I thought . . .' Surely the Countess had indicated that the girl was with friends, and would return that night?

'London it is, living it up in style with Lord Talland. The Countess would never have allowed her to go without him there to keep an eye on her. Right little minx she is with the men, and poor Mark eating his heart out over her . . .'

'Mark?' Roxanna felt as if she was floundering in deep water.

Rosie gave another giggle as she made towards the door. 'Mark Talland. Handsome devil, and he knows it. If Lord Talland had half his charm, he'd be married by now. Not that he's ever short of feminine company, you understand. He has a way about him, but not like his brother. He's always out racing that devil of a black horse of his, or fighting duels . . . He has quite a reputation in London. We call him the "the devil of Talland". Never make him angry . . .'

So, in the final analysis, it would be Lord Talland who approved—or disapproved—of the Countess's choice. This was his house, not hers as she had supposed. Left alone, Roxanna fell to the last of her unpacking, although, when she thought about it, there was no great hurry now. She would have little or nothing to do until Lisette de Villon returned from London.

She was disappointed at the long wait. How frightful it would be if the Master of Talland did not approve of her upon his arrival, and she had to leave. Had she made a mistake? No, she was certain the Countess had intimated that she would meet Lisette in the morning. Why, when she had departed for London hours before? Perhaps she was over-tired, over-reacting to a simple misunderstanding. Tomorrow everything would become crystal clear, she told herself, as she sipped the hot toddy a young maid brought.

'Shall I close the shutters for you, miss? There's going to be a storm tonight.' The girl hovered by the tall french windows.

'Oh, no!' Roxanna said, not wishing to shut out the last of the daylight until it was absolutely necessary. It was still quite early in the afternoon, but already grey shadows were lengthening about the room.

'You won't forget, will you, miss? These old rooms can be very cold when the mists come down.'

'You mean it can get worse than now?'

'Sometimes the whole house is hidden in it. It can be very dangerous then. People have been known to take a wrong path and go over the edge of the cliff on to the beach below. And then there is always the "devils" to contend with. They don't take kindly to strangers walking near their places.'

'Are you trying to tell me there are ghosts in this area? Nonsense! You are not serious, are you?' Roxanna asked, wide-eyed. What kind of a place had she come to?

'The old church is haunted, miss. On a clear day, if you stand behind the spinney, you can see it. Terrifying apparitions have been seen there. I've seen them myself, coming home late one night with Jeb from the village—he's my sweetheart. Fair gave us both the quivers. Ghastly, they was! And then there's old Jakey's hearse. He was a smuggler who used to keep people away by driving this awful black-draped hearse down the village streets whenever there was a cargo to be unloaded and transported overland. Never seen him myself, but my aunt Emmie has. Struck her dumb for two whole weeks. Best thing that ever happened to her—gave me a bit of peace.' The girl paused, a saucy look on her face. 'Haven't scared you, have I, miss? But if you are going to stay, you should know all about these things. I wouldn't like you to wander away from the house and—Well, I just wouldn't.'

'You need have no fear that I shall venture ouside the door after dark,' Roxanna assured her, adding firmly, 'Not that I believe a word of it.'

'Good night, miss. Pleasant dreams.'

If she slept tonight it would be a miracle, Roxanna thought, quickly finishing her toddy. Rubbish, all of it. Such tales were known to be put about by smugglers and wreckers to keep people away while they went about their business. 'Devils of Talland'! Silly men in sheets scaring away innocent villagers. Most of the latter were probably reared on such tales from the cradle, and never had the courage to dispute them. What was it Rosie had called Lord Talland? 'The devil of Talland'. Another coincidence? Had she landed herself in the middle of a nest of law-breakers with the master of the house at their head?

Oh dear, she thought, what nonsense. I am truly exhausted or I would never even consider such a likelihood. Unpinning her hair, she allowed it to fall past her shoulders, and a smile touched her lips as she caught sight of her reflection in the ornate gilt mirror on an inlaid mahogany table beneath the window. And then, as the pain of memory returned, she quickly turned away to clear the last items from her trunk.

A combination of the warm room and the spiced toddy soon made her drowsy. It had been her intention to read a book before going to bed, but she found it impossible to resist the temptation of climbing into the large four-poster and allowing her aching limbs to sink into the thick feather mattress.

For a few minutes she sat with her knees drawn up underneath her chin, surveying her surroundings. Never before had she been afforded such pleasant, comfortable rooms. Adjoining the bedroom she had discovered a small dressing-room, which she surmised she was intended to use as her own personal bathroom, for there was a blue and white porcelain bath in the middle of the floor. On a marble-topped washstand, a jug and basin containing fresh water. Across a small stool, several heavy towels. Such luxury for a companion!

The bedroom was decorated in pale grey, the starkness of two of the walls broken by large paintings of country scenes, the other two by heavy wooden panelling which went round the back of the bed where she sat. The floorboards were of oak, once again polished to a high degree, as was every piece of wooden furniture she had so far seen in the house. If Lisette liked her—if Lord Talland liked her—and she stayed, Roxanna knew she could be very happy here, regardless of the devils and ghosts!

Contentedly she slid down beneath the sheets, pulling the heavy covers up round her shoulders. Something dug painfully into her breast, bruising it through the thinness of her nightgown. Her fingers encountered the ring Ross had given her and pushed it quickly away. This night, she wanted no memory of him. She wanted only to sleep, to forget—and, on the morrow, to start anew.

She awoke with a start to find the room chillingly cold. The top cover had slipped to the floor, and in what must have been her restless sleep, most of the other bed-clothes had followed suit. The room was in pitch darkness and she groped for the candle she had left on the table. Unable to find it, she hurriedly climbed out of bed, pushing her feet into the slippers she had luckily thought to leave beside it, and hurried to throw another log on the fire and rake the dying embers. Why had she not thought to remake it before she retired?

The flickering flames, which sprang to life, sent weird shadows around the room. Although not a nervous person, Roxanna was glad when she had managed to locate and light the candle. A small clock on the mantel showed eleven o'clock. Had she been asleep over six hours? Yet it was little wonder, for she had not had any rest the night before.

Everyone had been right about a storm, she thought, as gusts of wind rattled the windows. She inspected them to make sure they were fast and was just about to close the heavy shutters, which she had forgotten about, when a flickering light outside caught her attention. She blinked, not sure if she had seen it or not, and when she tried to find it again, it had vanished.

No, wait, there it was again. She had no idea in which direction her room faced, but the sound of the breakers was so clear that she felt sure it must be towards the headland. Then the light was at the top of the cliffs, near the church—the church supposedly haunted by ghosts and demons who kept Godfearing villagers well away with their presence.

Whoever would be out on a night like this? Rain was lashing at the windowpanes. The mist seemed to have dispersed, but even so she could not see anything in the darkness outside—except the light.

Wreckers! Oh lord, was her imagination running riot again? It was probably no more than someone making his way home with a lantern. Why, then, did it not move? Her heart began to beat so loudly that it thudded in her ears. She flung the shutters closed, and ran back to the bed, to huddle in it beneath the bedclothes as if Rosie's demons were about to come through the door and devour her. In the morning she would take a walk and look around. Doubtless she would find a perfectly harmless explanation for the light. A house, perhaps? Of course, she would find a house . . . . Nevertheless she left the candle burning.

'Miss Dane?' The liveried footman who stood in the doorway was the one who had met her when she arrived. 'I am Russell. I hope you slept well?'

Roxanna, who had been standing by the window, staring out across carefully tended gardens to the solitary building which stood out across the cliffs, turned with a smile and nodded. 'Thank you, yes.'

'The—wind did not keep you awake? Sometimes it is difficult to sleep the first night in a strange house, and this old place does tend to be rather creaky in bad weather, even with a good slate-hung roof to keep it out.'

'It reminds me of a fortress,' she returned, wondering if her well-being was his only concern. Everyone was going to great lengths to tell her tales of ghosts and hob-goblins—how dangerous it was to walk after dark— not to worry about strange noises in the night. What was it she should not see, or hear?

'The room is comfortable?' Another polite question. She looked into the placid face before her searchingly, but could see nothing in the grave grey eyes to give her any cause to wonder at his concern. After all, she was a

newcomer, and being extremely foolish over nothing!
Pull yourself together, Roxanna Dane, you have work to
do.

'Very. I—I did not expect such luxury, I admit.'

'His Lordship takes care of all who live and work at
Talland, Miss Dane.' In the days and weeks to come, she
was to find he was the only servant always to refer to her
so formally. To all the others she became just Roxanna.
To Rosie—Roxy. She was not sure if she liked that or
not, but she liked the girl and her cheerfulness, and
so said nothing. 'Unfortunately, this morning, the
Countess finds herself somewhat indisposed; the return
of a chill which she recently suffered. She wishes me to
tell you she will be remaining in bed the whole day, and
perhaps tomorrow, if it does not improve. You are to
make yourself at home until she sends for you.'

'Oh! Please convey my regrets for her indisposition. I
hope she is soon better. I—I am at a loss. I have no Miss
Villon and now no Countess either. I have never had so
much time on my hands before,' Roxanna said with a
soft laugh. 'But it will give me time to explore a little.'

'Explore, Miss Dane?' Was it her imagination, or did
those granite eyes narrow just a fraction. 'If you are
planning to go on a walking tour, I suggest you acquaint
yourself first with the countryside. I am sure Rosie or
one of the other girls will be only too happy to show you
round, or tell you where it is safe to go.'

'Safe?'

'Over the years there has been a great deal of mining
in this area,' Russell told her. 'Copper. But when the
price fell so alarmingly, not many landowners, Lord
Talland, among them, could keep all the mines going at
full production, but there are many unused shafts, overgrown and dangerous. There is one mine at the moment;
enough for the villagers to have a fair living. He has
made himself responsible for each one of them, you
understand. Fishing hereabouts is not what it was, and
with the Channel such a dangerous place, full of British
men-of-war and French frigates thinking to make a

surprise attack on our coasts, the fishermen have all but given up their trade. It will be a good thing when this war with Napoleon is over and we can all get back to living normal lives.'

'That would not please the contraband-runners, would it?' Roxanna shot the question at him without warning, and this time there was a reaction. A faint nerve twitched at the corner of one brow—for an instant only, but it was sufficient to tell her the question had gone home.

'Smugglers—at Talland, Miss Dane? Dear me, have you been listening to Rosie? She will have you seeing old Jakey driving his hearse past the house, if you listen too long to her tales.'

'Are you telling me the men hereabouts don't turn their hand to smuggling now and then? Why, everyone knows Polperro and Looe breed the most daring race of seafarers in existence,' Roxanna persisted.

'Indeed.' The tone told her that she would learn nothing from him. 'Lord Talland may turn a blind eye to a few of the village men bringing in the odd kegs of rum and brandy, but nothing more than that. The coast is patrolled by a revenue cutter, and soldiers come this way without warning, searching and questioning. Once, perhaps—a long time ago—it might have been as you say, but not now. Will you take your breakfast in here, Miss Dane?'

'Yes, I think so, it is pleasant and warm. Besides, I have no one to share it with, have I? Then I think I shall go for a walk—after talking to Rosie, of course.' She had not the slightest intention of doing so.

'If you notice men on the beach below, stay clear.' Russell turned at the door and looked at her. 'A ship went on to the rocks last night. The bodies of the poor souls drowned are just being brought in on the tide.'

'A shipwreck!' Roxanna gasped, a hand going to her mouth in horror. 'Then that light . . .'

'What light, Miss Dane? Did you not sleep the night through, after all?'

'Yes—Yes, I did. I must have been dreaming. How silly of me not to have realised it.' She quickly turned away, afraid to look into his eyes, knowing that if she did she would betray herself. When she turned back, he had gone.

She stumbled to a chair and sat down, shivering. A wreck—and she *had* seen a light. No dream, no hallucination. She *had* seen it! So Lord Talland turned a blind eye to a little smuggling, but was otherwise a strict landlord. Why, then, as soon as he was away from the house, did this happen? Or was that his way? By being absent from the house at such a time, he would never be connected with the wreckers and their diabolical work.

She forced down the breakfast which arrived, toast with butter made in the village, she was told. Rashers of bacon and egg. And a small porcelain pot of honey. If only her father could be with her now to share in this good fortune. Could she remain, knowing what she did? Yet what business was it of hers? She had foolishly given herself away to Russell, who, she was sure, knew something. He would not allow her to gain any further knowledge. Not that she wanted to. The whole business was repugnant to her, as it must be to most townspeople. To the villagers of Talland, it was probably a way of life handed down from their forefathers.

No wonder the village had looked so desolate. The men did not need to work on the land or in the mines when they could earn money carrying contraband. Few would be afraid of the soldiers. Born and bred in this wild, rugged countryside, they would know paths and tunnels that the revenue men could never discover if they searched for a whole month.

How different it is today, Roxanna mused, looking out through the windows as she fastened the ribbons of her bonnet beneath her chin. There was no sign of any dark clouds, and although the breeze seemed quite fresh—she could see it bending the tops of the trees in the garden—a watery sun was doing its best to brighten the day. Perhaps the bad weather had passed. She hoped so. She loved to walk, and with so much time on her hands at the moment, she intended to make the most of the opportunity afforded her.

The breeze was indeed fresh, she found, as she stepped outside. She had managed to leave the house without being seen, much to her relief. For a while she would linger in the gardens and try to get her bearings from the house. That mysterious light could have come from only one place, the building some half a mile away round the headland. The church!

The gardens were beautifully cared for. She walked down neat paths, without a sign of a weed, and marvelled at the green fingers that had produced such a variety of sweet-smelling, multicoloured flowers and shrubs in such a desolate spot. In turn they would be lashed by rain, wind, heavy gales from the sea, yet from what she could see, all seemed quite hardy and would blossom profusely when the warmer weather arrived.

Near the house there were four rose arbours, more protected than anything else, where sweet-smelling honeysuckle bloomed around the wooden supports. The fragrance as she passed was heavenly, and she resisted the temptation to reach out and pluck a bright yellow sprig to pin on her cloak. She would ask if anyone would mind some being put her in her room. Once, her father had been a gardener, and his flowers had been the envy of the tiny Suffolk village where they had lived before moving to London after her mother's death.

Vivid yellow daffodils tossed their heads in the breeze, beside clusters of anemones. There was more honeysuckle creeping over a stone wall leading down to the cliff. The path led right to the very edge . . . She came to an abrupt halt, staring down at the yellow sands below, the white-topped waves breaking over them. There were uniformed men on the beach, moving backwards and forwards to the water, dragging from it . . . Quickly she turned away. The luckless souls drowned the night before, she realised with a shudder, and hurried back the way she had come.

Another path led off from the drive, through a mass of green thicket towards the very place she wanted to see. Gathering her cloak tightly round her, she set out towards her goal. For her own peace of mind, she had to find the explanation for the light. How convenient it was that the Countess was confined to bed with a cold. Roxanna could neither unburden her soul to her, nor question her about the mystery of Lisette's whereabouts. Was that the intention of this sudden ague? How suspicious she was! But then she had no cause to trust anyone. Her father, the most mild-mannered of men, had once been trusting and had almost ended up in prison a convicted thief because of it. With her alongside him as his accomplice. She trusted no one, accepted no one at face value any more. She would never allow herself to be vulnerable again!

It was a pleasant walk, and she found that the warmth of the sun on her face dispelled a little of the apprehension she had been feeling. By the time she reached the church, for that was what the building did indeed turn out to be, she was beginning to wonder if she had not come on a fool's errand.

It was not large—she doubted if it could accommodate more than twenty people . . . but she had not seen even twenty people since she had arrived. She had passed only one woman, with a baby wrapped in a shawl tied to her back, who stared at her with suspicious eyes and made a wide arc to go around her, neither answering her polite good-day nor indicating by even a slight smile that she was anything but an stranger, an interloper among the community. Would everyone outside the house treat her like this, Roxanna wondered?

It was a mixture of the old and the new, she discovered, as she stepped inside. Most of the church appeared to have been recently rebuilt with the now familiar grey Cornish stone, but there was a dilapidated old tower at one end that looked far older. Thirteenth or fourteenth century, perhaps. Her father would be in his element here! It had a cradle roof, and carved benches

before the altar. Set in the chancel floor was a stone slab
with an inscription on it to the effect that here lay a
well-known smuggler from nearby Polperro who had
been shot while plying his trade. The interior was rich in
wooden carvings. Cherubs heads were everywhere—
plump-cheeked, smiling cherubs, whose eyes seemed
somehow alive, following her as she inspected every
nook and cranny with more than a casual interest.

The one thing she did not find was a lantern. There
were wrought-iron candlesticks, and gigantic holders to
take candles which must have been six feet high, but no
lantern. Had she missed one outside?

She stepped back into the sunlight, and moved in the
direction of the graveyard. No lantern over the door, as
far as she could see. So someone had been standing here
holding it—deliberately! Nearly every tombstone had a
stone cherub carved over it, or angels with huge wings,
their heads bowed in prayer. At any moment she felt she
might hear a heavenly choir begin to sing. The graves
looked very old; some of the headstones were unread-
able, weathered with age and the continual salt winds
from the sea.

She looked up, away from the graveyard, and in the
distance saw what was invisible from the house: the ruins
of another place, set back amid windswept trees so that it
was almost hidden from view. Her curiosity not yet
satisfied, she headed in that direction. These ruins were
far older than the church, she saw. Years and years of
grass had penetrated what walls remained so that they
looked like elongated bushes. Wild flowers peeped at
her here and there, alive with insects. An old castle,
once, and well fortified, she guessed, by the ancient
cannon now half buried by fallen masonry. She wiped
away some of the grime with the edge of her cloak and
could just make out a date—1588. Why, that was the
year of the Spanish Armada. Two hundred and sixteen
years old! How she wished it could talk!

As in that year, England was at war. Not with Spain
this time, but with France, where Napoleon reigned

supreme as First Consul, and the exiled Bourbons plotted and schemed to get one of their own back on the throne. He had so far survived two attempts on his life, supposedly by members of their faction. French spies were rumoured to be everywhere in England, preparing plans of the chief ports, the coastlines and defences. Before she left London, there had been gossip that military preparations were well advanced in both France and Holland for an attack.

Roxanna turned and looked out over the shimmering sea, cold and grey despite the sunlight. No ship could approach here without being seen, and as for landing . . . She thought of the ships which had foundered on the rocks the night before . . . No French man-of-war would stand a chance!

'What the devil do you think you are doing here? Spying?' a harsh voice demanded behind her. She swung round to find herself face to face with a young tousled-headed man, whose pale face was bleak and unfriendly. 'This is private property. Be on your way.' He moved towards her, his fists clenched menacingly.

'I'm sorry.' She stepped back in alarm. 'I did not know. No one told me.' But then she had not asked.

'Well, *I'm* telling you. Nosy little miss, aren't you? Thinking of earning yourself a few coins off the revenue men, are you? I'd think twice before you say anything . . .' A balled fist was shaken before her face.

'I don't know what you mean . . .' Roxanna gasped. 'I'm sorry. I won't come here again.' She turned and fled through the mass of tall grass and weeds, trampling underfoot, unnoticed, the bright yellow primroses growing there in her haste to be gone from the place.

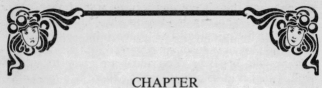

CHAPTER
THREE

IT WAS four days before Roxanna next saw the Countess
Elizabeth, and then she was summoned to her bedroom
late one afternoon. Her employer was sitting up in bed
looking remarkably well, to Roxanna's way of thinking,
and certainly not the invalid she had been expecting. She
was enjoying a herbal infusion.

'Sit down, Miss Dane. You are well? You look well.
All those invigorating walks you have been taking, no
doubt?'

'Thank you, I am in the best of health. And you,
madame? I hope your cold has not worsened.'

'Thanks to Agnes and her brews, thank God, it has
not.' Agnes was the Countess's aged maid who had been
in attendance since the day she set foot in Talland some
twelve years before, a fugitive from the bloodshed in
France. Roxanna had only to show a hint of curiosity
about anything at all, and Rosie was quick to fill in the
background for her. Instead of four short days, she felt
as if she had been part of the household for four years!
'You have not been bored, then, with so much time on
your hands?'

'Goodness, no! I have found plenty to do. I have
walked a great deal, and I read.'

'Ah, yes. Russell tells me you have spent every afternoon in the library.'

'I hope you do not mind?'

'Why should I? When Lord Talland is not at home, the
room is never used. You seem to appreciate books as he
does. That will please him. Lisette's head is full of
nonsense. Mark thinks of nothing but gambling and

women, and there's not one servant in the house, save for Russell, who can hold a decent conversation for more than five minutes.' The Countess pushed away her cup, and Roxanna rose and removed it to a side-table. 'Thank you, my dear. You and I are going to get on well, I feel it in these old bones. There is a quietness about you I like . . . and you do not have the airs of other companions I have dealt with.'

'I know my place, madame,' Roxanna said, paling slightly, and the woman's eyes were intent on her face. 'I am aware how much I am in your debt.'

'If you are referring to that unfortunate affair concerning your father and Lady Carsewell's necklace, I think it better to let the matter rest, don't you? As long as you do nothing while you are here to displease me—or rather Lord Talland, for it was he who instructed me to engage a companion for Lisette—it need never be mentioned between us again. I shall, of course, acquaint him with all the facts when he returns, but I am sure he will be guided by me in this matter.'

'From London? With Miss Lisette?' Roxanna asked, and the Countess gave a short laugh.

'*Bien!* I like a girl who speaks her mind. Rosie has been talking to you? No matter. You arrived at rather a critical moment, Miss Dane. I had brought my scatter-brained granddaughter back here from London in disgrace. She had just tried to elope with . . . someone totally unsuitable for her. Lord Talland stepped in just in time to make her a ward of court. Lisette, sweet child that she can be sometimes, is totally without a brain in her head, so like her dear mother. She is easily led, but when she does not have her own way, oh, *mon Dieu!* The tantrums that one can fling! She was in a most rebellious mood when we returned home, threatening to run away again at the first opportunity, and as Lord Talland was unfortunately not here to put her over his knee as she deserved, I decided to send her away with friends for a week. Give her a chance to get over this young man, you understand. She is with a family who will watch her night

and day, at the same time indulging her every whim, or
at least seeming to. They are *emigrés*, as I am, from my
beloved France.' The Countess sighed, and stared out of
the window, lost in her own thoughts for many long
minutes. 'Twelve long years since I last saw Paris.
Lisette was a child, a mere seven years old when they
dragged her poor mother to the blade of *Madame la
Guillotine*. Her father—my son—escaped, but he too is
an exile, in another land. One day, God willing, we shall
go home. One day that little Corsican upstart who
calls himself Napoleon, First Consul of France, will be
toppled from his perch—and we shall go back.'

She broke off and looked at Roxanna seated on a chair
beside the bed, hands resting loosely in her lap, totally
engrossed in what was being said.

'Yes—a quietness about you I find soothing. You may
read to me, Miss Dane. It is too much to hope that you
read French, I suppose?'

'My father did begin to teach me once,' Roxanna
admitted. 'But when my mother died and we left our
home to live in London, there was much that had to be
put aside for other things.' Like earning a living, which
she had never had to do before. Being a servant to
others, when once she had had a maid of her own. But
that was in the past, and she had promised herself to look
back no more.

'I shall ask Lisette to teach you. It would be pleasant
to converse with someone in my own tongue. Lord
Talland is fluent in it, but of course he would be. He will
be here in a few days. Perhaps, then, this house will
assume some sense of normality again. I swear, whenever he is away, the servants conspire to confuse me with
their Cornish words. There are times when I can scarce
understand that cheeky maid, Rosie! And as for Mark
. . . You have not met him yet, have you?'

'Mark Talland? No. Is he away too?'

'Heaven only knows where he is. At the bottom of an
empty keg of rum, I wouldn't be surprised. You watch
out for him, Miss Dane. If possible—and I say if,

because he will take one look at that pretty face and consider it another conquest—keep your distance from him. He's a plausible, charming good-for-nothing.'

'Elizabeth, how can you speak so ill of me?' a voice declared from the bedroom door. A slim, tousled-headed young man advanced into the room, and Roxanna, as she looked up into the smiling face, went suddenly cold. It was the man who had spoken to her so rudely on the cliff-top. This was Mark Talland? 'I have just heard you are indisposed . . . Or are you sulking because my brother has done you out of a wedding?'

'You young rogue!' The Countess frowned at him; nevertheless she extended a ringed hand and allowed him to touch it to his lips. 'There will be the devil to pay when he gets back, and you know it. I can't help you. I warned you not to go against him, and you refused to listen to me. Persuading the girl to elope with you! I should have you horsewhipped . . .'

'You are not in France now . . . and is it our usual practice to discuss family business before the servants?' Mark straightened, and his cold gaze settled on Roxanna's astonished features. *He* was the one who had eloped with Lisette against the wishes of his brother. She was not so sure if Elizabeth was totally against the match. She did not appear to be too angry. 'This one I have already found to be exceedingly curious.'

'Explain yourself. Miss Dane has not been here long. To what are you referring?'

'We—We encountered one another while I was out walking one morning,' Roxanna said quickly, bristling at his continued rudeness. She had given him no cause to be so with her. 'I had found these old ruins and a cannon . . . I was examining it when—when I was rudely told to go away . . . not to spy . . . I am still at a loss to understand what was meant by such words. I was not aware I was doing anything wrong.'

'So that's where you've been hiding yourself—the ruined castle,' Elizabeth murmured. 'In the company of a good few bottles, no doubt.'

'With the thought of facing my illustrious brother soon—a good few,' came the dry retort. 'Perhaps I was a little harsh with the girl, but she—startled me.'

'Your apology is accepted, sir.' Roxanna said with a forced smile. 'Have you a book in mind for me to read from, madame, or shall I fetch one from the library?'

'Go and choose one.' Roxanna had the feeling that she wanted to be alone with the newcomer, and was relieved at the suggestion. 'Pick several. Come back in half an hour.'

Roxanna was to spend many afternoons reading to the Countess after that. She found her an easy listener—or was it that her employer's thoughts were often far away, not on the book being read to her? Roxanna often suspected this was the case.

Mark Talland, having returned to the house once again, made his presence known in no uncertain manner. He was, without a doubt, the rudest, the most arrogant man she had ever known, Roxanna decided. He barely conversed with her at all. A curt nod whenever they met, and nothing more. Rosie, after being in his presence for only a few minutes, would come scurrying downstairs, her cheeks flushed, clothes awry, the most mischievous of smiles on her face. The housekeeper would rebuke her, and the other young maids gather about her eager to learn what had happened, and she would draw them into a corner and whisper what had taken place upstairs in the young master's rooms.

His reputation for tumbling the housemaids was common knowledge, Roxanna discovered, and hoped he would look no further afield for his pleasure. Although, from the way he treated her, it was obvious that she was not of the slightest interest to him.

She discovered differently, however, one afternoon after leaving the Countess's room and making her way to her own on the floor above. As she reached the door, she heard a soft footstep behind her and turned, expecting to find one of the servants. Mark Talland stood behind her.

From his reddened cheeks and unsteady gait she knew he had been drinking—and for some considerable while.

'You wish to speak with me, sir?' Her heart was in her mouth as she spoke, not liking the way his eyes raked over her body in the most searching fashion.

'I am in need of a friend, Miss Dane. Will you be my friend?' His speech was slurred, and her anxiety increased. She slipped her hand on to the door-knob. One quick turn, and she could have it open and be inside. He gave a short laugh, and his hand covered hers. It was exceedingly hot and unpleasant on her cool skin. As he came closer, she could smell the aroma of drink on him—brandy and wine, so strong that it made her turn her face away in disgust. 'Come now, what have you to be so coy about? Surely I'm not the first man to be interested in you? You're quite pretty for a servant . . . In other households, were there no amorous sons or husbands to dance attendance on you?'

'No! You are impertinent, sir!'

'And you forget your place, girl. But for the good grace and kindness of the Countess, you and your thieving father would be languishing in a prison now— doubtless where you belong.'

Roxanna gasped as though he had struck her. He knew! How many more would learn of her sordid background before much longer? She tried to push past him into her room, but he blocked her path. His hands went about her waist, sliding upwards to cup her breasts beneath the plain cotton blouse she wore. For a brief instant she remembered the last—and only—man who had ever touched her so boldly and the pleasure he had brought her . . . and then she struck out at the face nearing hers, twisted away from the mouth intent on seeking hers.

'Let me go this instant. I—I am not Rosie!' she cried indignantly, and Mark laughed at her anger. He was far stronger than he looked, she discovered, as his arms went about her, effectively pinning hers to her sides. His

lips covered hers, hotly, greedily. She had been slyly
pinched before by the men in the households where she
had worked, and once kissed quite ardently until the
man's wife came upon them and instantly dismissed her.
She had come to accept that, no matter where she went,
there would always be someone who thought her an easy
conquest. Those that had tried had discovered that she
was not easy and not to be conquered—at least, not by
them. Only one man could ever have done that to
her . . .

She came back to reality with the realisation that
Mark was trying to unfasten her bodice. She went limp in
his embrace as if near to fainting, and then, as he drew
back from her, bent her head and fastened her teeth in
the hand seeking her breast. He swore and snatched it
away. In doing so, his fingers entangled with the chain
about her neck and ripped it from her throat. The ring
from it fell to the carpet and lay between them. Before
she could retrieve it, Mark had scooped it up with
another oath. It lay in his palm, the dull gold gleaming in
the candlelight.

'Once a thief, always a thief, eh?' he snarled, eyes
gleaming.

'I—I don't know what you mean. Give it to me! It is
mine.'

'Yours? Yours, Miss Dane? How can it belong to you
when it bears the personal crest of my brother, who, as
far as I can gather, you have not yet met?'

'Crest . . . brother . . .' Roxanna reeled back from
him, eyes dilated. It was Ross's ring! How could it
belong to his brother . . . Lord Talland! Ross James
Talland? Was that whom she had married? Dear God,
then he was not even aware that his brother was dead?

'How did you come by this, girl? Speak true, or I'll
have you whipped—and I shall personally apply the
lash . . .'

'May I be of some assistance, sir?' Russell came out of
the shadows to stand beside them. How long he had
been there was not apparent, for he never betrayed

anything on those taut, grey features. 'Is something wrong?'

'We have a thief among us, Russell. Is this not my brother's crest?' Mark thrust the ring under the man's nose. His eyes flickered just once to where Roxanna stood or rather leaned weakly against the door of her room, before he nodded.

'It is, sir. He always wore it, as I remember.'

'Then how came this girl by it?'

'It was given to me . . . by a dying man!' Roxanna cried. 'I tried to help him, and this was what he gave me in return.' How outrageous and unlikely her story would sound if she told the whole truth, she realised, as Mark exploded into high laughter. 'It's the truth! At an inn the other side of Liskeard . . .'

'By God, girl, you can lie with the best of them, and mix a little truth to make it sound plausible.' He caught her wrist in a grip that made her wince. The brown eyes were suddenly cruel as they gazed at her. 'How you knew that I was there, I don't know, but I swear . . .'

She had never seen the face of Ross's assailant. Now she knew without a doubt that she was looking at him. Mark Talland had attempted to kill his own brother? As Nicholas had said! Why? As revenge because Ross had spoiled his elopement plans? No wonder he had been in such a mood when he flagged down the coach!

'You—were the other man?' Her words were hardly audible.

'And who will believe you—a proved thief? By to-morrow, Miss Clever Dane, you will be on your way to gaol in Liskeard. If the Countess won't press charges, then I shall.'

'Why do we not leave it up to Lord Talland to judge, sir?' Russell asked in a quiet, yet authoritative tone as Mark glared at him. 'After all, it is his ring that Miss Dane is said to have stolen. If he did indeed give it to her, he will confirm it.'

'He can't confirm it, you fool,' Mark snapped, and then stopped as he heard Roxanna's sharp intake of breath, and realised he had betrayed himself.

'Why not tell him why?' she whispered, and the grip on her wrist tightened until it felt as if it would break. 'You shot him. I saw you. You shot your own brother! I nursed him. He died early the following morning.'

'No, Miss Dane,' Russell said. 'Lord Talland will be home the day after tomorrow. We received word less than fifteen minutes ago. Dead men do not rise from the grave, despite all the old smuggling tales. I can assure you that he is alive.'

For the whole of the next day, Roxanna was scarcely aware of time. After an uncomfortable interview with the Countess in Mark's angry presence, during which he accused her time and time again of being a thief and a liar, she was told she would remain in her room until Lord Talland arrived.

'Ross, Lord Talland?' Roxanna had asked in a small voice, and Elizabeth de Villon had nodded, frowning. She had come to like this young English miss and did not want to see her go the way of all the others who had come in contact with Mark Talland's displeasure. But the story she told . . . of Mark shooting his own brother, of Ross giving her his ring in gratitude for her help . . . It could be the truth, of course, or she could have found it . . . or stolen it from his room. Only Ross alive and well, confronting her, would give her the answer to so many questions.

'I suggest you spend the time until Lord Talland returns rethinking your explanation to me, Miss Dane,' the Countess said with a sigh. Was this house to be forever plagued with problems? 'I wonder what you will tell us when he appears without a mark on him? The man has been in London these past four weeks.'

Only Roxanna saw the shadow which crossed Mark's face. She was in no doubt that her story would be substantiated . . . Where would that leave Mark? Yet uppermost in her mind, as she sat miserably in her room, was another thought. Ross, Lord Talland, was her husband! The annulment could not have been completed in so short a time. She would not be able to stay beneath the same roof—she would be forced to leave.

Alive! But Nicholas had told her he was dead. But then she had not looked for herself, he had made sure of that. He had deliberately lied to her. The act of a protective, true friend—he would never know the anguish he had brought her.

When Rosie found her in tears, the girl was most sympathetic. Only when she had gone did Roxanna realise she had probably thought that the tears were in fear of what was to happen to her. Did everyone in the house believe she was a thief? As they had believed her father to be one . . . and he the most trustworthy of men, without a dishonest thought in his head. He had been disgraced on circumstantial evidence too . . . concocted through the vindictiveness of a lecherous husband. It would not happen to her, she decided. She would run away . . . The thought of staying and facing Ross again was unbearable. To live beneath his roof, a mere servant, and he her master. Never daring to look at him as she had looked at him that night, or touch him as she had then . . . Was this really her? Level-headed Roxanna Dane, without a romantic bone in her body—mooning over a man who would not look twice at her once he had discovered her true station in life. What had he done to her with his devil's touch?

The devil of Talland! Was he the one Rosie had meant, with a temper so terrible that everyone was afraid of him? Was he, as Roxanna suspected, not ignorant of the events down on the beach? Was it possible for the gentle man who had held her, stroked her hair, and then without warning roused her to ecstatic heights to be capable of cold-blooded murder? For, as a wrecker, that was what would be on his conscience. Why not? She was an ignoramus where men were concerned. What few experiences she had had during her working life had left her with a sour taste in her mouth. Mark Talland had only been one more example of how a 'gentleman' behaved with those inferior to him.

As she had stood before Elizabeth de Villon and listened to his accusations, the blackening of her character—spotless still, despite the past year, of trials and tribulations which had plagued her life since the day her father had been branded a thief—she had had the urge to speak out, to tell him the truth. Tell him that she, Roxanna Dane, whom he was so maliciously maligning, was in reality his sister-in-law, the wife of his brother Ross. Not once, during all those months after her secret had been discovered, did she succumb to the veiled threats, the plausible endearments, of husbands or sons who thought to take advantage of what had befallen her and her father. Her refusal to become 'accommodating' had resulted in the loss of three situations during that time. She had been desperate—for the last of their money had gone and her father had fallen ill again—when the Countess sent for her. It was like a miracle from heaven. She had begun to make such plans . . . Now, once again, she would be forced to leave. It might be months before anyone else engaged her as a companion, during which time she would be forced to take any job open to her, however menial.

'Wind's coming up again,' Rosie remarked, coming to fetch her dinner tray and finding the food hardly touched. She clicked her tongue in a reproving manner, and Roxanna looked across at her from the chair where she sat beside the fire. 'This won't do, you know. Don't worry about him—Master Mark, I mean. Lord Talland has him pegged. He can't keep his hands off any of the servants, and everyone knows it—most of all his brother. Flutter those fascinating eyes at the one who matters, and you'll have no trouble getting him on your side.'

Roxanna inwardly winced at the suggestion. How many times had she been given the same advice by those who had already learned and taken advantage of the little rewards that came their way once they had become more amenable to the demands made on them. Be nice to Lord Talland! Rosie had no idea what she was asking.

'I thought Mark was the one with all the charm?' she said quietly, and the girl giggled as she closed the shutters over the windows.

'But you chose the elder brother. Did he really give you his ring for helping him?' Roxanna nodded. 'Honest? Russell was the only one who believed you . . . and me, of course. All the others thought you must have done a bit of wandering about the house while you had nothing to do. Gave it to you, did he? Well, now . . . Mark won't stand a chance, will he? Seems like the two of you are already quite well acquainted. Lord Talland's known to be quite a gay blade in London—you should hear some of the tales Miss Lisette tells about him—but he's never laid a hand on any of the women in this house. Never even looked twice at any of them.'

'He had no idea who I was,' Roxanna intervened, wishing the girl would stop speculating and go away. Her head was aching abominably at the prospect of the encounter with Ross the following day. 'I think I shall go to bed.'

'Best place for all of us tonight, if you ask me,' Rosie declared, staring back at the shuttered windows. The howl of the wind was growing with each passing minute. 'God help those who are at sea tonight. They'll be out for sure in weather like this.'

'Do you mean there will be another light in the church?' Roxanna asked without warning, and the girl's face blanched. 'Another wreck?'

'Don't ever tell anyone you saw a light, Roxy. It's more than your life is worth!' she replied, backing quickly to the door. 'Not a word, or you'll find yourself down by one of the stakes, watching the tide come in.'

She was gone before Roxanna could ask her what she meant. It was clear that she, too, knew something, but was far too frightened to speak. What stakes did she mean, and what had they to do with the tide? The only stakes or long poles that Roxanna had seen were down on the beach, just below the overhang of the cliff where the house stood.

Too obsessed by other problems more pressing to ponder it further, Roxanna began to undress. Why, oh why, did she not have the courage to run away, which had been the first thought to enter her mind when she learned who the master of Talland really was? She would have to walk or beg a ride into Polperro and find some kind of work to earn enough to get her back to her father in London, but at least she would be out of the house, and away from *him*!

She unwound her long hair from the severe coil in which she always wore it during the day and brushed it loose about her shoulders. 'Like the mane of a wildcat', came Ross's whisper to her ears, so clearly that he could have been standing behind her. Angrily she threw the brush down and buried her face in her hands. She could not leave because she wanted to see him again, even though she knew that what had passed between them at the inn could never be repeated. He was Ross, Lord Talland, Master of Talland, and she was a mere companion. As she had so often reminded herself, men of his breeding did not marry beneath them.

Yet, when he found her beneath his roof, what would he think? That she had somehow discovered his identity and come seeking more payment for the aid she had rendered? The Countess could prove she had been engaged in London, a full week before they had met. But then he might suspect that she had known who he was from the very beginning and agreed to the marriage only because she intended to blackmail him when he came back to Talland. But she had thought he was dead . . .

The thoughts struggled and reeled in her tired mind until they exhausted her. A fierce gust of wind shook the house, for all its thick walls, and she remembered Rosie's words. 'God help those who are at sea tonight. They'll be out for sure in weather like this.' They? Did she mean wreckers? Extinguishing the candles, Roxanna went to the window and pulled back one of the shutters a chink. Bright moonlight flooded the room and then was abruptly curtailed as heavy cloud obscured the moon. The window-pane shook under the fury of the gale. She stepped back, flinching as something struck them, and then realised it was the branch of a tree, bending in some unnatural dance in the garden outside.

Never had she known such storms as had swept the coastline hereabouts since she had arrived. Often her sleep had been disturbed by the lashing of the wind and rain against the windows, the banging of an unshuttered door somewhere outside. Often, in the morning, a broken branch on a tree, a shutter hanging loose on its hinges or driftwood coming ashore on the beach below would indicate the fury of the unsettled night. The hours of daylight were sunny and growing warmer as March came to an end. Soon the flowers in the garden would begin to come alive with a hue of colours to gladden the eye. She learned that the Countess had created the gardens exactly as they had been at her château in Provence. Even the marble statue of Cupid in the midst of one of the rose arbours was an exact copy of the one which had graced an elaborate network of connecting paths and herbaceous borders.

Roxanna strained her eyes as she peered into the darkness. A hand flew to her throat in a gesture of horror. It was there again! Faint . . . but it was there. Another light to guide another ship to its doom on the craggy rocks below the house! She paused for a moment longer, to ascertain that it was not moving, before fetching her cloak and fastening it about her shoulders. She had to find out if what she suspected was in fact true. If the villagers from Talland were waiting on the beach to haul away the cargo of a wrecked ship when it went aground, she would be there to see it. When Ross Talland returned, she would have a few accusations of her own, should he think her a thief and a liar and send her for trial! She was innocent. Was he?

The house was in darkness as she came softly to the

head of the stairs. The Countess was still in her room, and Mark Talland had left the house before it grew dark—Roxanna had seen him from her window, riding away. The servants' rooms were mostly on the far side of the house, so it was not difficult for her to slip silently down the stairs to a side door. She drew back well-oiled bolts and opened it just enough to get through, then closed it firmly behind her. With luck, no one would notice it until much later when Russell, who always made an inspection of the house before retiring, did his rounds. By then she would be back—with the truth. So he had believed her story about the ring. She wondered why—as of all people, he gave her the impression she did not meet with his approval at all.

She was forced to grab at her cloak and hug it tightly about her as the wind whipped at it, threatening to tug it from her back. She pressed herself close against the house to get her bearings, at the same time pulling the hood well over her face and tucking her loose hair inside as best she could. She had gone only a few yards when it was swept back and her hair was blown into her face, almost blinding her.

Minutes later, she started off again, found the path leading across to the church and began gingerly to advance towards the light in the distance. It was a clear path, although very twisting, she remembered from her walks. No reason why she should get lost, even in the darkness. She prayed it would not rain, or she would be soaked to the skin before she had gone half way.

The moon came out of the clouds for a moment, and she sighed with relief to find that she was indeed going in the right direction and was well away from the edge of the cliff. The sound of the sea was deafening in her ears, as it pounded over the beach below and crashed mercilessly against granite rocks in the bay. The moon began to fade again behind cloud, but not before she had glimpsed something else out on that silvery-grey expanse of water besides the white-crested breakers. Had it been a ship or her imagination? It was too dark to see, and the only sound she could hear was that of the sea and the wind. This was truly a place for devils and ghosts, she thought, and for a moment her courage almost failed her. Then, pushed on by the thought that she might discover something which would allow her not to be sent from Talland in disgrace, facing a possible charge of theft, she headed determinedly towards the church.

There was not one light, she saw as she grew nearer, but several, all carefully shrouded. She crouched behind a tombstone, hardly daring to breathe, as a bearded man loomed up out of the darkness ahead of her and went into the church. The lantern was gone, now! Was it not meant to lure a ship to disaster tonight, but to be some kind of a signal, perhaps? Another shape passed so close by that dirt was scattered over the folds of her cloak by the man's boots. He, too, went into the church. The signal for a meeting?

Daringly she sidled closer to the building. Within, she could hear the sound of voices, and froze as a man demanded, 'Where's Rawlings? Damn the man, I said nine o'clock, and I meant it.' 'I'm here, keep your fancy shirt on,' came a sarcastic voice some minutes later. This was followed by guffaws of laughter.

She did not know the owner of the second voice, but the other man . . . She would know those arrogant tones anywhere—they belonged to Mark Talland! Rosie had been mistaken. It was Mark, not his elder brother, who led these scoundrels. She was so relieved that not for a moment did she consider they might be in the whole enterprise together. The wind buffeted her body, making her almost lose her balance as she leaned on tip-toe against the window, trying to peer inside, but all she saw were blurred shapes through the thick, coloured glass. She stole back to her hiding-place behind a serene-faced angel, whose wings gave her ample shelter and effectively hid her from the view of anyone leaving through the front door. She must wait until Mark Talland left and be sure it was him she had heard; not that she doubted her own ears.

No wonder he had been angry to find her wandering about the cliff-top that day. Had she been close, unknowingly, to where the smuggled goods were kept? The ruins would make a perfect hiding-place. A penetrating cold began to steal into her bones. She hugged her arms about her for warmth, feeling less brave as time slipped past. How long should she stay? She did not want to be missed from the house and cause more problems for herself. Neither did she want to leave before she had established the identity once and for all of the man who led the wreckers.

Her hair was torn free of the cowl again. She was vainly trying to push it back out of the wind when the church door opened. Voices came clearly to her ears as men approached, and halted not a few feet from where she crouched, petrified now, not with cold, but terror.

'I'll be back in the morning.' It was Mark Talland's voice. She risked a quick look between the angel's wing and its head and saw him standing before her—so close that she could have reached out and touched him. 'Be sure those kegs are well on their way by then. We're behind with our order to The Ship and The Hole In The Wall. Prentiss isn't a man who takes kindly to late deliveries—he has customers waiting, as we do. See to it, Griffith. We've a shipment coming over in four days. Alert everyone that was too lazy to come tonight, and warn them I'll not tolerate disobedience in the men who work for me. If you think my brother has a temper, you should try mine! God help whoever does.'

'Yes, my lord. I'll see they understand.' Roxanna decided that the man Griffith's voice was decidedly insolent. 'Will you be needing the light to find your way to your horse?'

'Keep your light,' Mark snapped. 'And you'd best tell everyone else to walk home in the dark unless they want the revenue men on us next time. The whole place looked like Halloween when I rode up.'

She heard Griffith chuckle deeply as Mark strode off. He passed her and made off in the direction of the ruins, not without some difficulty in the dark, for she heard him swear as he stumbled and fell against a headstone.

'Yes, milord. No, milord. High and mighty young pup,' the remaining man growled, then raised his voice. 'Come on, lads, let's away to our beds. The kegs can wait until tomorrow. We'll do it in the light of day, and there'll not be a soul to challenge us. Isn't it the day the Master of Talland returns? They'll all be too busy grovelling at his feet to wonder what we are about. He'll soon bring that prize cockerel to his knees. Giving me orders . . .'

'Pays you well, though, don't he?' sneered someone who had come out to join him.

'Not well enough. If it wasn't for the little extra on the side, we'd all be in the poorhouse. Never fit in his brother's shoes, that one. Home, lads . . . but first . . . Grab her, Dick!'

Roxanna screamed as a hand fastened over her arm, dragging her from her hiding-place. The man who had grabbed her was a giant in height and strength, she discovered, and easily held her small wrists coupled in one hairy hand, thrusting the other over her mouth to silence her cries of pain and fear.

'So we have a spy in our midst, have we?' The man facing her she knew to be Griffith. He had the air of a leader about him, she sensed, more so than Mark Talland. All the men, some five in all, were watching him, waiting to see what he would say or do to her for daring to eavesdrop on their conversation. She knew that to try and explain away her presence would be useless. They would not believe her even if she could free her mouth from the cruel grip of the burly giant who held her, oblivious to the pain he was causing her. 'Anyone know her?'

'I know her. She's the new companion for Miss Lisette.' Roxanna sagged weakly in the grasp of her captor. The man who had revealed her identity was none other than Mark Talland's valet!

She made protesting noises behind the hand across

her mouth. Griffith, whose cold eyes made her realise that Rosie had not exaggerated when she said her life would be in danger if she spoke of seeing the light, faced her, hands on thick hips.

'Let's hear what the wench has to say, Dick. Well, out looking for a little excitement, were you?'

Mutely Roxanna shook her head. Her lips were so numb she could not speak directly. 'I—I was running away.' she stammered. His eyes narrowed sharply, in disbelief. 'It's true . . .'

'Don't tell me young Talland's amorous advances have made you skittish,' Griffith growled. 'Your sister likes 'em well enough, don't she, Geoff?' And he looked significantly at the valet.

'And one day he'll pay for laying his filthy hands on her. Wait a minute . . . I heard the old woman talking with him this afternoon—about her.' He nodded towards Roxanna. 'Perhaps what she says is true, after all. There's some uproar over a ring. She was wearing it round her neck, Master Mark says, and it belongs to Lord Talland. Has his personal crest engraved on it. He says she stole it. Wants to take her before the magistrate, he does.'

'So you're a thief as well as an informer, are you?' Griffith murmured.

'I am neither,' Roxanna declared vehemently. 'The ring was given to me by Lord Talland, and he will confirm that when he comes back.'

'And then you will tell him about tonight, won't you? For another little reward. What did you do for the last one, warm his bed?'

'I won't! I swear it! I'll not say a word about any of you,' she cried, as the men exchanged knowing glances. 'I don't know you—any of you.'

'You know me,' the young man broke in, but of all of them, she saw that Geoff was the only one who had any sympathy for her plight. 'Let her go, eh, Griffith? I can watch her. Maybe she was running away . . . You know how vindictive Master Mark can be if he's riled.'

'Why should she run away when she knows full well that Lord Talland can clear her, boy? She was spying—on us. She must have heard everything said back there. What if she's lying? Have you thought of that? If she is a thief and gets taken before a magistrate, what better way of getting off light than telling her little tale about us. She don't know names, but she knows our faces. And she knows you! I'm not risking my neck just because you are squeamish.'

'What—What are you going to do with me?' Roxanna asked in a trembling voice, and Griffith smiled at her. A slow, knowing smile that brought his lips back over his teeth, to remind her of a snarling dog with his back against a wall.

'Women are such unpredictable creatures, don't you agree, lads? This one looks a shy little thing—rather nervous. The strain on her over this stolen ring must have been too much for her. Why else would she go an' drown herself during the night?'

'No!' Roxanna's cry was abruptly silenced as the giant thrust a piece of rag into her mouth and tightly secured it behind her head. She fought him like a tigress, scratching at his face as he reached for her hands, kicking and twisting, but she was caught and held—her hands tied behind her—and she was helpless. Hot tears scalded her cheeks. Her eyes pleaded with each of the men in turn, but they stared back without pity. Only Mark's valet turned away, swallowing hard at the sight of her tear-streaked face.

Griffith stared at him in disgust. His smile widened. 'You, Geoffrey. You can introduce the girl to the tide stakes. The water will be high enough within the hour. Come back at first light and free her and leave her on the beach. When they find her . . .' He gave a laugh which made Roxanna's blood run cold. She was going to die! 'Such a pity that one so young should be driven to such desperate measures. Take her down, Dick and see he ties her well. Leave the gag.'

Roxanna was swung up into the air and over the

shoulder of the man called Dick as if she was a sack of potatoes. The breath was knocked from her body as she came down across a hard, unyielding shoulder. Her hair, falling past her face, blinded her vision. She had no idea in which direction they were heading, only that they were descending at a rapid rate, her captor slithering and sliding over rock and shale and, finally, sand.

Sand! They were on the beach. She fought to keep her senses. Perhaps there would be a chance for her to run? There was not. She was deposited on the ground and pushed back against something hard again which dug uncomfortably into her back. The wind freed the hair from her face and she saw that the sea was not two feet from where she stood. Even as her hands were untied, then retied round the tall stake behind her, a heavy wave crashed on the shore and the water crept higher and higher until it soaked the hem of her cloak.

'I'm sorry, miss.' Geoffrey stepped back from her, his young face betraying the anguish he felt at this moment. 'I didn't know it would come to this. I wouldn't have said anything otherwise . . .'

'Back at first light, remember?' Dick was without compassion as he checked the gag in Roxanna's mouth. 'Carry her further down the beach; don't leave her here. Understood? And make sure there's no marks in the sand afterwards.'

'I hear you. I'm not a fool. It's my neck too.'

'No, but you're soft. That's why you're going back up the cliff ahead of me. Move, boy, the water's coming in fast. She'll be gone within a few hours.'

Roxanna moaned behind her gag, but the feeble sound was whipped away by the wind. Neither man looked back as they climbed the cliff path and disappeared from sight. She was going to die!

She wrestled with her bonds, but they had been tied by an expert. She sagged weakly against the stake. Now she knew what Rosie had meant. This was how the smugglers disposed of informers, of traitors. No one would ever believe she had been murdered. Under a cloud of suspicion, she had taken her own life. Would *he* believe it when he returned to Talland and found that the girl he had married, and used for his own ends, was dead—had committed suicide because she had been accused of theft? The theft of the ring he had given her. Would he care? Why should he? He would be free of her and any unpleasantness she could have caused to him with her presence at the house.

She grew rigid with terror as water soaked her shoes and the hem of her dress. She was near fainting with the cold, let alone anything else.

When she was dead there would be no need for Ross to seek an annulment to the marriage. She thought of the papers she had signed which had immediately transferred all her rights to a man in London, whose name she had never known, so careful had Nicholas been as she signed them. There was also a paper drawn up to the effect that both parties wished the marriage to be annulled forthwith. She had not given it thought before. Why should that be necessary when Ross was dying? Nicholas had known that was not so. Had her husband also known? Used her while he spoke sweet words in her ear? Words no other man had ever used with her . . . had made her feel a woman? He had, she concluded. He had deliberately deceived her. And, knowing he was not about to die, it would have been necessary to have her permission for an annulment. Then why the marriage in the first place? She was too cold, too frightened, to unravel the mystery.

The magic was gone from those hours spent with him. He had played a game with her. A game a gentleman would no doubt find amusing with a girl of her lowly station. She could not believe she had allowed herself to be used by an unscrupulous man who had given no thought to the pain and anxiety he had caused her—or would cause in the future. A few kisses, a few searching caresses, and he thought she had been paid an additional bonus to the money.

She must have lost consciousness for a while—she had

no idea how long, but when she became aware again of the howl of the wind and the roaring of the sea, she found the water was lapping about her legs and rising at an alarming rate. She fought against the bonds which held her, until the pain in her wrists caused by the chafing ropes forced her to be still again. She could not free herself, or cry for help. And who would hear her if she could, on such a wild night? The moon came out from behind cloud, and she watched it dance across the water in front of her, feeling as if part of her was detaching itself from the pain and fear. She no longer felt the cold which had numbed her mind and body, or the water creeping slowly up around her thighs. She closed her eyes, drifting away from the prospect of death . . . remembering things from her childhood that she had not recalled in years . . .

Was she dreaming? Someone was unfastening the ropes about her wrists!

'We're in time! She still has her wits about her, God knows how.'

That voice—it could not be! It was a hallucination, because she wanted to see him again. A dark shape loomed beside her, and tilted back her chin to stare down into her ashen cheeks. She could not clearly see the features, but she would never forget the voice. He—He had brought her to this, she suddenly reasoned, and as strong arms went round her, she tried to pummel at this chest with small, hard fists.

'Stop it, you little fool! You're safe now. Be still, for the love of heaven! I'm still as weak as a kitten and I can't hold you.' There came a fierce oath as she ignored him. 'Take her, Nicholas, before this damned side opens up again. I'll personally deal with Griffith in the morning.'

Him too! As she was seized from behind with no more gentleness than she had been treated with at the hands of the smugglers, Roxanna gave a cry and folded in the arms that held her, her senses leaving her at last.

CHAPTER
FOUR

SHE RECOVERED to find herself lying on the bed in her own room. The fire crackled and leapt in the hearth. Some-one had recently piled on more logs to make it blaze. Instinctively her hands went to her wet clothes and found that someone had removed them. She was wear-ing only a woollen dressing-gown. Rosie, of course, she thought, tentatively sitting up. By morning the whole household would know what had happened to her. Slowly her wits began to function again.

It could not have been him, she reasoned . . . not Lord Talland. Why should he have been on the beach when he was not due home until tomorrow? She swung her legs over the edge of the bed, but they began to shake as she stood up, so she quickly sat down again. She was safe! It was a miracle, but she was safe! Tears stung her eyes, coursed down over her pale cheeks. As relief flooded over her she gave way to them, rocking silently backwards and forwards, hugging her arms about her cold body.

'Reaction. It will pass when you have had something to warm you,' a voice remarked to her left. Her head jerked up, her eyes flying to the door, but it was still closed. Ross, Lord Talland stood a few feet away from the bed, a decanter in one hand. Before her disbelieving gaze, a panel in the wall behind him returned noiselessly into place. 'Have you a glass? No, don't get up, I see one,' he added, offering no explanation for his mode of arrival.

He fetched the water-glass from the washstand and poured a large measure into it from the decanter.

'Brandy. Compliments of Napoleon.' He gave a humourless smile as he held it out to her. 'Drink it, Roxanna Dane. You have some questions to answer for me.'

'The war must have curbed your activities somewhat.' She could not resist the taunt as she took it and sipped the brandy. She had never had brandy before, and found it not unpleasant. Ross's eyebrows arched sardonically as she finished the rest of it. Almost immediately she found a fire in her body, sweeping away the numbness and the cold which plagued her feet and toes.

He poured a drink for himself and tossed it back in one swallow.

'On the contrary, I find it has greatly enlarged them,' he returned coolly. He wore a dry pair of breeches. Her eyes widened slightly as she noticed that his feet were bare. He had changed his shirt, too. Hurriedly, it seemed, for it was open to the waist, revealing a chest dark with hair and a heavy swathing of bandages!

Roxanna quickly averted her gaze, lifting her eyes to his face. It was grim, unsmiling, as he regarded her, the thick, crisp hair still damp from the night air. At the nape of his neck tiny curls were pressed tight against his skin. She remembered how she had run her hands through them . . .

'You should not be here,' she said in a small voice. 'Someone may come. Rosie . . .'

'No one except Russell knows I am home. And Nicholas, of course, and he has gone back to the village. We shall not be disturbed.'

'Then who . . .?' Her voice trailed limply off into an embarrassed silence as she came to understand it was he who had removed her wet clothing. 'I—I suppose I should thank you for saving my life.'

'Do you not consider it worth saving? After all the trouble you have gone to setting up this little charade, I should have thought it very valuable to you,' Lord Talland said bleakly, helping himself to another brandy. 'You are shivering. Go and warm yourself by the fire and dry that hair, or you will go down with the ague.'

'Your concern is touching, sir.' She rose stiffly to her feet, stung to retaliate by his harshness. 'But is it not a little out of character? You were not so concerned for my welfare the last time we met. I was a useful tool in your hands and you saw fit to take advantage of that.'

She swayed unsteadily, put out a hand to catch at the bedpost, and encountered his outflung arm. His fingers closed round hers and, as before, his very touch seemed to burn her skin. He appeared to notice nothing amiss, however, as he led her to a chair before the fire, fetched a towel and proceeded to dry her wet tresses.

'You must not,' Roxanna protested in horror. What was he about? 'Please give me the towel. What are you doing?'

'Did you not expect me to play the considerate husband, my little cat? Isn't that why you are here—to line your pockets with my gold? Someone should have warned you that I am not an easy mark.'

'I don't know what you mean!' she gasped. She would have sprung from the chair to face him, but his hands descended on her shoulders to hold her fast.

'Are you going to tell me you did not know who I was at the inn? Why else did you agree to marry me? Why are you here? Have you told anyone what happened between us? If you have, by God, I might just take you back down to the beach and tie you to a tide stake myself,' came the chilling threat, and she gave up struggling against his hold. He sounded so angry. Why was he angry? It was she who had been used and deceived!

He flung the towel into her lap and came to stand in front of her. The firelight flickered over the sun-bronzed features, now as black as the devil's countenance itself. Her chin jutted stubbornly. She would not allow his high and mighty manner to browbeat her. If anyone was owed an explanation, it was she.

'I married you because I needed the money,' she said in a quiet, clear voice, and saw him flinch visibly. She would not give him the satisfaction of knowing the truth

. . . that she had looked on him and her heart had gone out to him in his need. That what she had done had been done out of kindness and pity, not greed! 'My father is ill in London, and I thought to use it to pay for a good doctor.'

'Nicholas told me you knocked it out of his hand. Hardly the act of a girl desperate for money? You've got your sights set on something higher than fifty pounds, haven't you, my girl?'

He did not believe her! Her lips tightened.

'He also said you were dead. He—He insulted me. He had no cause to do that. I had asked for no payment for my help . . . That was his idea. And yours, no doubt, sir. You both thought to have some sport with me.'

'I do not consider wedding myself to a perfect stranger to be sport,' Ross snapped, but she saw his eyes were puzzled. 'Either you are an innocent, Roxanna Dane, or those eyes are beginning to bewitch me, for I am inclined to believe you. Answer me this, then. You left the money behind, but you did not go back to London. So what was your destination? Why did you come here instead?'

'But I was coming here from the beginning,' Roxanna cried, gripping the towel in her lap so tightly that her knuckles grew quite white. 'I was engaged in London by the Countess to be companion to Miss de Villon. I want nothing from you. I shall leave first thing in the morning.'

'Why?' he countered, with a searching look.

'Why?' she echoed hollowly. 'Because you have come home. Because you are not dead. Because of what happened that day.'

'What happened that day concerns no one but you and me,' Ross said, frowning slightly. He watched her pass a shaky hand over her eyes. When she raised her head again, she found he had half-filled the glass with brandy and was holding it out to her. 'Drink it. You have had an unpleasant night, and much as I would like to let you go to bed and sleep, we have much to talk about yet.'

She obeyed him in silence. He drew up another chair and sat waiting until she had finished.

'Now,' he said, as she put aside the glass. 'Russell tells me there was a shipwreck last week. That you saw a light up in the church. Was there one there again tonight? Is that why you so foolishly went exploring at the dead of night?'

'Do you not know, sir?' Roxanna decided it must be the effects of the brandy which made her speak to him so boldly. 'Is the "devil of Talland" not the leader of those—those murderers, along with his brother?'

For a moment she thought he would strike her. His hands curled into tight fists. She saw the dark hairs grow taut against the back of the skin. In the narrowed eyes which glared at her was a blackness so terrifying that she drew back in her chair.

'Be glad you are not a man, or I would face you across a blade in the morning for such an accusation,' he said cuttingly, and in that moment she knew he had nothing to do with the wreckers. He was innocent of that, at least.

'You forget I was there—that I saw them,' she answered bravely. 'I saw your brother with them, giving them orders.'

'Mark? With a man named Griffith?' He looked startled as she nodded, shocked. A fierce expletive exploded under his breath. 'The young fool. Will he never listen? Who gave the order for your death? God in heaven, not Mark?'

'No, he had gone before they discovered me hiding in the graveyard. It was Griffith. Your brother's valet recognised me . . . I think he was the only one who didn't want me to die.'

'Don't spare him another thought. I'll deal with them both personally. So you think I am the leader of a band of wreckers, do you?' He looked her full in the face, and the intent gaze of those dark eyes sent a strange thrill through Roxanna. Black, bottomless depths that threatened to drag her down into them if she dared to look into them, yet she could not take her own eyes from them. She felt her breath quicken. It was as if he had cast a spell on her. Nothing was clear in her mind any more . . .

'Yes . . .' She had to fight him. A gleam sprang to his eyes at her answer. Anger? Amusement? She knew not which. 'No, I'm not sure. I only know you lied to me . . .'

'When? Tell me.'

'At the inn.' Why did he not go away and leave her in peace? She would leave in the morning and he would never see her again. 'You pretended you needed me. Why . . . Why did you make me marry you?'

'Because I had to ensure that Mark did not inherit on my death. Whether you believe it or not, I was in God's hands for a good many hours.' A faint smile softened the harsh line of his mouth for a moment. The mouth that had plied hers with such persuasive kisses. Roxanna dragged her gaze away, and concentrated on her hands locked in her lap. 'I did need help and you gave it to me. Then, I had only money to offer in payment. Now, there is more, and I intend to see that my debt is paid in full. You left before I could do so, thanks to Nicholas.'

What did he mean by that? She wondered, stifling a yawn. A combination of the brandy and the roaring fire was making her exceedingly sleepy. Nothing seemed important any more. She had so many questions, but they would never be asked now.

He leaned towards her, and took her hands in his. Roxanna watched his fingers rove over the red marks still visible on her wrists from her attempts to free herself from the ropes binding her to the stake. His mouth tightened once more.

'Lisette has some salve for these. I will have it brought to you in the morning.'

'But—But I am leaving,' she protested drowsily.

'If you attempt to leave this house, Roxanna Dane, I shall have you brought back. You and I are not meant to part company yet. What is this nonsense about my ring?

Russell tells me Mark has accused you of stealing it. What answer did you give him in your defence?'

'What could I say? I have no defence. I told him and the Countess the truth, that I had helped a man who was hurt at an inn, and in gratitude he had given it to me. Neither believed me. Not after what happened before . . .'

'The stolen necklace in London. Yes, I know about that. Russell is my eyes and ears when I am away, as well as when I am here. He overheard Elizabeth and my brother talking. You gave Mark good ammunition to use against you. I wonder how he will feel after I get through with him? This side will slow me down, but he's going to pay for what he has put you through with his lies. What prompted it? I suppose he tried to seduce you?'

'He—He was drunk. He did try to kiss me,' Roxanna admitted, blushing furiously. The Countess had brushed aside her own condemnation of Mark's actions as if she was not only aware, but very tired, of these repetitious occasions. Roxanna wondered what she would say to see the companion now, sitting before the fire in her room, her hands being held by the Master of Talland himself—and both of them in a state of *déshabillé*.

'For once his taste was excellent, but he will have to accept that you are not available. You need not worry about his preposterous charge. Tomorrow I shall deal with it. I shall corroborate your story, and we shall leave it at that—for now. Do you agree?'

'Why—Why do you want me to stay? I am—an embarrassment to you,' Roxanna stammered, suddenly aware that his fingers had been stroking the backs of her hands for some considerable time. It was a most pleasant feeling, but she quickly jerked them free and he straightened with a questioning look.

'You were engaged as Lisette's companion. Believe me, she is in need of one. A level-headed young woman, such as you seem to be, will do wonders for her. She is due home tomorrow, I believe. You will like her, I am sure.'

'If you insist,' she said in a small voice, hardly able to hide her joy. To stay and be close to him.

'No more talk of running away?'

'No, sir.'

'Good girl. One more thing before I leave you. Say nothing of tonight to anyone. Only Russell is aware you have been out. Thank God I came back earlier than expected! If there was to be another wreck, I wanted to catch Griffith on the beach. Instead, I find a half-drowned wildcat.' He gave a soft chuckle and touched the hair flowing past her shoulders, almost dry now with the warmth from the fire. 'I am many things, Roxanna . . . many things, but I am not and never have been a wrecker. A few illegal shipments now and then . . . more than a few . . .' He laughed again, but there was no humour in the sound. It was as if he was trying to put her at her ease, but without allowing his own guard to drop. She could feel that he was tense inside, with anger, perhaps, for his brother—or with anxiety that she might reveal their secret? 'There is much you do not know about me. One day, I shall unburden my heart to you, but not tonight. You are nearly asleep, and I shall not place your life in danger again. It would be, if you knew the secrets I carry with me . . .' He broke off abruptly, and once more the eyes were narrowed and searching.

'Will you give me your solemn word not to speak to anyone of tonight? Nor of what took place between us at the inn? I have good reason for asking this of you.'

'Of course,' Roxanna replied dully. 'You would not want it known that you were wed, even for a few short days, to a girl like me. You have my word. I shall keep it.'

'For your sake, I hope so. You would not like me when I am angry.' Before she could guess his intentions, he had swept her up into his arms and turned towards the bed. For a brief moment before he laid her down, her cheek rested against his bare skin. He drew the bed-covers about her, smoothed the hair back from her face. 'Tomorrow all this will seem like a dream—a nightmare which will vanish as light appears. Go to sleep, little cat. No one will harm you now. The devil looks after his own,' he added mockingly, as her lids began to droop.

She forced them to open as the panel swung ajar. Tomorrow she would find out which one it was, and place a heavy piece of furniture against it. She could not have him coming and going from her room at will—it was unthinkable! His voice seemed to come from a long way off as she relaxed her aching limbs, but it was not for some while that the meaning behind them sank into her, to bring her sitting up in bed, her cheeks scarlet with confusion.

'I meant what I said, Roxanna Dane. My debt to you will be paid in full. There is to be no annulment of our marriage. You are my wife, and it is my intention to keep the *status quo*.'

Roxanna had just finished breakfast when Russell came to tell her the Countess required her presence in the library. She rose apprehensively to her feet, aware of Rosie's gaze intent on her pale face.

'Don't look so worried. He's back, isn't he? To tell the truth for you?' she muttered, as Roxanna smoothed down the skirt of her pale grey dress and arranged a stray lock of hair behind her ear. She must show a calm countenance, she had decided, allow nothing to ruffle her. Yet to stand before Ross Talland and remember what he had said to her . . . How could she stay calm? He intended her to remain his wife . . . to become his wife in every sense of the word. It was preposterous! Unbelievable! He could have his pick of any London lady he chose, so why would he want her, plain Roxanna Dane, a nobody? Grateful he might be, and she had now come to believe he sincerely was glad of her help that day, but gratitude did not stretch that far. He had no reason to commit himself to the extreme, like this. She had been prepared to leave . . . Why did he not allow her to do so?

How could she face him? And meet the intense scrutiny of those devil's eyes and think of those strong arms enfolding her, his lips taking command of hers, as they had done once before? His knowledgeable hands would rove over her body, exciting her, promising untold delights which lured her to the very brink of disaster. She could not—would not—accept his terms! He must let her go. It was the only sane, reasonable thing to do.

'I think she's been struck dumb,' Rosie giggled and Russell glared at her.

'Get back to the kitchen, girl! There is still work to be done.' As she slipped past him, still grinning, he turned to Roxanna and took a small jar from his pocket. 'I believe this may be of some use to you, Miss Dane. Lord Talland had me fetch it from Miss Lisette's room. It has special healing qualities, I believe.'

The salve for her wrists! Roxanna thanked him and placed it out of sight in a drawer until later. Ross had hinted he had very little hidden from his personal servant, and this seemed to bear it out. She looked at the man, so stiff and formal in her presence, as he was always with everyone she realised, and a faint smile touched her lips.

'I would like to thank you for your faith in me, Russell.'

'Miss Dane?' He gave a look which she should have taken to be ignorance, but she knew better. She suspected he was totally in his master's confidence.

'I believe you were the only one who did not think I stole the ring. But then you are Lord Talland's confidante . . . You know the truth, do you not?'

'I know only what I am told, Miss Dane. You are keeping the Countess waiting, you know. And His Lordship. Don't you think it better to get this whole unfortunate incident over with as quickly as possible? It cannot have been pleasant for you.'

'No,' she admitted, 'it was not. You are right. The sooner I face them, the sooner I shall know if I have a future or not.'

'I doubt if you have that to worry about, Miss Dane,'

came Russell's quiet answer behind her. She wished she could have been so sure.

Ross had been right about one thing. In the light of day, the nightmare of last night had receded to the back of her mind. But reality was still with her and could not be put aside as easily. She had yet to face him and the Countess—and Mark Talland. How would he handle his brother? He wished the liaison between them to be kept secret, so what tale would he invent to satisfy him?

Her steps faltered as she reached the door of the library. Russell gave her no time for second thoughts. Swinging open the door, he ushered her in and closed it behind her. Elizabeth de Villon looked up from across the room, and beckoned to the slight figure hesitating on the threshold.

'Come in, Miss Dane, and sit down.'

Roxanna was aware of Mark watching her from the sofa where he sprawled, one booted leg over the other. His expression was contemptuous as she sat on the edge of a chair, betraying the nervousness raging inside her.

'Look at her,' he snapped. 'Her very countenance betrays her guilt! Why are we wasting our time here? I say we take her before a magistrate and have her charged with theft. After all, it is not the first time.'

'In Talland, I am master. I say what will or will not be done.' A tall figure turned away from the windows and came into view. Roxanna felt herself instinctively grow rigid. She had not noticed him when she came in.

How different he looked this morning. His clothes were the latest London fashion: a cutaway coat in plain black cloth, sage green knee-breeches and a white waist-coat. On his feet, black leather shoes. Last night they had been bare . . . like a peasant's! Quickly Roxanna averted her gaze, knowing she must not dwell on those hours they had spent together. Whatever his reasons for wanting her as his wife, she knew affection did not come into it and therefore she must not allow her own feelings to become confused . . . more confused than they already were where this man was concerned.

Slowly she lifted her eyes to the face of Ross, Lord Talland. He was not even looking at her, but at his brother, and the fierce gleam in those eyes made her fear the temper she herself had never seen. There was an arrogance about him which seemed somehow out of character with the man she knew. But then, she told herself, she did not really know him.

'Before everyone begins to lose their tempers,' the Countess began, and Ross wheeled on her with a disarming smile.

'Don't take our harsh words to heart, Elizabeth. You know how Mark and I cannot bear to be in the same room together, let alone settle an argument amicably. He is a fool, and a mean one when he is crossed. The girl repulsed him, and he is seeking to have his revenge on her. My brother is not accustomed to having a pretty girl reject his advances.'

Roxanna drew a sharp breath as Mark stiffened in anger. If this was the way the conversation had proceeded at the inn, no wonder he had been provoked into the foolish act of trying to shoot his brother. It was as if Ross had no regard for him at all . . . That conversation between them was a trial to him and, if possible, he would bait him with more skilful rhetoric and so provoke him. What had taken place between them to bring about such enmity?

'Miss Dane has told us you gave her the ring she carried, Ross. Is this true?' The Countess was obviously accustomed to these exchanges, for she ignored his words. 'It bore your crest. Your personal crest.'

'The galleon? Of course I gave it to her. She is no thief. We met at an inn the other side of Liskeard. The weather was atrocious, and I should not have been riding in it, but I was in a hurry to get back . . . The matter of Lisette, you understand? That brute of a horse of mine threw me right in front of the coach. I was lucky not to have been killed.'

'How many times have I warned you that it will happen one day if you do not get rid of it!' Elizabeth said in an exasperated tone. 'This is the fourth time.'

'My own fault entirely. I rode him like a fool. I was in a foul temper,' Ross continued with a rueful smile. Not once had he looked at Roxanna. Mark, however, was watching her like a hawk. If she so much as batted an eyelid at the wrong time, he would see it. He was just waiting for some sign that this whole story had been concocted between them. Thrown by a horse? He had been shot by his own brother! She did not know how one could lie so blatantly, and the other sit a few feet away, looking at her as if she were somehow the cause of all the trouble. 'Anyway, I was taken into the inn, luckily close by, and Miss Dane happened to care for me until the doctor arrived. I was out of my head for a while, I believe. She was a veritable little saint . . . She stayed with me all night long, and then was simply going to leave. We didn't even have an opportunity to exchange names. I remember taking off the ring and pressing it into her hand before I lost consciousness. It was a small thing . . . I am glad I now have the opportunity to thank her for the concern she showed that day. I was in no condition to appreciate it, unfortunately. Only afterwards, when the fever abated, did I remember her at all.'

He came across the room and stood before Roxanna's chair. Not one flicker of recognition was in those eyes as he bent and took her hand and touched it to his lips. Nothing to betray those intimate moments they had shared the night before. Nothing to betray the fact that she was his wife!

'Miss Dane, you have been treated most unfairly. Allow me to apologise for my brother's boorish behaviour. I am sure, as a gentleman, he will do so later himself. This is yours, I believe.' He held out the crested gold ring to her.

Roxanna swallowed hard and shook her head. 'I—I cannot take it, sir. Not now. No payment was necessary for what little I did for you.' Now I am a liar too, her eyes cried as they met his. His hand took hers and pressed the ring into her palm.

'Take it—in the spirit it was given—and let us say no more about this affair.' He was not about to let her refuse him!

'If you insist.'

'I do, Miss Dane, I do.' And, at Talland, I am master, the look he gave her said. My orders will be obeyed. And for all the politeness of tone, it was an order, not a request.

From the direction of the sofa came a snort of disgust as Mark leapt to his feet and headed towards the door.

'I think you owe Miss Dane an apology.' Ross's cold tones halted him, one hand on the handle. 'You have maligned an innocent girl, Mark. Does that not concern you? Would you have done so had she not known me?' As he asked the last question, Roxanna watched his features grow taut with anger as he stared at his brother's back, and saw the stiffening of Mark's shoulders, the defiance in his expression as he swung round to face them all.

As he opened his mouth to speak, the door was abruptly flung open. A pink-cheeked, breathless girl with flaming red hair descended on the room. She flung her arms about Mark's neck and kissed him soundly.

Then Elizabeth rose from her chair in horror, and said sternly, 'Lisette, behave yourself, young woman, or I shall send you to your room this instant. You were not expected until late this evening.'

The girl turned and effected a most elaborate curtsy to her grandmother before running to Ross's side and kissing him warmly on the cheek.

'I am so glad you are back. Grand-mère has been horrid to me! She sent me away so that I could not be with Mark. I hope you will be angry with her. Where have you been? I have so many questions I want to ask you.'

'Enough, you little baggage,' Ross thundered, but there was a smile on his face as he did so. Her unexpected arrival had greatly reduced the tension in the air,

Roxanna thought, sinking back in her chair in relief.

She stole a look at the man standing in the open doorway, who was staring at the newcomer with such a tender expression in his eyes that she could hardly believe this was the same malicious person who had so falsely accused her of theft. Anyone could see he was enamoured of Lisette de Villon. Why was his brother so against the match?

'You were sent away—as you put it—on my instructions. After your unseemly conduct in London, I decided you should remain out of everyone's way for a while. I have enough trouble on my hands just now without you adding to it with your scatterbrained ideas of being in love.'

Lisette stepped back from him with a tiny gasp and moved closer to her grandmother. From the doorway Mark gave a hollow laugh.

'Doesn't he put things so charmingly?' he drawled. 'But then I suppose it is difficult, for someone who has never known love, to understand the feelings of others who are fortunate enough to enjoy it. You have to have a heart to be able to love, so that excludes you, does it not, brother?'

Ross's eyes narrowed to dangerous glittering slits as he stared across the room. For an instant Roxanna felt his gaze alight on her, but she dared not look back. Whatever it was he felt for her, it was not love. From what she had heard of the Master of Talland, she was beginning to wonder if he was not what everyone said he was . . . a devil . . . a devil without a heart. Only someone totally without a conscience, without regard for another human being, would force her into accepting his outrageous terms. And force was what he would use, she was sure, if she did not agree.

Yet last night she had sensed a strange kind of loneliness about him—a need to sit and talk with her. Need? He needed no one!

Mark's eyes fastened on Roxanna and his lip curled. 'They are well matched. A devil and a liar. He's trained

her well from the beginning. Shall I tell you what
happened at the inn that day? There was no riding
accident . . . I did it.'

'Have you no pride, man? Hold your tongue!' Ross
demanded. His words were ignored. Both Lisette and
the Countess were staring at Mark as if he had taken
leave of his senses.

'I shot him.' There was a satisfied note in his tone that
made Roxanna inwardly wince, at such hatred between
brothers. Even Ross had grown quite pale. One hand
had gone, perhaps unconsciously, to his side where the
pistol-ball had entered. She had an urge to run to him
and put her arms about him. How foolish she was
becoming about this man! 'I told you I would pay him
back for parting us, Lisette, and I did. I meant to kill
him. I wish I had.'

'Mark . . . No!' the Countess cried. Lisette turned and
buried her face against her grandmother's shoulder,
unable to stand the wild stare in the eyes of the man she
loved. He was like a stranger.

'So now you turn away from me! You would not do so
if I was master here; if I had the money and the title.'

'You have said enough,' Ross thundered, and this
time his voice halted Mark's wild tirade.

For a moment he looked quite startled, as if he had not
been aware of what he was saying. Then a slow flush
crept up over his neck and cheeks, and he ran a hand
through his tousled brown hair with a shaky laugh.
'Well, now you know how I feel. I'm glad it's out in the
open.'

'You and I have to settle this.' There was a flicker of
pain in the depths of Ross's eyes as he spoke. Was she
the only one to notice it, Roxanna wondered?

'I'll be up at the ruins if you think you can take
me—with that wound! You may have all the women in
this house under your thumb, Ross, but you'll never get
me there.' The answer was defiant and challenging. He
was no coward, Roxanna knew by the tone of voice, yet
he had shot his own brother. It did not make sense!

'I have always wanted you at my side,' came the quiet answer. 'It was you who chose otherwise. I shall be there, wait for me.'

For a long moment brother measured brother, then Mark gave a strangled oath and slammed out of the room. For a while no one spoke.

Elizabeth sank into her chair, a hand against her throat. 'Will someone please pour me a glass of wine? I feel quite faint.'

Ross turned away to the sideboard and poured dark red claret into a crystal glass and gave it to her. Of all of them, only he remained completely in control of himself.

'He surely did not mean what he said? He did not shoot you?' Lisette whispered, and when he nodded, she covered her face with her hands. 'It is my fault. I was so cross when you parted us. I love him so much, and he loves me, Ross. He does, he does! It is unfair . . . You care nothing for him.' She fell back into French, which Roxanna thought sounded much more natural for her, although her English was perfection itself. The Countess tried several times to interrupt her, but she was ignored. Roxanna saw that Ross was beginning to have difficulty in retaining his temper.

His eyes flashed, his mouth tightened, and then he answered the girl in her own language, as faultless as her English, even though it was not his tongue.

As he did so, Roxanna found herself remembering the Countess's words to her not long after she had arrived at Talland, '*It would be pleasant to converse with someone in my own tongue. Lord Talland is fluent in it, but of course he would be.*' Why should he be? Was this another mystery to which she would never know the answer?

Lisette burst into tears, knocked away his outstretched hand, and ran out of the room. Ross gave a sigh as he poured himself some claret. For several minutes he stood staring moodily out of the windows.

'Ross . . . Ross, what are we going to do with that

child? We cannot watch her every moment of the day,'
Elizabeth said anxiously.

'I'm afraid we must. Mark is not my prime concern
just now, as you must realise. There are others who
would like to get their hands on Lisette. With Miss
Dane's help, we shall keep her safe, Elizabeth. I promise
I will allow no one to come within a mile of her.'

'Dear Ross, what would I do without you?' The
Countess extended a jewelled hand, and he came to her
side and kissed the wrinkled fingers. As he raised
his head, he found Roxanna's eyes on him. She was
beginning to wonder if she had been forgotten.

'Please do not question me now, Elizabeth, but accept
what I tell you,' he said quietly. 'Roxanna Dane is
utterly trustworthy. I know. Do not be afraid to speak in
front of her, or to give way to a few of your fears. Who
knows, one of her tender years may well have the answer
to love's young dream gone wrong.'

Tender years! Roxanna felt the colour surge into her
cheeks. He was laughing at her immaturity as he had
done at the inn. Was he reminding her of that moment
when he had kissed her? Her first real kiss. How she
wished she had never admitted the fact to him.

'I am nineteen, sir. As I have never been in love, I
regret I am unable to be of any assistance in this matter.
It looks a good match from where I am standing,' she
added boldly.

'Does it, now?' Only the glint in those dark eyes
betrayed his annoyance at her answer. 'When you
know my brother better, you will not think him such a
charming young man. He is a fool, and a reckless one
at that.'

'And you, sir, seem to me to be exceedingly stern with
him. Were you not once his age yourself? Were you not
a little reckless? Are you not now?' She heard
the Countess give a little gasp at her audacity. Instead of
anger at her presumption, Ross burst into laughter,
which ended in a groan as he clapped a hand against his
side in pain.

'Roxanna Dane, you know me too well already! We shall take up this conversation at a later date . . . When I have settled things with my brother.'

'You cannot mean to fight him,' Elizabeth gasped. 'You are hurt, and he *is* your brother, no matter what he has done.'

'You do not know the half of it, my dear,' Ross replied with a dry smile. 'This fight will be not only about Lisette . . . He has other things to answer for.'

'You go to the ruins?' Roxanna asked, suddenly remembering the conversation from the night before between Mark and Griffith. 'But . . .'

'I do.' He eyed her searchingly. 'What do I not know?'

'The man Griffith was told to unload the kegs and dispose of them last night, but after—after your brother had gone, he sent the men home, telling them it would be done this morning. They will be there now . . .'

'Griffith on the end of my blade,' Ross murmured. 'I could not have planned it better. My thanks for the warning.'

'And you still mean to go?' the Countess asked in astonishment. 'I know these men work for you at times, Ross, and that their—and your—activities are not always, shall we say, inside the law . . . And I know why you risk so much. But to involve yourself with Bob Griffith! Everyone knows, not that they have the courage to say it openly, but they know he has a most deplorable sideline.'

'Wrecking.' Ross nodded grimly. 'I know. I've been trying to catch him red-handed for the past six months, ever since he came back to this area. But when things began to happen to take me away from here . . .'. He shrugged broad shoulders. 'You know my villagers, they are not murderers like he is. I am the only one who can deal with him, and I shall. If I do not see you before, I shall join you for dinner. And tell Lisette I expect to see her at the table too, acting like a lady instead of a spoilt child. Perhaps you can acquaint her with the difference,' he said to Roxanna, and she nodded mutely, trying to keep her thoughts away from a picture of him facing Mark—and Griffith. Perhaps the two of them against him—and him wounded. Had he no fear?

'As reckless as my brother, perhaps, despite my many years,' he murmured softly. 'Don't look so worried, Miss Dane. The worst that can happen is that Talland has a new master.' And you, his eyes said mockingly. 'Or I may end up in need of your nursing skill again. From what I remember, that will not plague my life unduly. In fact I think I would find it quite a novel experience.'

Neither of the two women left in the room spoke for some considerable time after he had left them. They heard him call for his horse to be saddled, and not long afterwards he cantered past the windows astride an enormous black stallion, which took the jump over the wall at the end of the side gardens without pausing in its magnificent stride.

With a heavy sigh, the Countess rose to her feet and stared at the girl whose eyes were still transfixed on the fading pair. 'I think we should go upstairs and deal with Lisette and her tantrum, do you not agree, Miss Dane?' She suddenly sounded very tired.

'Yes, madame.' Roxanna was glad she was not to be inundated with questions, which was what she had expected as soon as they were alone. Obviously Ross's declaration as to her trustworthiness was enough—for the moment at least.

'Would you prefer me to go to her alone?' she asked, seeing the Countess sway slightly. 'You do not look at all well. You are upset.'

'Two brothers. Two fine young men determined to kill each other. It grieves me to hear them tearing each other apart. Why can they not live together in harmony? Yes, my dear, I think I would prefer to stay here. Lisette is your responsibility, after all, now. Go to her and do not allow her to deceive you with her tears. She uses them as a weapon. Only Ross is immune to them. I wonder if any woman will ever touch that one's heart.'

'So he does have one?' Roxanna thought she had gone too far, as the woman looked at her sharply.

'Oh, yes, he has one. Would you could know him as he really is . . . Go to my granddaughter, Miss Dane. I shall see you at dinner.'

CHAPTER
FIVE

'Go away! I will see no one,' a quivering voice cried out in response to Roxanna's knock on the door of Lisette's room.

'It is Roxanna Dane. I am your new companion. Please open the door.'

The only answer back was a loud thud against the wooden panels as something solid hit them. She knocked again. No answer. Taking a deep breath she opened the door and went in.

Lisette sprang up from the bed. Her face was puffy and red, her cheeks wet and almost the colour of her hair. Her fingers reached for the glass ornament on the table beside her, as Roxanna closed the door and came nearer.

'If you don't go away, I shall throw this at you,' she threatened.

'And I shall throw it back,' came the quiet reply.

'Then I shall break everything in sight until you leave.' Lisette's bright blue eyes sparked rebellion. The glass was flung from her with all her might and shattered against the far wall.

'Go ahead. My father always used to say it is best to get anger out of your system.' Roxanna sat down on a blue velvet button-backed chair, determined not to allow herself to be provoked by this headstrong young girl.

'Your father is a fool. My grandmother will hear of this. How dare you give yourself such airs! I shall have you dismissed.'

Roxanna smiled slightly, wondering what Lord

Talland would say to that? If she believed him, she was to be a permanent resident at Talland.

'I do not think that will happen, and I am here because your grandmother sent me. The unpleasantness of what happened downstairs has upset her.'

'Not her. She's as hard as—as the granite stone which built the house. As for Ross, I hate him. *Cochon!* I shall never speak to him again. He will kill Mark, I know it. I think he wants to marry me himself . . . that's why he is keeping us apart,' Lisette declared, seizing another ornament, this time a beautifully carved little horse. It received the same treatment as the last object, and lay shattered on the pale blue carpet. Roxanna stared at it in dismay, but said nothing. Long ago she had learned the wisdom of patience.

'Are you dumb? I don't think I like you, Roxanna Dane. Roxanna—I think that's a silly name,' Lisette sneered.

'It is a Persian name. It means "dawn". My father gave it to me because that was the time I was born. Far from being a fool, he is a very clever man. A scholar.' Her temper flared at the insult, but she did not retaliate.

'My father never comes to see me.' Another piece of glass smashed against the wall, and another. If she went on like this, there would be only the furniture soon, Roxanna thought, sitting quite still and showing no sign of agitation. She noticed that Lisette's tears had stopped, and that once or twice she had looked across at the new companion in obvious puzzlement. 'Oh, I wish I could go home. I do not belong here.'

'Do you not think of Talland as home?' Roxanna asked in surprise. 'Surely you have been here some considerable time—since the Reign of Terror, isn't it?'

'Grand-mère wanted to stay, and so did I. I wanted to be with my mother, but they took her away one day and I never saw her again. Ross told me a long while afterwards that they had—had guillotined her. She was so beautiful. I have her hair and her figure . . .' Lisette was near to tears again.

'And her temper?' Roxanna ventured to ask, and
Lisette glared at her.

'You are laughing at me. I allow no one to laugh at
me.'

'I do not think you are at all funny,' Roxanna said with
a sigh. 'An intelligent young woman of your background
behaving like a spoilt child. It is little wonder that Lord
Talland does not consider you adult enough to take on
the responsibilities of marriage.'

'I have told you—-he wants to marry me himself!'

'That is quite out of the question.'

'Why? I shall inherit a large amount of money when I
am twenty, and I have estates in France. When the
people overthrow Napoleon and put a Bourbon king
back on the throne, I shall be an heiress. Ross knows
this.'

Mark also, Roxanna thought, but wisely did not say
so. 'I think Lord Talland is already married—to Talland
itself,' she said instead.

'He does think a lot of this horrible old house,' the girl
admitted. She seemed to have forgotten she was holding
another ornament, ready to throw it across the room to
join the others. 'And he is good to the villagers. But for
him, they would starve. Since he had to close down one
of the mines, things have been very difficult. Did Mark
really shoot him?'

'Yes, I am afraid he did. I saw it happen. I was not
near enough to overhear their conversation, but I think
they had been quarrelling for some time before I came
upon them,' Roxanna confessed.

'What came over Mark?' Lisette whispered, tossing
the ornament she held on to the bedcover without
another glance. 'He is kind and gentle. I know there is no
love lost between them, but to try to kill him . . . It is too
horrible. Yet I still love him. I would go away with him
tomorrow if he asked me. We almost managed it the last
time, but that wretched man Russell somehow found out
about it and Ross locked me in my room so that I could
not go to Mark. They had a terrible quarrel that night,

too. I could hear them, even upstairs. Rosie said Ross hit him . . .' She broke off, staring wide-eyed at Roxanna who had not spoken a word during the confession. 'Why am I telling you all this? You are a stranger.'

'Because you need to talk to someone; and perhaps, because I am a stranger, I can see things a little differently. I am not involved.' Roxanna was pleased that there was to be no more broken glass.

Not involved! She was totally involved, albeit against her will. And even that was debatable. She would stay because she wanted to be near *him*, but when it came to meeting his demands, could she?

'Perhaps I shall like you, after all. Usually, when I get angry, the servants all run for grand-mère, or Ross. She scolds me, and he loses his temper. Once he even put me over his knee. He was sorry afterwards, of course, and bought me the prettiest little bracelet to make amends. The brute! I had to use a cushion to sit down for three whole days.'

'How undignified for you.' A smile twitched at the corners of Roxanna's mouth. Lisette considered the memory for a moment, and suddenly burst into laughter so lighthearted and infectious that Roxanna, too, found herself laughing. In the space of a heartbeat the girl's character had changed completely.

Running to the window, she stared out towards the church, clearly visible on this bright, sunny morning. 'I can't see them. Do you think they will fight? Ross is weak . . . He cannot win. Mark is no mean swordsman.' She wheeled about and her pretty face was now wretched in its misery. The laughter of a moment ago was wiped away, leaving no trace of the warmth Roxanna had glimpsed. 'I could not bear it if either of them is hurt. It will be my fault. I shall go and stop them.'

'No!' Roxanna barred the way to the door, took the girl gently but firmly by the hand and looked into her troubled eyes. 'You would only anger Lord Talland further if you tried. Whatever this—this enmity is between them, it must be settled. Please be guided by me.'

'Settled. By the death of one of them? That is how it will end,' Lisette cried. 'Mark has his pride too, and Ross . . . he does not know the meaning of fear. He will not cry enough! If only Mark had some of his ruthlessness, his arrogance, his ability to command . . .'

If only you knew, Roxanna thought, recalling Mark's leadership of the wreckers. Whatever else lay behind the fight, she suspected this was the prime cause for it. Ross apparently was not averse to a little smuggling, but he drew the line at the deliberate wrecking of ships, the murder of innocent men and women. His younger brother, it seemed, did not. Ross could have denounced him and had him arrested, but he had chosen this way of dealing with him. A chance to fight—to defend himself, which was more than he had allowed the poor souls who had managed to reach the shore. In this way, no scandal, no slur, on the name of Talland. She wished Ross could have found another way, even so. Did he think more of his name than of his brother's life? Where was the heart the Countess had spoken of?

'Will you be my friend, Roxanna? May I call you Roxanna?'

'Please. I would like that.' Her heart went out to the girl in her misery.

'And you must call me Lisette. I insist. We must stand together, must we not, against these men? Will you go after them?' she pleaded. 'Make Ross listen to you. Tell him I shall do anything he asks of me. Anything . . . if he does not fight Mark.'

'I cannot,' Roxanna protested. She had no sway over him! 'You really love him, don't you?'

'He is not strong like Ross, or clever, but given a fair chance . . . Ross allows him to do so little here. Mark is a little wild, I know it, and reckless, but I shall always love him. If Ross harms him, I shall never forgive him. Please, Roxanna, help me? I am so unhappy.'

'Very well, I shall try.' Roxanna disengaged herself from the girl's fierce embrace. 'When I come back, I want to see that face washed and hair combed. There will be no more repetitions of scenes like this. You must show Lord Tallard that you are willing to abide by his decisions. Perhaps a little meekness, good manners and patience may help to achieve your purpose. Who knows? If Mark sees that you are prepared to be sensible and bide your time, loving him all the while, perhaps he will not always seek to antagonise his brother by opposing him. Between you . . .'

'Stand together, you mean, but not appear to. How clever you are. Did your father teach you that?' Roxanna nodded, her eyes clouding for a moment as she thought of that sick old man alone in a tiny, uncomfortable room in London. How she missed him! 'I am sorry I said he was a fool. It was horrid of me. He is a clever man. Please go, Roxanna—run like the wind. Stop them!'

Roxanna did indeed run up the grassy slopes, cutting across the cliff instead of taking the path, to save time. If Ross had gone directly to the ruins . . . His black horse was tethered by some bushes. She heard the distinct sound of steel clashing against steel as she paused, panting. She was too late!

Rounding a corner of a fallen wall, she saw them. Just two men, no more. Where were the villagers who were supposed to be disposing of the hidden contraband? Watching, waiting to pounce? She glanced quickly about her, shivering despite the warmth of the sun as she looked across at the graveyard and remembered what had taken place there a few short hours ago. There was no one else. Just two men intent on killing each other.

She stumbled and almost fell, grazing her hand on a sharp piece of rock as she began to run again. There was only one way to stop them. She did not consider the danger to herself as she cried out, as loudly as her bursting lungs would allow, 'Stop! Stop it, both of you!' She ran between them.

Ross swore at her. She screamed as his blade flashed past her. Without ceremony, he pushed her to the ground to one side of him, and said tersely. 'Stay put, you little fool.' To his brother, 'Yield, man. We shall continue this some other time.'

'Now.' Mark's face was white, wet with sweat which ran in tiny rivulets down his cheeks and soaked the cravat at his throat. Both men had discarded their coats. Roxanna had seen these on some fallen masonry, where they had been flung in the heat of those first few minutes as the two brothers came together. To fight, perhaps to kill. Certainly with the intent to wound each other, she thought, staring at them in horror.

There was a long rent in one of Ross's sleeves, and he fought with one hand pressed constantly against his side. It must be causing him agony! Yet it did not show on the set, grim features, or in the dark eyes that watched his brother grow noticeably greyer, his movements more erratic. He countered a lunge, and attacked with a suddenness that took Mark completely by surprise. His sword was sent flying and came flashing down to earth, to stand quivering, its sharp point buried in the ground.

Ross's own blade was at his brother's throat. A wild look flashed in his eyes that so frightened Roxanna that she thought he intended to take his life.

'No, for the love of heaven, don't kill him!'

'He would have killed you,' Ross thundered, and she trembled at the fury in his voice. 'Show him your wrists! Do as I say, girl,' he ordered as she made no move to obey him, then slowly she unfastened the buttons on her sleeves and drew them back as far as the tight material would allow. 'Look, brother! Do you see those marks? She saw the light last night, as she saw the last one—the one you and Griffith hung outside the church to lure the *Charlotte Dee* on to the rocks . . .'

'I knew nothing about that . . .' Mark began, then broke off, a bitter smile twisting his wet features. 'You won't believe me, so I'll say no more. I'm not a murderer. I've used Griffith while you were away, I admit that. If you can get away with it, so can I. And I have, very successfully for the past four months!'

'You damn idiot!' Ross spat the words at him. His

sword was flung aside, and his open palm lashed out and caught his brother a stunning blow across one cheek. As Mark reeled back, there came another and another until he lost his balance and fell to the ground, blood seeping from a cut at the corner of his mouth.

'Griffith is a cold-blooded killer. I warned you about him. I warned everyone. By God, whoever threw in their lot with him will face me for it! You will give me their names.'

'No. I gave them their orders—if they went against me, then it is my place to bring them to account, not yours.' Mark wiped his hand across his mouth. It came away streaked with bright red blood. 'You can hit me as many times as you like, but I'll not betray them. Although I doubt if they'd do the same for me. I'll deal with them. They will not work for me again.'

'It's nice to know you're not a coward, at least.' Slowly Ross's anger seemed to be diminishing. Roxanna gained her feet, but did not dare approach them.

'I've walked for so long in your shadow that I've forgotten what it was like to be a man,' came the bitter reply. 'You could have killed me. Why didn't you? You wanted to, I saw it in your eyes! Now I know why they call you a devil. It was like looking into the fires of hell. I don't think I've ever really known you.'

Ross turned away, a strange expression on his face, and saw Roxanna watching them. He said in a voice weary with pain, 'I did not take your worthless life because she is still alive. Had she been dead, as Griffith planned, I should have killed you without a qualm. They caught her last night after you had gone. Griffith had her tied to one of the tide stakes to drown. Afterwards they would have made it look like an accident.'

'Suicide,' Roxanna said quietly, as she rolled down her sleeves and fastened them again. 'Everyone was to have thought I killed myself rather than face an accusation of theft.'

'My God!' Mark ejaculated. 'And I . . .'

'You would have been as responsible for her death as

if you had tied her down there yourself,' Ross snapped.
'Be grateful to her. She has saved your life—as she once
did mine, when you meant to take it from me,' he added
meaningfully.

His brother flushed, and looked uncomfortable. 'You
goaded me. You always do—as if you take delight in it!'

'Perhaps one day I am hoping you will stand up to me.'

'I shall never be as you want me to be. Even wounded,
you are still a better man. My woman didn't run after
me . . .'

'I would not let her,' Roxanna said quickly. 'I came in
her place to beg you to stop for her sake. Did you not
think how she would feel if you were hurt—or killed?
You bear her a strange kind of love.'

'Even a man in love has his pride,' Ross drawled.
'Where are the men, Mark? Why are they not here as
you ordered?'

'So she told you everything, did she?' Mark sneered.
'Where, in your bed?'

'Unless you want the flat of my hand about you again,
there'll be no more talk like that. Roxanna is not my
mistress. Nor will she be.'

'So it's Roxanna now, is it? This morning it was Miss
Dane. So polite. So formal. Where did you find her,
brother? Some waterfront tavern on one of your trips to
London? You have your pleasures but you deny me
mine!'

Roxanna marvelled at Ross's control. The black eyes
blazed, but no anger registered on his expression. Why
should it, she then thought, realising he had no reason to
be annoyed at such a remark, for she was nothing to him.
Mark was baiting him now, and he did not like it.

'I suggest you use your skill, such as it is, with words to
deal with your men. I want a meeting this evening, or
have you forgotten that we have a consignment due
soon?'

Roxanna could hardly believe her ears. Was he so
confident of her that he now openly discussed his activities in front of her? She felt Mark's eyes search her face.

He, too, looked taken aback by Ross's frankness.

'For all our sakes, I hope she keeps her mouth tight shut,' he snapped.

'She will. Leave her to me. One more thing. She is not available, Mark. Touch her again, and you *will* have my blade in you.'

'So you lied. She does belong to you. Your personal property! I should have realised there had to be a good reason for her to carry your ring. I've never known you take it off your finger these past ten years, since Father died. Alicia Brandon will have your eyes out when she knows. Discarded for a common little servant-girl! I shall watch with interest when the two of you meet again. Did he tell you about Alicia?' Mark's eyes flickered maliciously to Roxanna. 'A perfect match, so everyone says. She expects to be the next mistress of Talland. The two of you will have to share the house and take turns in his bed . . .'

'You go too far . . .' Ross began, taking a step forward. Mark backed away, his mouth tightening into a bleak line. Once again they were contemptuous of each other.

'I go to do your bidding, master. I leave you in the hands of your shabby little helper.'

'One day I shall surely kill him,' Ross muttered after the departing figure. They both watched him snatch up his coat, fling it over his shoulder and start along the path which led over the slopes to the village, a mile away.

'No, you will not,' she said, and he turned and looked at her questioningly. 'For all the enmity between you, there was a moment when you were brothers again . . . I felt it.'

'Did you, now?' His smile was sardonic, but then he nodded. 'Yes, I felt it, too. If I had held out my hand to him at that moment, I wonder if he would have taken it?' Then, with a shrug, 'No. He would have laughed in my face!'

'Perhaps the next time . . .' she said, and he gave a hollow laugh.

'The next time, you will not be around to stop us. Give me your arm—this side is paining me. Help me back to the ruins, and I shall rest there a moment before riding back.'

He slipped an arm about her shoulders, leaning heavily on her as they made their way slowly back to where he had left his coat. Without thinking what she was doing—the coat was of the most expensive material and brand new—Roxanna set it down on the ground for him to sit on. He propped himself against a piece of fallen wall, and said with a strange smile, 'So you came for Lisette. I am devasted. I thought you had come because you were worried over me.'

'You are quite capable of taking care of yourself, sir,' she replied in an aloof tone. Now that they were alone, there was again that gleam in those eyes she had seen not long ago . . . and his manner was too friendly. The atmosphere was becoming too intimate. She must not allow it to happen—must not succumb to the over-whelming charm this man could radiate at will. It was reaching out now, as he smiled and motioned her to seat herself close by him.

'I think I should go and fetch Russell to help you back to the house,' she said, making no move to do so.

'Nonsense! Sit down. You were so tired last night that we never did get round to half the things we have to discuss.'

'Discuss?' Roxanna placed herself carefully on the grass, keeping a good distance between them. The lazy smile hovering around his lips grew as he saw how deliberate her actions were. 'We have nothing to dis-cuss, sir. I have agreed to stay—or rather, you have made it possible for me to stay by clearing me of your brother's accusation.' She would not give him the satis-faction of knowing that his threat had had anything to do with it. She would not be under his thumb as Mark said Lisette and the Countess were. Master of Talland he might be, but she was still a free spirit. He would not bind her if she did not want it. Yet was he not doing so already, with every smile, every gesture, every touch?

'Do you remember what I said to you last night, as I was about to leave?' Ross asked softly, laying his hand over hers. She snatched it free. He laughed. 'You do. I meant every word. You are my wife, Roxanna, and I intend you to remain so. You will be my wife before God and man one day, but until then I shall have to find ways of . . . making amends for keeping our marriage in secret.'

Roxanna dared not ask what kind of amends he had in mind. 'You—You cannot mean to hold me to our marriage,' she gasped. 'Why? I am nothing to you! There—There is this other woman, who expects to be your wife.'

'Why she should is beyond me. I have given her no cause,' Ross returned with a shrug. 'Yes, I do intend to hold you. I suggest you consider the prospect most seriously. My reasons for what I do are my own. You would not think them important . . .' He paused, staring into her indignant features. 'Very well. Shall we say that I want to settle down. I am tired of society life; it bores me. I am tired of the knowledgeable, overdressed, painted women who follow me in droves.' The arrogance of the man, Roxanna thought, too astounded to speak. 'What happened at the inn has provided me with the answer to my problem. I have a wife who is, I believe, quite intelligent and with whom I shall be able to converse. She is pretty, but not a striking beauty, so I shall not have to kill the men who dare to woo her behind my back.' Roxanna gave a choked cry, and he looked at her in surprise. 'You asked for my reasons.'

'You are insulting, sir. I would rather be married to—to a farm-hand than to such a braggart!' The laughter in his tone stung her.

'No, Roxanna Dane, you shall remain married to me. In time you will grow to accept that I am not quite as bad as you believe. You might even begin to like me a little.' His tone changed, no longer suave and velvety soft, but dangerously low, challenging. 'I am not endowed with the patience—or the virtue—of a saint, so do not make me wait too long for your answer.'

'You can have it now,' she flung back, tossing her head in disdain. 'No!'

'I will not accept that. Don't you understand, you foolish girl, that there is only one course open to you—acceptance. I am not a bad catch, or so I have been told. You will not find the situation unrewarding, I assure you. Think of what you could do for your father. He is in bad health, is he not? I could have him brought to Talland. The sea air can cure many ailments.'

'Not a broken heart,' Roxanna replied angrily. Was she going out of her mind? He was serious! He intended to make her his wife. Did he think he could buy her? 'You are cruel to bring him into this.'

'I shall use whatever methods—fair or foul—to have my own way. I could, of course, simply enforce my rights as your husband, but I prefer you to come to my bed willingly. However, if you make me wait too long . . .' The threat was only too clear. 'Think on it carefully. Think of the advantages. The long-term advantages.'

'Of allowing you to come to me by way of a secret passage so that you are never seen?' Roxanna declared contemptuously. 'I may be unable to prevent you from taking what you consider yours—by force. But I will never—never!—take anything from you. It would make me feel . . .'

Before she could utter the word, he had thrust a hand over her mouth. His eyes glittered at her, and as she looked into them she found herself growing weak at the naked desire lurking there. He made no attempt to hide it; how sure he was of himself! Of her!

'You will take what I give, be it money, jewels, clothes. From what I have seen of you so far, you are in dire need of all three. And one day I shall show you off to the world, never fear. When the time is right.'

Roxanna struck his hand away, hardly aware of what she was doing, so embarrassed was she. 'Do you think I don't know what you really mean? That I shall be your—your plaything until you tire of me, and no one will know of it. Who would believe a mere servant-girl against the Lord of Talland? When you were tired of me, you would send me away. Do you not think I have heard of things like this happening before? Do you think me a fool?'

'A fool—no. Unwise to speak to me in such a fashion? Yes, very unwise.' Ross's hands reached for her, and fastened over her shoulders before she could move. 'Be still,' he warned, as she twisted to be free of him, and thrust her to the ground, his weight pinning her beneath him, holding her immobile. 'This side is hell enough.'

His face was close to hers. His eyes burned into hers as his fingers slid over her body, as they had done that night at the inn. She closed her eyes to escape his burning gaze. 'Shall I remind you how it was between us, little cat?' came the mocking whisper in her ear. 'You liked my kisses then. You will again. No other man shall ever rouse you as I do.'

Her body went rigid with fear—and shock as his mouth closed over hers. She forced herself to stay taut, unyielding, her lips closed, but he forced them apart with a ruthless pressure that made her moan in despair. She had not forgotten the ecstasy of those kisses, but had thought only to have memories for the rest of her life. Now . . .

His mouth touched her cheek, the smooth hollow of her throat, wandered teasingly over her tightly closed eyelids and back to her mouth again, parting her lips easily this time, devouring them with bitter-sweet kisses that once more rendered her incapable of thought. She was lost. She had no weapons with which to fight him. What an easy conquest he must think her! A few kisses were all it had taken to bring her to surrender. As it had at the inn.

'I hate you,' she said, emerald eyes blazing as he drew back from her, her soft lips bruised and quivering.

'I can live with that,' came the low, amused retort. He eased himself upright against the stone again, the blood suddenly draining from his face. Roxanna's vexation died as she saw his lips compress in pain. He gave her a one-sided grin. 'I am being paid for my rough handling of you. Be a good girl and bring my horse, or I'll not make it back to the house.'

She did not think to argue. She ran and brought the huge black horse, and helped him, not without great difficulty, for he was so much heavier and bigger than she was herself, to mount. He clung fast to the pommel, reeling unsteadily. Snatching up the reins, Roxanna led them both as quickly as she dared back to the house, where he was at once carried inside by two of the servants and put to bed.

Roxanna did not see Lord Talland for two days, and when she did it was purely by accident. It was Elizabeth de Villon's birthday at the end of the month and Lisette had persuaded her to celebrate it in style—with a *bal masqué* during the first week of May. In France, she had been told by her young charge, already brimming over with excitement at the prospect of having the house full of friends, that anyone who was anyone in society always attended one of the Countess's balls.

And so it was that Roxanna had risen earlier than usual, for they were going to Plymouth to choose materials for new gowns. She would have to make do with last year's gown again, she decided. Perhaps with a little alteration, no one would notice. A provisional guest-list had been drawn up, and already the numbers were over one hundred. From as close as Polperro and Looe, as far as Exeter and even London. Lisette's excitement was infectious, and Roxanna could not help beginning to look forward to the occasion.

The house would soon be in an uproar, for there were spare bedrooms to be opened and dusted, beds to be aired, warming-pans collected and cleaned. The kitchens would begin stocking up with food and wines to sustain the guests who stayed over for breakfast, perhaps lunch . . . even dinner, for days afterwards.

The first thing Roxanna saw as she opened her eyes

that morning was the leather money-pouch on the bed-side table. She recognised it immediately as the one Nicholas had held out to her—then she had knocked it from his grasp and sent the contents flying across the floor. With trembling fingers she opened it, and on to the bedcover there poured a stream of coins. There had to be at least fifty pounds, she thought, gasping at the wealth before her. And then her head jerked up, her eyes flying to the panelled wall beside the bed. She ran to it, her fingers probing and searching; but as before, each oak panel was set firmly in place and she could find no opening.

He had come to her room while she slept, and had left the money! He had stood by her bed and looked down at her, and she had been unaware of his presence! She touched her fingers lightly to glowing cheeks. So close, yet he had gone away without waking her—without touching her! The knowledge stunned her.

She washed and dressed, her mind a jumble of confused thoughts and emotions. She had tried not to think of his ultimatum, but his words haunted her day and night. *'You are my wife, Roxanna, and I intend you to remain so . . . I suggest you consider the prospect most seriously . . . I shall use whatever methods—fair or foul— to have my own way . . . Think of the advantages. The long-term advantages.'*

She dared not, for if she did, she was honest enough to admit that they were most attractive. Not only would she have a position and a name—which, she had discovered, carried much weight in this part of the country—but she would be able to provide for her father. He could be moved to a fine house and have a maid to look after him and she could afford to pay for a good doctor. Ross had spoken of bringing him to Talland. How wonderful that would be, to have him with her again!

Angrily she brushed the thought aside. She had money now; enough to move him to a more comfortable place. She would take this money and use it well, perhaps even take a little to buy material for a ball-gown. More than enough would remain for her father's needs. But she would not accept Lord Talland's offer, or bow to his threats. She could never be his wife.

As she was finishing dressing, the sound of voices below her window drew her to look out curiously. It was barely seven-thirty. Apart from the servants, there was never anyone about at this time. Below her, beneath one of the arbours, were two men. One was hunched inside a heavy jacket, the collar turned up about his neck to keep out a chill breeze which stirred the thick mop of sandy hair. She recognised that weathered face immediately— Nicholas. And then his companion turned slightly in her direction. It was Lord Talland. He wore thick hide knee-breeches and boots that came almost up to his knees, and a black leather coat. From his waist hung the long, slender sword she had seen him use against his brother. Russell had gone up to the ruins that day to bring back both discarded weapons.

His wound had healed remarkably quickly, Roxanna thought, watching them stride at a fast pace down the path which led to the beach. Had he been pretending that day, hoping to gain her sympathy, perhaps? To make her more receptive to his advances? He was limping slightly, she noticed, but there was also something very purposeful about his stride. Where did they go at this early hour? It was as she went down to breakfast, some while later, that she happened to look out of one of the landing windows. She could clearly see the headland and the beach below. There was a ship anchored in the bay. A longboat had just been lowered from it and was heading towards the two men who waited on the sand. Nicholas and Lord Talland!

She did not linger, for Russell appeared at the end of the corridor. He gave her a searching look as she passed, and when she risked a quick look over her shoulder as she reached the head of the staircase, he was standing where she had been, looking out towards the bay. If anyone knew what was going on, it was he, Roxanna thought as she continued downstairs, but she knew he would betray none of his master's secrets. When the carriage turned out of the drive on to the Polperro road, an hour later, with Lisette debating whether or not she should wear blue and have her hair loose or white and have it curled, topped with her mother's diamond circlet, Roxanna looked down into the bay below. There was no sign of the ship. If Lord Talland had returned to the house she would have seen him, she reasoned, therefore that left only one answer. He had sailed on it. But where? Mark had spoken of frequent trips to London. Surely to travel there he would use his carriage?

The next four days gave her little chance to dwell on the mysterious ship or the comings and goings of her employer. They stayed overnight in Liskeard, at the house of an old family friend, before continuing on to Plymouth. The brief sojourn turned into the busiest hours Roxanna had ever known. First, visits to the draper to see what new materials were about. Lisette moaned at the short supply and was told it was the fault of the French. Since the outbreak of hostilities between England and France in May 1803, no trading had been possible. Roxanna knew she was dying to know what the French ladies were wearing this year, and in particular the wife of Napoleon, Josephine, who was well known for her sumptuous array of clothes.

Only those dealing in contraband were doing any trade, Roxanna thought to herself as she chose several yards of pale yellow muslin and some gold braid. The Countess nodded approval at her choice, and urged her granddaughter to hurry and make her selection as they had many more calls to make.

After the draper, there were gloves to be bought, shoes to match the new materials, jewellery and a hundred and one other little things that resulted in both Roxanna and Lisette returning to Talland laden down with parcels and boxes. That very afternoon Lisette's sewing-maid began on her gown. Roxanna had insisted on making her own. It was a simple garment after all,

and she was an excellent needlewoman. She sat and
sewed while Lisette and the Countess went over the
guest-list for what must have been the twentieth time.
They would delete three names and add another ten! At
last it was finished, and the writing of the invitations
began.

Her wrist aching from so much writing and the ad-
dressing of envelopes, Roxanna was glad to retire in the
evenings and sit in front of the fire for a while before
going to bed.

She awoke with the realisation that someone was in
the room. At the same time as she opened her mouth to
scream, she saw the dark face of the man standing by the
bed, his features illuminated by the candle she always
left burning on the table. The panelled wall behind him
was open. Four panels away from the bed, she counted,
as he moved away from it to toss something on the bed.

'What—What is it?' she asked, drawing the sheets
high about her shoulders. He smiled slightly at the
gesture and came no closer. When had he come back?

'A peace-offering. I meant to leave it without disturbing you,' came the quiet answer. She saw grey shadows
of tiredness beneath his eyes as she sat up and reached
for the package, wrapped in coloured paper. 'You enjoyed Plymouth? You have not been there before, have
you?'

'No, it was very pleasant.'

'And you did some shopping.' His eyes alighted for a
moment on the uncompleted dress lying across the back
of a chair. 'I am glad you have been sensible and
accepted the money. It did belong to you, after all. You
will not need that—the yellow thing you are making.
I have brought you the gown you will wear at the
Countess's *bal masqué*. A gown to show off that hair to
perfection, and those eyes.'

Roxanna sat in stunned silence. She found herself
looking down at the most exquisite creation she had ever
seen. From the paper she carefully drew out a gown so
light that it could not have weighed more than a handful

of thistledown. And so transparent that she could see right through it.

'Not silk as I wanted, but the colour is right, and you will be the envy of every woman, for it is the latest style in Paris. Josephine wore one exactly like it to the Opéra last week.'

'Jo-Josephine!' she stammered, her cheeks the colour of a scarlet poppy. Napoleon's wife! Was he intimating that this gown came from France? How could it?

'There is a cashmere shawl to go with it. The genuine article, not one of these poor imitations everyone is wearing in London. I've brought one for Lisette too, lest she feels I am favouring you unfairly.'

Roxanna ran her fingers over the jade green muslin. She had a slip of watered silk which she could alter to go underneath it, thus making it more respectable. Only as she looked up and found Ross's eyes on her, glinting with wicked lights at her obvious delight in his gift, did she know that she could neither wear it nor accept it. She rewrapped the gown, aware of his gaze narrowing.

'What's wrong?' he demanded, as she pushed the parcel away, her mouth a tight, firm line. Stubborn! 'Don't you like it?'

'It—It is beautiful, but I am sure Lady Brandon would look so much better in it than I. I cannot accept it, sir. You were kind to think of me, but I shall wear the yellow.'

'The devil you will!' he exclaimed, giving her a fierce frown. She did not flinch before his anger. 'You will wear it—even if I have to put you into it myself—and I will, if you force the issue,' he threatened.

Roxanna held her ground, even though she did not like the way he was looking at her. She had no doubt he was perfectly serious in what he said.

'Are you not afraid of what people will say when they see me so attired?' she asked. 'Apart from the obvious conjectures, they might begin asking where and how you acquired such a piece of merchandise. And cashmere shawls, which everyone knows have not been brought into this country since the beginning of the war.'

'Why, little cat, are you concerned for me? Rest assured, their questions cannot harm me. Most people know that anything can be acquired at the right price. Everything—and everyone—has a price. Even you. It seems I have yet to find out what it is.'

Roxanna gasped at the insult. Without thinking, she grabbed up the parcel and flung it at him. It came open, and the muslin fell in a tiny huddle at his feet.

'I don't want your gift. I cannot be bought. Not by your money or your favours. I will never be your wife. Never!'

'Damn your cold little heart,' Ross said harshly. 'If I was not so tired, I'd show you you have no choice in the matter. I will be obeyed, in all things, Roxanna.'

'Nor am I afraid of your threats,' she added bravely. Afraid? She was terrified of them. No one would ever accept her word over his, and they both knew it. 'If you persist in trying to make me agree to something totally repugnant to me, I—I shall tell the authorities what you and your village friends are about.'

She knew immediately that to threaten him was the worst mistake she could ever have made. His eyes raked her from head to toe in a look so insolent, so blatantly suggestive, that she drew back from him, even though he had not made a move towards her.

'No, I'll not touch you now. I would bruise that soft skin. I might even have an impulse to put my hands around that little neck and squeeze the life out of you for daring to make such a suggestion. Turn me in, would you?' He gave a mirthless laugh and bent to pick up the gown from the floor. 'I am a fool to think a mere bauble like this could buy a girl of your character. I should have made it a diamond brooch, perhaps. How would you have reacted then, Roxanna? Would you like me to shower you with expensive jewellery? Would that ease your conscience and bring you to my bed? I shall, if you ask it. When you have what you want, I shall have what I desire.'

'I want nothing from you,' Roxanna repeated in a trembling tone, and his eyes gleamed once again as he heard the tremor there. 'Go away. Please go away.'

'I'll go, and I'll take my gift with me. I doubt if Lisette will turn up her nose at it. You and I shall continue this conversation at a later date, when I am less tired—and less angry. Do not make me angry again. And do not ever consider betraying me to the authorities, or you will find yourself in gaol.'

'Why?' Roxanna demanded, as he turned away from her. 'I have done nothing wrong.'

'If you malign my character, I shall deal with you most severely. I shall say that you are indeed a thief, and I only corroborated your story at first because I felt sorry for you. Then I discovered, to my chagrin, that you intended to continue your thieving ways. It would be so easy for a few of my close friends to lose some jewellery, some item of importance. I would make sure you had been visiting them with Lisette, of course. With their testimony and that of Nicholas . . .' He paused, his eyes on Roxanna's ashen cheeks. He had frightened her badly, he saw, but she had brought it on herself. There was too much at stake to risk her going to the authorities about him. He could have exerted some influence if she did and questions began to be asked, but that would mean involving people in high places who would not like it known that they were involved with him. And it would take money, too, to bribe the necessary law officers. He had the local constable well in hand, but his superiors might not be so obliging as to turn their backs as often as he did. 'Do I make myself clear, Roxanna? One word about my activities, whatever you think them to be, and you will find yourself in a very uncomfortable position and for a long time. Who will care for your sick father then, girl?'

The panel swung into place behind him, and Roxanna was alone again. Hot tears came into her eyes. With a sob, she threw herself on to the pillows and wept miserably. She was trapped. She could no longer deceive herself with the thought that she could somehow escape what he had in mind for her. He *would* make her his wife, and there was nothing she could do about it! He was a devil, and she was being made to dance to his tune. It was over an hour before she fell into an exhausted sleep, the pillow beneath her cheek wet with her tears. Ross's dark countenance followed her . . . menacing, mocking, the firm mouth twisted into a cruel smile as he chanted over and over again in her ear,

'You are my wife, Roxanna. You are . . . You are. My wife . . . My wife . . .'

CHAPTER
SIX

'GOOD HEAVENS, you do not look well, Roxanna. Are you going down with a chill?' Lisette declared when she saw her friend the following morning. 'Why, your eyes are all red. Have you been crying?'

'I awoke in the night with a streaming nose,' Roxanna said, aware of the Countess listening to every word. She had gone to the library directly after breakfast, to complete the writing of the invitations. Lisette had taken a tray in her room and did not show herself until nearly eleven o'clock. 'Perhaps I have caught a chill.'

'Then you must return to your room and go to bed again. Must she not, grand-mère? We have almost finished here. I can ask Russell to take over from you, Roxanna.'

'I agree with my granddaughter, Miss Dane. Go back to your room. Rosie shall bring you up a hot posset. If you have not improved by the morning, I shall send for the doctor,' Elizabeth said, glancing up from her guest-list to inspect the pale-cheeked girl. If it were not for the tell-tale signs of weeping, she would have accepted that she had a cold, for the four days they had spent in Plymouth had been exceedingly grim as far as the weather was concerned. It had rained for hours during their shopping expedition, and later, a bitterly cold wind had prevailed for the remainder of the afternoon and all the next day. The journey home in the carriage had been most uncomfortable despite the abundance of rugs covering them all.

'I am sure I shall feel better in the morning,' Roxanna assured her, not wanting a doctor to call and find her out in her lie.

the peace of her room, she locked the door
Rosie had brought her posset and sat down to still
her wildly beating heart. She had a daring scheme in
mind to free herself from the clutches of Lord Talland,
and this was a heaven-sent opportunity to put it into
operation. While searching for the secret panel before
going downstairs, she had discovered a torn-off piece of
paper at the bottom of one wood insert, so small that she
had missed it several times. Finding a pair of scissors, she
now inserted one of the blades into the panel beading,
and applied some leverage. It refused to budge, and all
she achieved was to chip a tiny piece of wood from the
panel itself.

The scissors were stuck! She could not pull them out.
As she was waggling them frantically about, there came
a faint click and the panel above her swung silently open.
She knelt on the carpet, hardly daring to breathe as she
stared into the blackness beyond. Not a single glimmer
of light. She hesitated for a moment only, before lighting
the candle and stepping through the opening into the
passage beyond.

On each side of her the thick walls were heavily
cobwebbed. Strands brushed her face, as her hand
searched for the way ahead. The candle illuminated a
multitude of spiders running for cover as their domain
was invaded. She heard a scuffle of tiny feet, and something furry brushed her ankle. Somehow she bit back the
cry which rose to her lips. Mice! Or rats! Ross Talland
might not mind their company, but she did.

The passage, which was wide enough for her to move
quite easily without restriction, began to widen slightly.
She came to a halt before a spiral staircase hewn out of
the solid rock. The tunnel, too, stretched ahead of her.
Where did it go in that direction? she wondered, and
decided to mount the stairs first. She knew Ross's rooms
were on the floor above hers, and they were what she
wanted to find. She climbed twenty-four wide steps and
came to another narrow passage. Was the house
honeycombed with such tunnels? Holding the light

in front of her, she started along it, but had gone only a little way when a sheer wall loomed up ahead. She stopped in dismay. Would she have to turn back?

She was just on the point of doing so when she caught sight of a wall bracket in wrought iron. A candle had been inserted in it, and used, she saw, and her heart began to beat unsteadily. Someone had come this way recently. But why, if it was a dead end? Her fingers ran over the walls but found nothing, and then as before she must have touched some catch without realising it, for a section of the wall, just big enough for her to stoop through, swung open.

She found herself looking into a pleasant, well-lighted room, where a fire burned in a huge grate directly opposite her. It was larger than her own room, with a four-poster draped in indigo and gold, a solid-looking rocking-chair beside the latticed windows, and a spy-glass, such as sailors used, positioned on a tripod beside it. She had little doubt it was trained on the bay!

The furniture, as in most of the house, was mahogany, with a few pieces of rosewood interpersed with it. A shelf over the writing bureau caught her eye. It was lined with delicate pieces of French pottery. A woman peddling her oranges stood beside an old man mending fishing-nets. An exquisite little creature in a ball-gown of the Marie Antoinette period curtsied before an elegant man in full court dress. And then she realised that the long, tasselled sofa before the fire was of French design, as was the matching chair a few feet away. This was Lord Talland's room, for there was a coat flung carelessly across the unmade bed. A leather coat! What connected him so closely to France? How did he speak the language so faultlessly?

A tiny shiver ran down her spine. Was that where he went on the strange ship? Across the Channel to France, to an enemy country? For what—a few kegs of rum and brandy, and silks for his women friends? Why risk his life so recklessly, when all he had to do was wait for the consignment to arrive on English shores. Mark had told

Griffith, 'We've a shipment coming over in four days.'
Ross had said to his brother after the fight, 'Have you
forgotten we have a consignment due soon?' If the
contraband was being brought to them, why had he
sailed away? What was more important to him than his
life? No one risked the Channel these days, for fear of
encountering a French man-of-war. A spy going to meet
his paymaster might risk his neck, but otherwise . . .

What was she thinking? A spy? A traitor to his own
country? It was madness. Yet what other explanation
was there? If he was, there must be something she could
use against him to make him let her go away, and give up
the idea of remaining her husband.

Extinguishing the candle, she stole into the room.
From the direction of the dressing-room off to her left,
she could hear the splashing of water. He was taking a
bath. She might have but a few minutes. She tip-toed
across the polished floor, uncarpeted as her own room
was, to the writing bureau against the far wall.

A large map was unfolded on it, with several more
beneath it. She found herself gazing at the French
coastline, with several places underlined in red. Paris.
Boulogne. Havre. Dunkirk. Ostend. Boulogne, she
noticed, was more heavily underlined than any of the
others. Of greater importance, perhaps, but why? A
route had been traced, in pencil this time, from Brittany
to Paris. Who was to make the perilous journey across
country to the capital, and why? It was more than she
could fathom, but she would remember the names.
Perhaps she could use them to her own advantage.

'Spies are usually shot,' a harsh voice snapped behind
her. She wheeled about, her eyes widening in alarm at
the sight of Lord Talland standing in the doorway across
from her. The pistol he held in his hand looked deadly,
and it was aimed directly at her.

Fear gave speed to her feet as she ran for the opening
in the wall, but even so he was ahead of her. He moved
with incredible agility, and his tall frame blocked her
escape. His free hand fastened over one of her wrists,

spun her about and flung her with some force towards
the sofa. She lost her balance and fell on to it in a most
undignified manner, straightening in time to see the
panel close.

'Now, what shall I do with you?' He laid the pistol on
the bureau and gazed down at the map for a long
moment, his features bleak. Roxanna tried to speak, but
her mouth was dry with fear. Was he going to kill her?

'You—You are a spy!' she blurted out at last, and the
eyes which came to rest on her glinted warningly.

'Yes, I suppose you could call me that.' He folded the
map, placed it in a drawer with the others and the pistol
and locked it, dropping the key into the pocket of the silk
robe he wore. His feet were thrust into leather slippers,
his hair still wet from the water he had left when he
sensed someone in the room outside. He knew it could
not be Russell, for the man had gone on an errand to the
village. Although he had heard no sound, the strange
sixth sense that had so often warned him of danger in the
past rose up in him now, to rouse him from the hot bath
in which he had been relaxing. So now she thought he
was a spy—which in effect he was, Ross thought, a smile
touching the corners of his mouth. She would get no
explanations from him. He was still angry over her
rejection of the gown he had bought for her. All the way
into Paris, dressed like a French peasant, to see a friend
whom he knew could supply him with what he wanted.
And for what? To have it thrown in his face!

'You are not going to deny it?' Roxanna gasped.

He came to stand before her, his hands on his hips. He
had frightened her out of her wits with the pistol, he
realised. 'At this moment, I don't know whether to put
you over my knee and give you a good spanking for
daring to pry into my personal papers—or kiss you,' he
said, and she drew back to the far side of the couch.

'If you touch me . . .'

'No one will come. The whole household is being
instructed on the great occasion which is to come, and
are all downstairs with the Countess in the library.

Besides, the walls in this part of the house are very thick, as you have discovered on your way up here. By the way, how did you find the passage?'

'A piece of paper was caught in the door. I managed to get it open with some scissors.'

'What a resourceful young woman you are, and a foolish one. If Russell had found you sneaking about in my room, he would not have treated you so gently.'

'Gently!' Roxanna echoed, rubbing her bruised wrist where the marks of his fingers plainly showed.

'You are lucky not to have a pistol-ball in you,' came the terse retort. 'What the devil did you think you would find anyway? More money? You don't have to steal it. As your lawful husband, I shall not keep you penniless.' His smile mocked her fear and her anger, and the fierce colour which appeared to stain her cheeks at his words. 'Give me your hand.'

It was an order, not a request. In silence, Roxanna did as she was bid. He ran his fingers over the red marks and then bent his head to lay his lips against the bruised place. 'There, is that better? What were you after, Roxanna?'

'Something I could use against you to make you stop hounding me,' she cried, knowing it was useless to lie. She wished he would release her hand, but he showed no intention of doing so, and when she tried to pull it free, he only tightened his hold.

'Hounding you?' He looked surprised at the statement. 'Is that how you consider my proposition? I could name a dozen women that would like me to offer them the same thing,' he added with a frown.

'Then please feel free to do so,' she returned sharply.

'But I am not free, am I? And neither are you. We are bound to each other by the sanctity of marriage.'

'I signed papers . . . for an annulment,' Roxanna said breathlessly. His touch was beginning to affect her. She averted her eyes from his face, aware of his smile growing at her discomfort.

'I tore them up,' Ross said calmly. He came round to

the front of the sofa and lifted her to her feet as if she weighed no more than a feather. 'When I realised I was not to breathe my last for a while, I decided to try to find you. To offer you . . . shall we say . . . a worthwhile proposition. What is it about me which offends you so, little cat?'

'Don't call me that!' She dared not look into those burning eyes even when he came closer, so close that his body touched hers. She could not move away, for the sofa effectively barred her retreat.

Ross's fingers touched her hair, sought and found the pins confining it, and took them out one by one. As the tawny gold tresses fell past her shoulders, he sighed. 'That's better. Now I am looking at you as you were that first day. It is a picture I have always carried with me. Tell me why the prospect of remaining—nay, becoming—my wife offends you so?' he asked quietly. 'I will have an answer. So loosen that stubborn tongue and talk to me. Or must I shake an answer from you?'

'It—It is impossible,' she said hastily.

'Nothing is impossible. All you have to do is say "Yes" and the matter will be settled,' he drawled, with a seemingly indifferent shrug. He made it sound so easy.

'Until you tire of me and send me away . . . an unwanted annoyance to be discarded before anyone discovers the truth.'

Her chin was seized in a firm grip and tilted back so that she was forced to look at him. There was no anger on his face, as she had expected from her bitter words, but rather a puzzled expression, almost pained. She felt his hand go around her back and she stiffened as he pressed her against him, bending his dark features towards her.

'What an exasperating little creature you are! What must I do to convince you I shall not discard you? In you, I shall have all I want. A meek, docile, obedient homely little wife who will warm my slippers by the fire for me, fill my pipe and sit at my feet.'

'Oh, you are insufferably arrogant.' Roxanna could

contain her anger no longer. 'I shall not sit at your feet like a tame dog.'

'No, you will share my bed and give me fine, strong, healthy children to carry on the name of Talland,' he told her quietly. 'You will be mistress of my home, and we shall be content. Few people have more from a marriage. Is it not enough for you? Very well. I shall bring your father to Talland. He will want for nothing. He is not enjoying the best of health, I believe. It will improve here.'

'I do not think I shall ever forgive you for using such a weapon against me.' He had struck at her most vulnerable spot. If she refused him, her father would remain in London, in poverty, and his health would never improve. If she agreed, she would be the wife of a man who would never care for her, who would use her when it suited him and doubtless take other women to his bed, as most gentlemen did. The ties of matrimony would not bind him to one woman for life. But they would bind her with unseen chains to one man. Him. And the chains were made of love, more durable than any iron. 'My father is the most important thing in the world to me. I would do anything for him.'

'I am glad to hear it. It is settled, then. You have only yourself to blame, you know, for forcing such measures on me. If I could not charm you into accepting my proposition, I had to resort to other means of persuasion.'

Roxanna was having great difficulty in concentrating on all the arguments she had presented to herself against the proposed match. It was difficult even to think when he looked at her with such hunger in his eyes. The fingers holding her chin slid along her cheek, smoothed back a lock of stray hair, ran along her eyelids and back to the smooth line of her throat. She wished it was possible to hate him, but she could not.

'You will wear the green for the *bal masqué*, yes?'

No! she wanted to cry out, and found instead she was nodding agreement.

'Good. And no more nonsense about running away, or betraying me to the volunteers. If you do that, you will be doing more harm than you know.'

'Tell me, then,' she pleaded. Ross shook his head, but the misery in her eyes reached him and he cursed her under his breath.

'Damn you, woman, I'll not give my life into your hands or anyone else's. I'll tell you this only. The mine I have closed down . . . You have heard about it?'

'Yes. Only one is working now after the fall of the price of copper,' she said. 'Rosie said it had caused hardship for everyone, and that you lost much money over it.'

'That is true, but it is still working—with men from the village there. Very carefully, of course. The copper is shipped across the Channel to Brittany. In return, we get contraband goods sent back which, when sold elsewhere, provide enough money for those men, and the rest of the village, to go on surviving until better times. There, now, is that so wrong?'

She could only stare at him in amazement. 'Why— Why did you go to France?' she whispered. It was a guess, but an accurate one, she saw, as his mouth tightened and the hand on her shoulder bit suddenly into her skin making her wince.

'No more questions! You are too astute for your own good. You will have to trust me for the answers to all your questions. I will answer them—when I can.'

'How can I?' Roxanna said, torn with indecision.

'Must I remind you that a wife cannot give evidence against her own husband?' Ross drawled and her eyes went wide with shock.

'That's why you want me to stay! To keep me silent . . .'

He gave another oath. She cried out in alarm as his mouth descended on hers in a wild, savage kiss that sent her senses reeling. She fought a losing battle against the skill which threatened to subdue her in mind and body, to dominate her.

'This is why I want you,' he said, his lips against her ear. 'And I have been patient long enough, my wife.'

Roxanna was swung up into his arms and carried across to the bed. She had no chance to flee as he set her down, for he flung himself alongside her, gathering her into his arms again. He held her tightly against him, kissing her protesting mouth until he had silenced her, and her lips flared to life beneath him. He caressed the tense, trembling body until she lay quiet and acquiescent beneath him, every nerve fired to the response he sought.

She was conscious of him unfastening her bodice, planting teasing kisses along her bare shoulder, down over the rise of her breasts. She tried to push him away and found instead her hands locked about his neck, to draw his lips back to hers for more kisses that rendered her near-insensible with pleasure. She could fight him no longer. Fight herself no more. In her heart of hearts she knew this was what she had wanted from the very first time they met, when his touch had burned her skin like tongues of fire, when his lips had awakened hers as no man had done before. She was his wife . . . In truth, she was his wife now. The bargain was sealed! Why did she feel no shame at what she had done?

She heard his soft laughter in her ear, reminding her what was expected of her.

'You see, little cat. I am not an ogre after all, just a man.'

The fire in her body raged out of control. As it consumed her, she had a vision of herself at the *bal masqué* in the jade green muslin gown, all the way from France. What had he risked to get it for her, and why? She would never understand him . . . perhaps he never intended she should.

The days that followed that morning in Ross's room began to seem like a dream to Roxanna as she threw herself into the preparations for the *bal masqué*, now under way with full vigour. Whenever they encountered each other, he was as polite as always, but there was nothing in his manner to betray what they had shared for those few stolen, wonderful hours. At meal-times, Roxanna sat at the table and listened to him discussing the price of horses and grain with his brother, enquiring of the Countess if there had been more acceptances from the one hundred and thirteen invitations sent out. Chatting amicably to Lisette, asking what dazzling creation she was going to wear to the occasion to gather all the eligible young bachelors about her like bees to a honeypot. She saw Mark's face darken with annoyance at such remarks, and wondered if Ross knew that he had been meeting Lisette in secret?

Only by accident had she discovered the fact. She had taken to walking in the afternoons, when Elizabeth and her granddaughter often rested for an hour or two. Her favourite walk was over the cliffs towards the village, away from the church and the ruins. A mile away she had found a length of broken wall, some eight yards in length, still containing several small lancet windows. Russell had told her it was all that remained of the Monks' House, little more than a crude cell that had provided sanctuary for two monks who ministered to the church in early times. Before the rebuilt church she now knew, a small chapel had stood there, having been in the possession of Glastonbury as far back as 1144. Below the old ruin there was another small cove and an ancient quay, much overgrown and half covered in sand. After the long walk, she would sit on a stone by the water's edge to enjoy the peace and quiet, which was broken only by the shrill screeching on occasions from the cormorants and guillemots nesting on the cliff ledges far above her head.

On her return to the house later than usual one afternoon, she had seen Mark and a young girl entwined in each other's arms behind the stables. Not until she drew nearer, hoping she could enter before they saw her—for it embarrassed her to see him with another woman, knowing of Lisette's deep affection for him— did she see that his companion had red hair. She stood in a shocked silence, and watched Lisette break from her lover's embrace and run into the house by a side entrance. When Roxanna looked in on her several minutes later, she lay outstretched on the bed, apparently dozing.

She was in a quandary. Should she reveal what she had seen to Ross? And perhaps provoke another fight, this time one she would not be able to stop? Tell the Countess, which might result in Lisette being sent away? Mark might then follow, and that would certainly bring him to blows with his brother again. So she remained silent, awaiting the right moment to tell Lisette that she had been seen and must cease these clandestine meetings. Roxanna was in no doubt that they took place on most afternoons when she was supposed to be resting.

The decision was made for her. Having a little spare time before the evening meal, she took some writing materials down to the library, where she knew she would not be disturbed. Of late, Rosie had begun coming to her room to speculate on the forthcoming ball. Who would arrive with whom? Would Lisette make Mark jealous by dancing with other good-looking young men? Would Lady Alicia Brandon pursue Lord Talland all night, as she usually did whenever she came to the house? Roxanna had long ago decided she did not like the woman who, it seemed, had her eye firmly set on becoming mistress of Talland. And for all his talk of wishing to settle down, from the way Rosie had talked, Ross was doing little to dissuade her from her intentions.

Every other day she wrote to her father, but since her arrival at the house had received only one letter, and was beginning to grow worried. She intended to write him a long letter, telling him how pleased she was with her new position and that there was the possibility of his coming to Talland in the near future to be with her. She wished she could say definitely that he could come, but Ross had not mentioned the matter further to her. Surely he could not have forgotten? She had agreed to remain his wife only because of his promise to help her ailing father, to provide for him as she dearly wanted to, but could not. No, that was only part of the reason. Why did she continue to lie to herself? She was falling in love with the unpredictable Ross James Talland, and was more than a little afraid of the power her love would give him over her. He had proved already that he was ruthless enough to use any guile to get his own way.

Her father would love the library, she mused, as she sat down to write in a high-backed chair facing the window. The walls were lined with long oak shelves, and on these were every description of book to fire the imagination. A scholar like her father would be in his element here. She had discovered poems by many famous names, including Wordsworth and the German poet Goethe. In her room was a translation by Tobias Smollett of the fascinating *Don Quixote*. There were history books, first editions, and alongside these, books which looked as if they could fall apart with age. In this room she felt a different person. Someone of import- ance, as she browsed the shelves, remembering as a child, the vast amount of books which had been at her disposal. Lisette thought her selection of titles boring and dull, and admitted that she entered the library only to sit sometimes with Ross while he worked there.

Not so today, Roxanna heard the door behind her quietly open and close again. A soft giggle, and Mark's hushed order to be calm. She froze in her seat, and unconsciously slid down a little further so that no part of her showed outside the chair.

'I must go, beloved,' Lisette whispered. 'Grand-mère will be awake soon. Besides, I have a fitting for some clothes at four o'clock.'

'Come to me after supper. She will not miss you. Pretend you have another of your headaches.'

'I'm not sure. I do not think she is suspicious, but I am sure Roxanna has been giving me some very searching looks of late. Mark, surely . . .?'

'My brother's little amusement?' Mark gave a hollow chuckle that made Roxanna's blood run cold. He could not know anything? No one could know what had taken place, she thought, her heart beginning to thump unsteadily. 'She's set her cap at him, but she'll not keep him amused for long, and then you may well find yourself with a new companion.'

'Don't,' Lisette protested. 'I like her. We are friends.'

'She's a proved thief. You may have been taken in by that story she told, but I'm not. Ross is not immune to a pretty face, you know. He obviously felt sorry for her. I've had enquiries made about Roxanna Dane in London. Do you know that her father was accused of theft and she of being his accomplice? It's true! The necklace was recovered and no charges pressed, thanks to the benevolence of their employers, but for the past year he has been unable to find work, and she . . . Well, every position she has had after that has been abruptly terminated. The girl is not to be trusted. She's an outrageous wanton!'

'I cannot believe it! No, I will not . . .' Lisette's voice trailed off in horror as she saw the ashen-faced girl who rose before them. 'Roxanna, what are you doing here? *Mon Dieu!* You heard . . . Mark did not mean all those dreadful things! I do not believe them . . .'

'I meant every word.' Mark was quick to recover his composure, and there was no pity on his face for the misery in Roxanna's eyes. 'I know you for what you are, Miss Dane. Soon my brother will, too. Is that a new gown?' He eyed the one she wore. 'Did he pay for it?'

Roxanna opened her mouth to speak, but no words would come, so ashamed was she at his contempt. Did the whole household know of her past? The Countess had promised that, as long as her conduct remained impeccable, it would never go beyond the two of them. But now Mark knew, and with his hatred of his brother, any weapon was useful.

'I see you begin to understand. Anyone who is with my brother is against me.'

'Please don't talk to her like that. I don't like you in this mood—you remind me of Ross,' Lisette pleaded.

'For heaven's sake, don't compare me to him!' Mark snapped. 'Why should I be like him? I am me! I have a right to lead my own life, to take a wife without his gracious permission. I'm nearly twenty-five, dammit! I should have more responsibility here than I do. What am I?' Little more than a glorified mine manager. The allowance I have from our father's will doesn't even cover my losses at the tables for one night!'

'You could always give up gambling,' Roxanna suggested coldly, her composure returning at last. Why should she be afraid of this man's words? They could not hurt her. She was Lady Talland and, if she wished, she could order him from the house. The temptation to tell him how precarious his position at Talland really was almost overcame her, and then she saw the pleading look on Lisette's face and knew she would do nothing to hurt her. For her sake she would remain silent and bear his hurtful sneers.

'I am not in the habit of taking advice from a servant,' Mark snapped. 'And if you breathe one word to my brother or Elizabeth of having seen us together, I'll . . .'

'What will you do?' she asked, emerald chips of ice forming in the depths of her eyes. 'Hand me over to Griffith for another lesson at the tide stakes?'

'What does she mean?' Lisette gasped, as Mark went white with shock. 'Roxanna, you speak in riddles.'

'I thought you knew,' Mark said slowly, frowning. 'Griffith's body was washed up last week two miles along the coast. The volunteers found him on a routine patrol. Would you say his death is convenient, Miss Dane? I would, but then my brother is a very thorough man. He doesn't like to leave loose ends . . . or men who might talk and put his head in a noose alongside theirs.'

'And yours,' Roxanna reminded him, allowing the shock to wash over her without absorbing it fully. 'Remember that, sir. And yours.'

'Where are you going?' Lisette demanded in a tearful tone as Roxanna headed for the door. 'Not to Ross? Oh, please, don't tell him! We were doing nothing wrong. We love each other.'

'My brother is off on another of his mysterious little jaunts and is not expected back before the night of the *bal masqué*.' Mark's arm went round Lisette's shoulders defiantly. 'Didn't you know that either? Dear me, and I thought you were close to him. Be warned, Miss Dane, you will never know him. Many women before you have tried to trap him and failed miserably. He guards his secrets well, even from me, his own brother.'

'Perhaps I shall succeed where others have failed, because I ask nothing from him.' Roxanna looked into his glowering face and managed a faint smile, as if to suggest she was already in possession of a few of those secrets. 'Nor do I try to compete—as you do.'

Not until she reached the sanctuary of her room did she allow herself the indulgence of a few tears, but for a moment only. She did not want the Countess enquiring at supper whether she was going down with another cold. Griffith dead—and Mark suspected Ross of being responsible for his death! The chilling words he had spoken the night he saved her life returned to haunt her dreams later on . . . 'I'll deal with them both personally'—meaning Griffith and young Geoffrey, Mark's man. She rarely had cause to see the latter during the course of the day, and when they did encounter each other, the boy's eyes were evasive—ashamed, she suspected, at the memory of that night. They had never discussed it, for he would scuttle past her like a frightened rabbit, never giving her a chance to detain him.

But Griffith, the wrecker, was dead! For many nights afterwards she dreamed of being pursued across the sand by the men she had seen that night at the church . . . They drove her into the water where the heavy breakers threatened to pound her insensible. And then Ross was carrying her up the cliff path, but at the top he set her down and turned back. She cried out to him, but he ignored her pleas. Down again to the beach where Griffith waited for him . . . Griffith and Mark . . . Two against one . . .

She often awoke soaked with perspiration, and could find no rest again. Then she would rise and go to sit beside the fire until it grew light, afraid to try and sleep again for fear the nightmares returned. How she wished Ross was back. She would ask him for the truth, but would he give it to her?

The night before the *bal masqué* the dream recurred and awoke her just as a clock somewhere in the vast regions of the house chimed four solitary notes. Pulling on a wrap, she pushed her feet into warm slippers and went to a chair beside the fire. It had gone out, for she had forgotten to bank it before retiring. It had been well past eleven before she left Lisette, after hours of discussing the final accessories she would wear with her gown. Roxanna's mind was in a whirl when she finally fell exhausted into bed. White kid gloves or stark black to show off the perfection of the white silk and muslin she was to wear? Golden slippers or white or black? Her mother's diamonds, or pearls? Should she have her hair dressed on the top of her head, or in curls drawn to one side of her face? Nothing was yet decided even after all those hours of suggesting one thing after another. Roxanna fully expected her to change her mind about everything at least a dozen more times before she appeared before their guests.

Shivering slightly in the coolness of the room, she went to the window and opened one shutter. Thank God there was no light tonight. She had seen it twice since Ross had been away, and knew Mark had left the house furtively to rendezvous with the men awaiting him on the beach. With his brother away, he was in charge. She found herself staring suddenly at the wooden panel, behind which lay the secret tunnel to Ross's rooms. As if drawn by some unseen power, her fingers touched the place where she had chipped out a piece of wood. An inch or so above this was where she exerted strong pressure, and, as several times before, the panel swung open. This time she did not hurriedly close it again, afraid to step over the threshold, but slowly made her

way with the candle held high to the room at the top of
the flight of steps. She was drawn to it like a moth to a
candle-flame, knowing full well that the flame would
destroy it, yet unable to stop itself flying nearer and
nearer to certain doom.

Russell came out of the dressing-room as she stood in
the open entrance to Ross's room, noticing from the
unmade bed and the tidiness of the room that he had not
returned, and a great uneasiness took hold of her. Over
two weeks! He did not usually remain away so long. She
supposed he had left on the ship which came and went
from the bay at regular intervals. Was it coincidence or
careful planning, that the red-coated volunteers who
patrolled the coast were always miles away on those
days? She could be terribly wrong, she suddenly
thought. What if he had gone somewhere else? To
London, perhaps? To Lady Alicia Brandon?

As she stood hesitating, colour flooding into her
cheeks at the man's intense stare, he came forward and
helped her to step down into the room, for the passage
was a good foot higher.

'His Lordship is not back yet. I have no idea at what
hour he will return. To tell you the truth, my lady, I am
beginning to grow quite concerned. I expected him soon
after dark . . . Is anything wrong?' Roxanna was staring
at him with surprised eyes. He had addressed her as 'my
lady', not 'Miss Dane'!

'You know . . . that Lord Talland and I are married?'

'But of course. I am totally in his confidence. I hope
that you, too, will feel able to trust me.'

His manner was so pleasant that it prompted her to
ask, 'You knew I had seen the light? Did you follow me
that night?' She remembered how he had warned her so
gravely not to go exploring and seek an explanation for
what she had seen.

'I did not, my lady. When Lord Talland returned
home, I brought him up to date with everything that had
been happening while he was absent. About you. He
told me what had taken place at the inn—concerning his

brother and the young woman who had been so kind to him. He wished me to make enquiries about her—to find her if possible. When he gave me the name, I was astounded, as you can imagine. We both were. He went direct to your room and found it empty. That's when I guessed you had seen the light again and gone out. As we were on our way to the church, we saw two men going away from the cliff path—too distant for us to see faces then . . . Lord Talland went down that cliff face at such a reckless pace that I thought he would break his neck. As it was, he started that wound of his bleeding again. To fight with his brother was madness, but I've never seen him so angry. Like a devil he was . . .'

'Who gave him such a terrible name?' Roxanna asked quietly, sinking on to the sofa. Now that the man seemed willing to speak more freely to her, she was not going to let him stop.

'The old master, his father. Used always to remark as he watched young Ross ride, "There goes the devil again, Russell." Master Ross would always buy the wildest horses, you see, and break them himself. He'd laugh at his father, and retort that the devil looks after his own. As he grew older, he was a reckless young man, whereas his brother was quiet and studious.'

How they had changed, Roxanna thought, wise enough not to interrupt such a surprising statement. Mark, the gambler, the smuggler, quiet and studious! Would that he were. Perhaps, then, Ross would consider him a match for his ward.

Russell was suddenly quiet.

'Go on. Don't stop now,' she entreated. 'There is much more I must know.'

'Not from my servant, and certainly not tonight,' a familiar voice drawled behind her. Turning slowly, she found Ross standing just inside the secret entrance. He was not alone. 'What are you doing here? Looking for my maps again?' There was cool mockery in his voice, but the eyes which searched her face were dark with suspicion and anger.

CHAPTER
SEVEN

NOT WAITING for an answer, Ross stepped into the room.
Three men followed him, all clad in dark clothing, as he
was. All wore swords at their sides, and had an air about
them of men confident in the handling of them. Roxanna
had heard of Ross's prowess as a swordsman and the
many duels he had fought in London, and had herself
been witness to his skill that day on the cliffs when he and
Mark fought each other. The last man to step into the
room and close the panel behind him also had a brace of
pistols in his belt. Nicholas! His face was a picture! Had
she not been aware of Ross's underlying anger at her
presence, she might have laughed at the gaping mouth.

'You look like a fish out of water,' Ross remarked,
with a brief glance in his direction. 'Where else should a
loving wife be, but in her husband's room, waiting to
welcome him home? Pour us something to drink,
Russell, and then get our guests settled.'

'There was—some trouble, sir?' Russell asked, as he
filled four glasses and gave one to each man. Roxanna
shook her head when he looked enquiringly at her.
'Brandy, sir? You all look frozen.'

'As always, you anticipate my every need. Two bottles
of wine couldn't achieve what this will,' Ross remarked
drily. He unbuckled his sword and tossed it down on the
bed, peeled off the thick jerkin he wore over his shirt and
stretched his limbs as if they were cramped.

'Are we to understand that this young lady is your
wife, Ross?' The question came from the man standing
closest to him. A squat, red-headed little man with
coarse features. Peasant features, Roxanna thought, as

she looked at him. He was certainly not the most handsome man she had ever encountered. He scratched on thick red sideburns with his fingers, a smile tugging at the corners of his mouth. 'You are to be congratulated—and envied, *mon ami*! A veritable flower you have discovered for yourself.'

Roxanna found herself blushing furiously before his bold gaze, and gathered her robe about her more tightly, wishing Ross would answer the question Russell had put to him.

'Gentlemen, allow me to introduce you to this little baggage, who has forced my hand somewhat in her eagerness to see me again. For the moment, our marriage is known only to the people here in this room, and I am sure you will be discretion itself and adhere to my wishes that it remain that way. Roxanna, may I present Paul Lazaire.' The red-headed man bowed. 'My old friend, Nicholas Pendennis, you already know.' He did not even look at her, and so she ignored him. 'Richard Denning and the Comte de Villon. Lisette's father. They have all come for the *bal masqué*. Have you not, *mes amis*?'

'Do you think a mask will hide this ugly form?' Lazaire asked with a grin. 'A sheet perhaps.'

Each man in turn, except for Nicholas, came forward to kiss Roxanna's fingertips, while Ross watched, an amused gleam in his eyes. First he had been angry with her; now the situation amused him. To introduce her to his friends in such a fashion, and she in only her nightclothes! Whatever the reason for the presence of these men at Talland, she knew that the *bal masqué* was of secondary importance to them, if, indeed, any.

'Tomorrow is going to be a long day, gentlemen, so I suggest we all retire. Russell will show you to your rooms. From what I remember of Elizabeth's revels, none of us will be abed before dawn.'

'I shall console myself with the excellent contents of the casks we brought with us,' the Comte chuckled. 'As well as dancing with my lovely daughter and your very charming wife, Ross. I intend to monopolise her the whole evening.'

'You will have to stand in line,' Ross returned, throwing Roxanna a wicked grin. 'I have sadly neglected her, and must make up for it tomorrow.'

'We seem to be forgetting why we are here. We have business to discuss . . .' the man called Richard Denning broke in, his face grim and unsmiling. 'You all appear to have forgotten that our lives hang in the balance at this very moment! With Cadoudal in prison and the Duc d'Enghien dead, all our necks are at risk . . . And you talk of a ball!'

'None of which—apart from the ball—is any concern of my wife, and so we will not broach the subject again before her,' Ross interrupted with a hardness of tone that made the other man flush uncomfortably. 'To your beds, gentlemen. I shall see you in the morning. Sleep as late as you wish . . . if you can sleep with the hubbub of activity this place will see tomorrow,' he added, chuckling, and the men bade him good night and left the room, with Russell following.

'Now, young woman, I want an explanation for your presence here.' Ross spun round on Roxanna, and there was no friendliness in the eyes which looked down at her. Surely he did not really think she had come to spy on him?

'I—I . . .' She wanted to tell him the truth, that she had been concerned over his continued absence, but she knew he would not believe her. She had given him no cause to think she cared one jot for him. 'Your brother told me . . .'

'Told you what? Speak up! Why do you look at me so strangely?'

'Is it true that Griffith is dead?' The words came out in a rush.

'Dead? How? When? I know nothing of this . . . Should I? Is that it?' A fierce expletive broke from his lips. 'Of what am I being accused now, Roxanna? Murder?'

'I did not say how he died, so why should you think he was murdered?' she asked, and his eyes narrowed sharply.

'You are too clever by half, little cat. Tell me the truth—do you think I had a hand in his death?'

'I—I don't know. You said you would deal with him that night—personally,' she reminded him, and he nodded, grave-faced.

'I did, I remember. But I had other, more urgent, matters on hand. I went looking for him later, but he had left the village, Nicholas told me.' He broke off, running a hand through his thick hair. 'Damnation! I should have known . . . There was bad feeling between those two. Something to do with Nicholas's wife, a long time ago. She ran off with a man and has never been seen or heard of since. I've long suspected that the man was Griffith, but Nicholas has never confided in me. He is close-mouthed, that one, and shares no part of himself with anyone else. Perhaps you understand his manner with you at the inn a little better, now. He will never trust another woman. Poor Nicholas.'

He sat down on the edge of the bed and began tugging off his boots.

'Come and help me like a dutiful wife,' he commanded. Roxanna pulled a face at his manner, but went to do so.

'I am not meek, or docile, or dutiful,' she said, as he dragged off his coat and threw it across a chair. 'Your brother said that is how you are—like your friend Nicholas, I mean. He said you guard your secrets well, even from him. He thinks you killed Griffith . . . to dispose of any loose ends.'

'Does he, now? What else did he say to you? I didn't know you were on such friendly terms,' he drawled sardonically. Then, seeing the look which crossed her face, he demanded, 'He has upset you in some way. Tell me how, and I shall speak to him.'

'No—I don't want that. He—He did not mean what he said . . . Please, I don't want another fight.'

'Why, little cat, are you concerned for me? Or did you come here tonight just to ply my servant with questions? Do I not give you all the answers you need?'

'You tell me nothing,' she flashed, and he grinned, smothering a yawn as he did so. She watched him stretch out on the bed, not bothering to remove any more of his clothes. He would fall asleep at any moment, she realised, watching his eyelids begin to droop. He was exhausted.

'Come here. Stay with me.' He held out a hand to her.

'Why do you ask it of me? You do not really want me. Please let me go back to my room.'

'No. I want to feel you close to me. I want to feel safe . . . There was a time yesterday when I thought I might not gaze into those fascinating eyes again. Come here beside me, Roxanna, where you belong.'

She allowed him to draw her down beside him. He slipped an arm about her shoulders and laid his head on her breast. She could feel his breath against her skin.

'You don't know how good it is to be safe again. One day I shall tell you . . .'

She looked down at the dark face, and found he was asleep, all tenseness and strain wiped from it as he relaxed against her. Carefully she drew the heavy bedcover over them both and allowed herself to relax on to a pillow.

Suddenly she felt very, very happy, for as she gazed at him, studying the long black lashes, the tiny scar at his temple, listened to his slow, steady breathing, she knew she was not falling in love with this man who was her husband. She *was* in love with him. Deeply, passionately in love.

Only when she awoke in the morning did she realise that she had asked none of the questions which had pounded in her brain the moment they were alone. The Comte de Villon, Lisette's father. But he was an exile, living the life of a near fugitive, Lisette had told her, because of his close association with the Bourbons. It was his dearest

wish to see another king on the throne in place of the
upstart Corsican, Napoleon. She could not believe he
had risked his life to attend the Countess's *bal masqué*.
Then why?

Who were the men Georges Cadoudal and d'Enghien?
One in prison, the other dead? Nicholas Pendennis was a
seaman; perhaps Denning was, too. Very useful if they
had ships at their disposal.

'What is troubling that pretty little head now?' Ross
demanded quietly, coming back to the bed. He had
removed his clothes and donned a robe in preparation
for a bath. On the table beside her Roxanna saw a tray of
coffee and sweet biscuits.

'Help yourself, it's still hot. Russell brought it a few
minutes ago,' he said, and she sat up and did so. It felt
very strange to sit in his company, drinking coffee, as if
they had been married ten years and grown quite used to
each other.

'Well?' Ross prompted, pouring himself a second cup.
He took it black, without sugar, she noticed. 'You
haven't answered me.'

'You must realise that I am curious about those men
. . .' she began, only to stop as she saw his eyes narrow.
'Very well, I shall ask you nothing. Then you can hardly
blame me for what I think.'

'And what is that? I am a smuggler, possibly a
wrecker. I take human life without one iota of conscience. That I am a spy. But then I have never denied
that, have I?' As she blanched and quickly put down her
cup, he added, 'I shall do nothing to harm my country,
Roxanna, neither will the men I have with me, regardless of their nationality. Not all Frenchmen desire
Napoleon to rule them, you know.'

'So my father once told me. I know nothing of
politics.'

'That is as it should be. Listen to me. There will be
other men here, before the day is over, who will meet
with those I brought last night. There will be a time when
I must leave them in your hands, for my attention must

be divided between my business and my guests. I trust
you to care for them while I am gone, even though the
occasions will be short and few. Will you do that for me?
Ask no questions of them, but be gracious to them? I
need your help, Roxanna. Do this for me.'

'Very well. Does the Countess not know about these
other guests? Were they on her list?'

'Certainly not!' He chuckled, and kissed her lightly on
one cheek. As he drew back, Roxanna saw the gleam
which sprang to his eyes, and caught her breath as his lips
sought hers . . .

Rosie, noisily entering the room with a pitcher of hot
water in each hand, brought them apart instantly. Roxanna felt herself blush to the very roots of her hair, while
Ross merely drew away from her, his face registering
annoyance at the interruption.

'Your pardon, my lord . . . I've brought the water for
your bath . . .' the girl gasped. She could not take her
eyes from Roxanna in her wrinkled robe, which gaped
visibly to reveal her nightgown. Her hair all awry, and
those red cheeks which told their own story . . .

'In here, girl, and be quick about it,' Russell thundered, coming out of the dressing-room. 'Your pardon,
my lord, I did not hear her knock.'

'How could I, with both hands full,' came the cheeky
answer, and she was propelled so quickly into the other
room that she almost dropped both pitchers.

'I shall fetch the remainder myself,' Russell said,
ushering her out of the bedroom. Even so, Rosie managed to look back over her shoulder, and her grin was
positively mischievous.

'In less than half an hour she will have told everyone,'
Roxanna gasped, throwing aside the bedcover. 'What
will the Countess say? I shall be dismissed.'

'Roxanna, calm yourself. I shall not let you be sent
away, foolish child. Elizabeth will believe whatever I
choose to tell her,' Ross drawled.

'Your brother already says quite openly that he be-
lieves me to be your mistress. Would you have her

believe it also?' she cried, taken aback by his words.
'Will you not tell her the truth?'

'Should anyone know you are my wife, it would place
your life in danger. Anyone close to me at this time
would be in danger. Little fool, don't you understand?
My silence protects you,' Ross said, his tone harsh, and
the anger fled from her face. 'The life of every man you
met last night hangs in the balance, as Denning said, for
the next few weeks, at least . . . until a certain little
problem has been removed.'

'Napoleon,' she whispered. 'You mean to kill him,
don't you? Your life, too, then, is at risk.' It came to her
suddenly as she wondered why the Comte would leave
the safety of his home in Spain to travel abroad, leaving
himself open to the chance of being recognised by one of
Fouché's men, forever seeking to capture Bourbon sym-
pathisers, and return them for execution, no matter
where they were.

'And yours,' he admitted. 'I do not want the additional worry that you may be used against me, which is what I
have always feared could happen if the French laid
hands on Lisette. That is one of the reasons I watch
her so closely.' He did not answer her question about
Napoleon, but his gaze had narrowed sharply at it. 'I am
fast growing accustomed to your being here, and I do not
want an accident to take you from me. Now I have
frightened you,' he said, as she shuddered. 'That was not
my intention. Only to make you believe I have good
reasons for everything I do. Soon . . .' He bent and
kissed her trembling lips, but the kiss was without
passion. Had Rosie not come in when she did, Roxanna
knew that it would have been very different. She had felt
it.

'Does the Countess ever talk to you about France, and
what is going on there?'

'Sometimes. But mostly it is Lisette. She fears that her
father will become involved with his old friends again
. . . people who will try to rid France of Napoleon
and return a Bourbon to the throne. Like the Duc

d'Enghien,' she added. She had no idea who he was, but her shrewd guess proved more than a guess, for Ross gave a soft oath.

'The man is dead, God rest his soul. An innocent man. Napoleon needed a scapegoat, and chose him. There will be others, if Cadoudal does not break and talk.'

'The man in prison?'

Ross nodded. He was not telling her anything new, merely confirming what she had overheard. So there was a plot in progress—and it was her assumption that not only Ross, but the men he had brought last night, were deeply concerned in it.

'You will forget those names, Roxanna,' Ross said quietly, and she nodded. 'And their faces must not exist for you, even in your mind, once tomorrow is over.'

'I understand.'

'I wonder. It is no game. The stakes are our lives,' he returned grimly.

After leaving Ross's room, she returned quickly to her own to wash and dress, realising that the Countess would be expecting her to show herself for breakfast. She had no appetite, and excused herself on the pretence of a slight headache, saying she wanted to go for a walk. To her horror, Mark intercepted her as she was almost at her door.

'Please allow me to pass.' She looked into the cold eyes regarding her, and knew he was aware of what had happened. She had momentarily forgotten that Rosie was enamoured of him, and would doubtless relate every piece of gossip she thought worth while.

'You disgust me, do you know that?' he snapped. 'You have the gall to stand there and look at me with those innocent eyes when you have just come from my brother's bed!' A passing footman slowed his steps, and then hurried past as she turned to look at him. 'And you dare to stand in judgment on my love for Lisette! God, you are amazing. You may last longer than the others he has had, but I'll give you no more than another month.'

'You are insulting, sir. And totally misinformed.'

'Are you telling me Rosie didn't find you in my brother's room—in his bed—in his arms, half naked?'

With a gasp, Roxanna brushed past him into her room. His laugh followed her. An hour later Russell came to say that she was required downstairs in the library. She had spent the time standing by the window, watching the first of the guests arrive for the evening's festivities, envying the elegant women who alighted on the arms of handsome escorts. She should have been on top of the world—she was in love, and married to the man who had stolen her heart—but he would never look at her as many of the men she saw looked at their companions. He wanted a quiet, uncomplicated, married life. A wife who would give him children to carry on his name, but not make demands of her own in return. Who would have no fire, no depth to her own character but be totally dominated by his. And she loved him, so she would accept it.

Was she to be rebuked by the Countess for her seemingly wanton behaviour in the bedroom of the master of the house? For the gossip which now prevailed? The room appeared to be empty at first, and then from the very same chair that she had sat in and overheard Mark and Lisette discussing her, so large that it was hiding him completely as it had hidden her, rose a stooping figure which brought a cry of joy to her lips. She ran to him, flung her arms about his neck and smothered the drawn, grey features with kisses.

'Father! Oh, Father, he kept his word! You are here. Why did he not tell me you were coming? Oh, I am so happy! When did you arrive? You should have let me know . . .'

'Gently, my dear child! How can I answer you when you are near smothering me. Enjoyable as it is after all these months, I would like to breathe. There, now, that's better.' George Dane held his daughter at arm's length and surveyed her with shrewd brown eyes, as alert as they had been in his youth. They were all that

now reminded her of the vitality, the timeless energy, he
had once possessed. He had aged in the short space of
time they had been apart, she thought sadly, noticing
that the last of his hair was now completely white. Had
he been ill again? 'Let me look at you. The sea air agrees
with you; there is colour in your cheeks. So you have
settled here, then? You do not miss London?'

'No. You will like it here, too. We shall go for walks
together and I shall show you the interesting places I
have found. An old ruined house with a cannon dating
back to the Spanish Armada, and the sanctuary of the
monks who used to care for the chapel which was once
here, and . . .'

'My old legs will not carry me far these days,
Roxanna, you know that. Besides, I shall have far too
much work to do. You do know why I am here, don't
you?'

Roxanna realised that she did not know what her
father had been told. Of only one thing was she sure. It
was not the truth.

'It was meant as a surprise. Your daughter was not
even aware of your arrival,' Ross remarked, coming into
the room in time to hear the question, and seeing her
dilemma at once. 'You had a good journey, I hope? I am
Lord Talland. Your daughter told me of your love of
books—something we have in common. From all she
has told me about you, I am certain I have the right man
to catalogue all these for me.' He waved a hand in the
direction of the bookshelves. 'You are to take your time,
and consider yourself my guest. I am sure we shall have
many opportunities in the near future to discuss some of
these works.'

'You are most gracious, sir.' If George Dane noticed
the stunned look on Roxanna's face, he did not comment on it then, or later when they were together. He
was sure, however, that it was not just a common
interest in books which was the reason he had been
brought to Talland, at a salary far beyond his expec-
tations. And in style. His back rent had been settled,

and the outstanding fees for the doctor. New, warm clothing had been provided for the journey. A coach had collected him and conveyed him in comfort to his new abode. 'I sincerely hope my work will be to your satisfaction.'

'It will be,' Ross assured him.

Because it was not of the least importance to him, Roxanna thought, hating him for reminding her of the bargain she had made and spoiling the marvel of this moment. And then, looking into her father's face and seeing the lines of pain etched deep into it, she knew she had been right in her decision. For the remainder of his days, he would never want again. He had cared for her all his life; now it was her turn to do something for him. She would not count the cost to her pride or her dignity. They were small things by comparison with his happiness.

'Your father's room is prepared, next to your own. I thought you would like him near you,' Ross said, ringing for a servant. 'I am sure he would like to rest for a while after his journey.'

'You have thought of everything,' Roxanna returned, and an eyebrow arched at the frostiness of her tone.

'I should like a word with you before you go,' he requested, as she went to accompany her father from the room. She kissed his lined cheek and said that she would follow directly. Then, turning, she faced Lord Talland with a toss of her head to indicate that his company was not what she desired. 'I have kept my part of the bargain. Why do you not look more pleased? At least I expected the courtesy of a simple "Thank you",' he said bleakly.

'Thank you.' The words almost stuck in her throat. 'You brought him here to work . . . He is not well. Surely you can see that? How could you?'

'A few weeks of good food and your company, and I am sure he will feel stronger and in need of something to do. Pamper him for a few days, ensure that he does nothing strenuous, if you are concerned, and I shall ask the doctor to see him later today . . . For your peace of mind,' he added, a familiar mocking twist to his mouth. Her peace of mind! What did he care for that? She was under his thumb, now, like everyone else. 'If he has half your pride, which I am certain he has, he will accept the work I have offered. He will spend days, weeks, months—I care not—in here, cataloguing these books. The library is his domain, as far as I am concerned. He may come and go as he pleases, use it whenever he wishes. It will not be work to him, but a pleasure. Or do you not know your own father as well as you think you do?'

'I know him better than you ever will,' she flashed. 'I shall not allow him to be used—as you use others.'

'You, for instance?' Ross's eyes burned into her angry face, challenging the justness of her heated words. 'I think that, so far, I have given more than I have received. You have my name, and my confidence to the extent that I am able to give it. You hold my very life in your hands, and I bring your sick father to live beneath my roof. What more is it you want from me, Roxanna? My head on a platter, perhaps, because I expect my wife to share my bed in return for the advantages my name and position—and money—give her? That you will not have. Be satisfied with things as they are. I have no more to give.'

Not to me, Roxanna thought miserably as she went upstairs. To another, perhaps. To the Lady Alicia Brandon who chased after him so relentlessly. What kind of a relationship did he share with her? Tonight she would find out, for she knew that name had been included on the list of guests.

One look at her father's drawn features when she entered his room, and she knew that it was not the journey which had taken toll of his limited strength. She helped him to undress and climb into bed, over-riding his feeble protests that he should make himself known to other members of the household.

'You will do no such thing,' she told him firmly, tucking the clothes about him. 'Are you comfortable? I am going to fetch you some books. Lord Talland wishes you to make full use of his library, so you can begin over the next few days by staying in bed and reading what I bring you. This afternoon a doctor will come to see you. Please do as I ask, Father? Rest, and get well, and then you can think of work.'

'I did not come here to lie abed, my girl,' he reproved. 'I am not being paid to shirk my duties.'

Paid! That was something else Roxanna had been unaware of. She knew that a salary would make her father feel he was less of a burden to Ross. How she wished she could tell him that he would never want for anything again; that he had no need to work.

'What is it, Roxanna?' As she hugged him, he took her by the shoulders and held her away from him, his expression concerned. 'You come here as a companion, yet you speak with such authority in your voice.' He was interrupted by a knock on the door. Rosie came in, carrying a tray. The moment she saw Roxanna, she began to smile in a most knowing fashion, which caused her great embarrassment, which she barely succeeded in hiding.

'Lord Talland told me to bring this up. Some soup for the old gentleman, and hot buttered toast. There's a bottle of his best burgundy to go with it. Important, is he?'

'My father,' Roxanna replied stiffly. 'Thank you, Rosie, you may go.'

'My, we are getting above ourselves, aren't we? Fancies you, does he? Master Mark bet his valet you'll last a month. I think you stand more of a chance than that . . .'

'Out!' The girl retreated hastily before Roxanna's furious expression.

'Why am I here, Roxanna?' Her father's voice was stern, his face unsmiling, as she turned back to the bed with the tray. He watched her set it down beside him and take up the steaming hot broth and a spoon and prepare to feed him. 'I am quite capable of feeding myself.' She gave it to him in silence. 'Now, please tell me what that girl meant. What price did you pay to bring me here?'

'Lord Talland is not like that, Father. Believe me, it was his own idea, when I told him how difficult life had been for us this past year . . . of your bad health . . . and he learned that you were a scholar. I think he looks forward to the two of you having long, intricate discussions over his collection. Some of his books are first editions. He is very proud of them.'

'And he has made no . . . advances towards you?'

'Certainly not! He is not like . . . like . . .'

'Lord Carsewell? I have not forgotten what he had in mind for you. Had his wife not discovered his intentions . . .'

'Had I not repulsed him, he would not have had you accused of theft! Even when she found out, she did nothing! She could have cleared your name . . . she knew he was an odious lecher, but remained silent for the sake of her own selfishness. The thought of the gossip frightened her . . . the loss of friends, when they discovered that her own husband was prepared falsely to accuse an innocent man because a servant-girl had slighted him. I was dismissed because she was afraid I might be believed. All his friends knew what he was like.'

'You were the first not to be afraid of his threats, and not to succumb to his offers of money and presents in return for your favours,' George Dane returned, patting her hand as he saw the distress in her eyes. 'Do you swear to me that this Lord Talland is an honourable man?'

'I am not his mistress, if that is what you are so tactfully asking, Father. Nor will I be. That I promise you. Now, have your soup and a little of this wine while I fetch you some books.'

She found she was trembling as she left the room. She had never lied to him in all her nineteen years. Servants hurried past her with armfuls of clean linen, towels and sheets for the guest-rooms. Every single one on this floor was to be occupied overnight, as well as all those on the one below. Only the floor above, which housed the private rooms of Lord Talland, was not to be invaded. She wondered if that was where he had placed his friends from France. If they did not want to be seen they would not be, for there was no reason for anyone to venture further than the second floor.

She spent some while in the library choosing her father an assorted collection of books to keep him occupied. She did not want him leaving his bed for at least a week. On the way back upstairs she encountered Lisette, clutching a pair of bright blue shoes in one hand, a simple golden circlet for her hair in the other.

'Where have you been, Roxanna? I have been searching everywhere for you. What do you think about these shoes with the white? And this for my hair?'

'I prefer the black shoes with the diamond buckles, and the diamond circlet, as I said yesterday,' Roxanna said, wondering if the next hours were to be spent on endless, fruitless suggestions yet again.

'Do you? Perhaps you are right. Come and help me choose . . . I really will this time. Oh, your things have arrived. Clementina brought them with my own.'

'Things?' Roxanna asked, looking puzzled. She had ordered nothing from the dressmaker that she could recall, even though she still had almost fifty pounds.

'Surely you can't have forgotten? I declare, Roxanna, you have excellent choice for someone of your station. I mean a mere companion . . . Oh, I'm sorry! That sounded so rude. I didn't mean it. But the things you chose are so lovely. You have an excellent eye for colour. The burgundy is simply stunning.' Her eyes alighted for the first time on the books Roxanna held under one arm. 'What are those?'

'Books for my father. Lord Talland has engaged him to catalogue his book collection, but I am afraid the journey has exhausted him, and he has retired for the remainder of the day. With Lord Talland's kind permission, of course.'

'Your father? Yes, I remember you spoke of his love of books. Ross will certainly enjoy his company. I shall come with you to see that you do not linger too long with him, for I am in dire need of your help.'

Roxanna was pleased to see that every drop of the soup had been consumed, most of the buttered toast and a glass of the wine, when she returned to her father's room. She introduced Lisette, and saw immediately that her father liked the bright-eyed young girl who was determined to drag her away after only two minutes.

'I must go, Father,' she said apologetically, fixing the pillow more comfortably behind the thin shoulders. 'I shall come back later. There is a *bal masqué* tonight given by the Countess de Villon, and we have much to do yet.'

'You are going?' Her father's surprise was not to be wondered at, for a mere companion was not normally allowed to join in such occasions, when there would be ample members of the family present to keep an eye on any unruly daughters.

'But of course,' Lisette declared. 'We are going to dance with all the good-looking men, are we not, Roxanna? Make them fall madly in love with us, and then run away before they can unmask us! It will be fun.'

'I hope you will both have a pleasant evening.' George Dane's eyes twinkled unexpectedly as he looked at the two of them. His idea of fun was to read a detailed history book or the translations of Molière. 'Run along to your duties, Roxanna. I am more than content here.'

It was over two hours before Roxanna was able to escape to her own room with the box Clementina had delivered. She had sat in a stunned silence as Lisette inspected every article, commenting again on her good colour sense, her appreciation of fine silks. She could not deny she had bought them, for the question then asked of her, would have been—Who did? Only one person that she knew of, she thought with fiercely burning cheeks as she laid across the bed a flimsy nightgown in white silk, embroidered with lace. Another in the sheerest chiffon—it was positively indecent, she thought, holding it up to the light and quickly throwing it down again. There was little difference between these and the four gowns which accompanied them. All were in the latest London mode, with the high waist actually beneath the bosom in a Grecian style. They were extremely *décolleté*, even in daytime. Did he expect her to wear such garments? Two were ball-gowns, one of burgundy silk, the other in pale blue, shot with silver thread at the waist and hem and round the small puffed sleeves.

She had never possessed such beautiful clothes before. There were dainty shoes to match, and, at the very bottom of the box, several silk underslips. An afterthought, Roxanna wondered, as if he knew she would not parade herself in such flimsy attire. Yet all the ladies of fashion wore clothes like these—some, she remembered before she left London, even more outrageous in their necklines than these she surveyed.

She would wear the burgundy tonight. Her yellow gown was finished, a modest creation in comparison to these, but the burgundy would show off her hair better. For a fleeting moment she thought of the lovely jade green gown Ross had taken back from her, and with a heavy sigh she carefully put away her new acquisitions. She would cause more of a stir when she appeared tonight, as elegantly gowned as any other woman, but he expected it of her. As she was to play hostess—albeit reluctantly—to his extra guests who knew the secret she carried with her, she must give them no cause to speculate on what they had been told.

Out of sight of everyone else, she would be his wife for the short time demanded of her. It might be some considerable while before the opportunity arose again, if ever. Mark's scornful words still lingered with her. He was so sure that Ross would abandon her before long.

She spent the best part of the afternoon with the Countess, who insisted on inspecting all the rooms prepared for the guests. After that, the kitchens and the enormous array of food being prepared there. Enough for three hundred people, let alone one hundred, Roxanna thought, watching the cook putting the finishing touches to a goose in aspic. It looked mouth-watering.

At last given leave to go to her room, to spend what little time remained on her own preparations for the evening, Roxanna gratefully made her way upstairs. In less than an hour the first carriages were expected to arrive, and the Countess had taken herself off to change and receive the influx of people. She looked exceedingly tired of late, Roxanna had thought, and more than once as they toured the house she had been aware of Elizabeth's shallow breathing, as if she was finding difficulty taking air into her lungs. She was quite old, and had suffered greatly in the Revolution which had swept her beloved France. All her family were dead except Lisette and her son Claude, the man Ross had brought to Talland last night. Roxanna hoped she would be well enough to enjoy the *bal masqué*.

Her footsteps faltered as she neared her room, seeing who lounged outside the door, a malicious smile on his face as he watched her approach. Did he mean to detain and insult her again, as he had done after breakfast?

'I hear you are acquiring quite a wardrobe, Miss Dane. What do you think of my brother's tastes?' Roxanna blanched, remembering that her father's room was only a few paces away. Lisette had told him, of course. She doubted if they had any secrets from each other. Ignoring him, she laid a hand on the knob of her bedroom door, but froze as Mark taunted cruelly, 'Come and look out of this window. Come and take a look at your rival, Roxanna Dane.'

She flung the door open and rushed headlong inside, slamming it behind her. A hand against her fiercely beating heart, she stood in the middle of the room, afraid to go to the window . . . afraid to see the face of the woman below. She knew full well whom he meant, but she could not resist the temptation to gaze at the woman who sought to have Ross James Talland for her own.

Lady Alicia Brandon stood in the garden, wrapped in a silk cloak trimmed with rich sable fur. Roxanna could see little of her, for the cowl covered most of her face, but then as the woman lifted her head to speak to the man at her side, she glimpsed a full, sensuous mouth and large eyes, framed by long black lashes. She heard her laugh softly, and watched mesmerised as she lifted a hand where rings flashed and shone on nearly every finger and drew his head down to hers. It appeared that the Lady Alicia had taken up where they left off the last time they were together, Roxanna thought, anger rising like a red angry mist to cloud her vision until she turned away, biting back her tears. But not before she had seen Ross—the man who was her husband, the man who had proclaimed that this woman meant nothing to him—take her in his arms and return the kiss.

She lingered in a bath of hot water that Rosie had brought without comment, wishing with all her heart that she could plead a headache and be excused from going downstairs that evening. The excitement of it all had long since left her. While she was entertaining his French guests, what would he be doing, she wondered miserably? Dancing with his true-love? Why, then, had he wished to remain married to her? Why had he bedded her? There was only one answer—and it frightened her and sent her plummeting into the very depths of despair. A wife could not testify against her husband. She could not give evidence against him. Whatever she knew about him and his activities, whatever she suspected he was involved in, what crimes he had committed, her lips would always remain sealed. That was the law! So long as she remained married to him, he was safe! And now her father resided beneath his roof—added protection against a change of mind on her part. What a devious, heartless, rogue he was. And she, God help her, loved him still! Her only consolation was that he would never know it.

When she emerged from her bath and sat down to curl her hair, her eyes through the mirror saw that the burgundy dress she had placed on the bed had been tossed carelessly on a chair. In its place lay the jade green muslin. Beside it a cashmere shawl, and on the floor, dainty green satin slippers with silver buckles. There was something else on the bed, too—a long, thin velvet box! She rose slowly to her feet, and picked it up with fingers that trembled violently. He had again come to her room while she bathed. Had she no means of keeping him out? She must block the entrance, somehow. She could not have him coming to her in this fashion. She was too vulnerable to those sweet endearments which dropped from his lips and were worthless, to his touch which roused her to such undignified passion. No, she would not allow it to happen again. She would not be used.

She gasped as she saw the opal necklace which lay on a bed of faded red silk. Hesitantly, she drew it out. One single stone set in gold lay in the palm of her hand, and reminded her of flames leaping in the hearth. There was red amid the blue and streaks of yellow. And earrings to match.

For a moment, rebellion rose inside her. Why should she obey this silent demand to wear what he chose? She knew why. Because her father was a pawn in his little game, to be used as ruthlessly as he was using her, and she had no doubt that he would do so if she disobeyed him. No, she would wear the green. She would bear the stares of the guests and the sniggers of the servants so long as her father remained at Talland. And she would do so with pride, she decided, returning to the complicated task of arranging her hair in the latest fashion. She would show him he could not take that from her . . .

Before she went downstairs, she moved a heavy oak chest from its place at the foot of the bed to a new home—against the panel which gave entrance to her room.

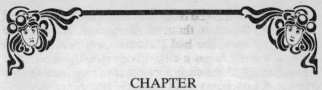

CHAPTER EIGHT

WHILE SHE was gathering sufficient courage to go downstairs, Roxanna looked in on her father. He stared drowsily at the slender, well-groomed young woman who stood by the bedside, bent to kiss his cheek and left an aroma of sweet perfume hovering in the air.

'My dear child, where did you get such fine clothes? You will outshine the finest lady tonight in that attire.'

'The Countess is very generous, Father. She has provided me with a complete new wardrobe and allows me to repay her from my monthly salary. I am treated almost like one of the family. I am very lucky.'

He gave her a searching look as if to ascertain whether Lord Talland regarded her as such. She pretended not to notice, tidied his bedcovers and said good night, promising to return before she went to bed.

Before descending the staircase to the mirrored hall, now full of beautifully gowned and bejewelled women and their companions, whose clothes in many respects rivalled their own for colour and elegance, she quickly put on the black velvet mask which, she prayed, would give her some anonymity until it was time to discard it at midnight. Now she could pass among them easily, she realised. Her gown was the height of fashion, and from the envious glances coming her way, it far outrivalled many around her. Her jewellery was obviously expensive, and in far better taste, to her way of thinking, than an abundance of shimmering stones which many of the women wore, which seemed to be intended to cover every inch of bare skin available.

She was acutely aware of the admiring glances

directed towards her from many of the men as she
ventured to the threshold of the Blue Room, where most
of the guests had gathered. The atmosphere was gay and
relaxed and she found it difficult not to allow herself to
be caught up in the pleasantness of her surroundings.
Musicians had come from Bodmin to play for the whole
evening, and already couples were dancing in the middle
of the floor. She shook her head, politely declining the
invitation of a young man. Would he have asked her had
he known who she was? she wondered. Perhaps he
would. A mild flirtation with a servant-girl amused the
kind of men around her, and the women were as lax with
their morals as were their husbands or lovers. They
thought nothing of arriving at such an occasion with one
man and leaving with another. Or at least dallying with
someone different, sometimes quite blatantly under the
noses of their escorts. She had been shocked when she
first went into service. It still made her very sad and
deeply ashamed to see women degrade themselves so
disgracefully.

A laughing couple brushed past her to join the dancing, and as she turned aside, seeking Lisette and the
Countess, she found her way barred by a tall man
wearing a burgundy-coloured satin mask. His coat was
of the same colour, and the collar which stood high at the
back of his neck was of velvet instead of plain cloth.
Beneath, his waistcoat was of white satin with gold
thread, the upper buttons open, as was customary, to
show off the heavily frilled shirt beneath. His knee-
breeches were also white.

Slowly Roxanna lifted her gaze to the gleaming black
eyes behind the mask. She would know those anywhere!

'I am pleased you saw fit to wear the gown I sent,' Ross
said quietly, aware of the people milling close at hand.
His eyes studied the mass of shining curls pinned to the
top of her head and surmounted by a plain ribbon of
green silk. He slowly considered her, from the top of
those gleaming tresses to where the fire opal rested in the
hollow between her breasts. 'A perfect setting,' he

added, bestowing a smile on her that, had she not known differently, she would have taken as pride. He wanted her to be at ease with him so that she would no longer question his demands on her. How she wished she could just accept her lot without the burden of a troublesome conscience. But she could not.

'Had I not, sir, I am sure you would have torn whatever I was wearing from my back,' she returned with iced sweetness, and the smile vanished from his face.

'Do not anger me this night, Roxanna. I have more than enough to contend with. Mingle with our guests.' Our guests! As if he meant her to be included in the words. 'Lisette and Elizabeth are over by the fireplace, should you wish to join them. It might be safer. I have noticed that you are already being eyed by several young dandies fresh down from London, eager for a new face, a harmless little flirtation. Do not even think of accommodating one of them!'

'If you do not wish me to enjoy myself, perhaps I should return to my room?' she suggested, and his eyes flashed a warning. 'You can always send for me when my presence is required.'

'Are you determined to anger me? I warn you, you will regret it. Do not think that the presence of these others will protect you from me if I choose to take you to task over your manners. You do not know me if you are relying on that.'

'No, sir, I do not know you. Nor do I have a wish to, outside the bounds of the bargain we made. With your leave, I shall join Lisette.'

She had slipped past him and into the crowd before he could stop her. She headed straight for the two women seated beside the roaring fire and placed herself alongside Lisette's chair. The girl stared at her for a long moment, then a bubble of laughter rose up in her throat.

'It cannot be! Roxanna—is it? It is you. Grand-mère, look! Is she not a picture? Where did you get that lovely gown? I do not remember seeing it this afternoon.' She wore white silk, edged with gold, her fair curls crowned with a diamond circlet.

'I hid it at the bottom of the box,' Roxanna lied with a wildly beating heart, for she saw Ross making his way towards them, and the Countess was staring at her too . . . No, not at her, but at the opal around her neck. 'I wanted to surprise you. I did not think you would recognise me. It was all for nothing, it seems.'

'Not at all. It is your hair . . . Very few women in the room have long hair such as yours; they prefer the shorter styles, these days. And the colour . . . it shines like the sun in all this candlelight. Did you recognise her, Ross?' She looked up at the man who stood before them. Roxanna dared not.

'Who? What puzzle do you plague me with now?' came the amused answer, and Lisette clapped her hands in glee.

'Look! It is Roxanna. I recognised her at once.'

'With so many beautiful apparitions floating past me, their faces so carefully concealed, I am at a loss to recognise anyone I know. There will be the devil to pay if I offend someone I shouldn't,' Ross chuckled.

Roxanna was sure he would recognise Alicia Brandon. Lisette's eyes sparkled at the declaration, and her next words confirmed that she, too, had had the same thought.

'If you do not recognise Alicia, Ross, she will scratch out your eyes!'

'Lisette, do not make such preposterous statements. Lady Alicia would never dream of doing such a thing. I declare the child grows sillier every day. You must take a firm hand with her, Miss Dane. I leave it to you to show her how a young lady should behave. Your manners and your decorum are impeccable. She can learn much from you,' the Countess remarked, frowning at her flippancy.

Roxanna risked a quick look into the dark face turned towards her. There was a look in his eyes she could not fathom. He was staring at her, yet it was as though his thoughts were a thousand miles away.

'Do you not agree, Ross?' Elizabeth asked, prodding him with her fan, and he gave her a slow, charming smile.

'I have every faith in Miss Dane's ability to curb the impetuosity of youth and tame the wildest of natures,' he drawled, and his sarcasm was not lost on Roxanna. 'However, I think it a great pity that she has obviously never experienced a little recklessness in her own spotless life. I always say there is no substitute for the experience one learns at first hand.'

He bowed and left them, leaving Roxanna wishing the floor would open up and swallow her. Experience, indeed! He had more than enough for them both, in so many things. And he knew that her character was far from flawless—Lord Carsewell had seen to that!

'I am sure he is dancing with Lady Alicia,' Lisette declared a few minutes later. 'There, by the french windows. Do you see the woman with him? Look at that dress and those jewels! Her first husband left her a very wealthy widow. Ross could use some of that money to reopen the old mine, could he not, Grand-mère? If he married her.'

'No, little matchmaker, he could not. In the first place, the mine is dangerous. He told me long ago that several of the shafts have collapsed from lack of maintenance, and, second . . .' She paused, her eyes resting momentarily on Roxanna's face. 'Second, Ross has never mentioned marriage. I think he is a confirmed bachelor.'

'Not while Alicia is at hand. Can you not see the way she is gazing at him, all dewy-eyed and innocent? Grand-mère, you know she can twist him round her little finger. Look, they are going outside . . . and on a cold night like this, too. Perhaps she has plans for keeping warm . . .' This time the look her grandmother threw her quelled the speculative remarks.

Unable to bear another word about the hateful woman, Roxanna accepted an invitation to dance. It was the first of many. She did not want to be still—or alone.

She must stop her mind from thinking about another woman with her husband. Yet she had no claim on him. Nothing had been said in the making of their bargain which gave her the slightest hope that he would ever care for her!

She took no interest in whom she danced with or who accompanied her to the tables of refreshment set out in the adjoining room. At first she drank lemonade, provided in abundance for the younger members of the *bal masqué*, but it did nothing to revive her flagging spirits and at last she accepted a glass of wine. And then another. After three of them, her head, unaccustomed to any strong drink, began to feel as if it were floating, and suddenly the evening took on a lighter, more relaxing tone. For the first time she noticed that more French was being spoken tonight than English, by most people. Half the guests seemed to be *émigrés*.

Whenever she looked for Ross in the throng, he was always—or nearly always—with the same woman, whose black hair gleamed beneath the candle chandeliers, whose black gown was lower, more outrageous, than any other in the room. Milk-white shoulders were left bare. Around her slender throat was a magnificent ruby. Similar jewels hung from her ears and encircled shapely wrists. As before, when Roxanna had seen her in the garden, rings of every description glittered on long fingers. She was the most beautiful woman in the room, Roxanna knew, and she accepted it. Men were clustering about her, even in Ross's company, like bees to a honey-pot.

She was jealous! And she could do nothing about it, but watch helplessly while he dallied with another woman. Russell found her in a corner some while later, in the company of a boring young man who had done nothing but boast continually of what a good catch he was and how he would like to take her back to London with him when he returned. He would be most generous with his gifts in return for her 'friendship'. Ordinarily Roxanna would not have stayed to listen to such talk—

she had heard too much of it before in the past—but she was not even listening to what was being said, and the man was so full of his own self-importance that he had no idea she was not engrossed with his proposal and considering it carefully—which was what her silence seemed to imply.

'Excuse me, Miss Dane. Would you come to the library? At once, if you please.'

Without a word she followed Russell out of the crowded room. Was this the summons she had been expecting all night? Ross had not been present for some time, and he was not with Lady Alicia, for she was dancing with the Comte de Villon.

Russell closed the door after them, and walked across to a section of shelves containing the works of Shakespeare. He touched the third volume on the left of the door, and Roxanna stood in silence as it swung open to reveal a black, gaping hole beyond. The man picked up a candle and motioned her to follow.

'Is this whole house honeycombed with secret tunnels?' she asked. As soon as she had stepped inside, the panel closed behind her. Russell held up the light to guide her way. She lifted the hem of her skirt to avoid it being trailed in inches of dust. Well-trodden dust, she saw, with the imprint of many feet.

'A veritable rabbit-warren, Miss Dane. His Lordship thought it better that I do not refer to you in any other way for the moment. I hope you understand? Too many ears about, although it is a perfect opportunity for people to come and go. People who do not want to be seen and recognised,' he added, coming to a halt. Obviously he thought she knew more than she did. They climbed a now familiar set of steps. Her heart began to pound.

Brilliant light blinded her for a moment, and then Russell was ushering her into Ross's bedroom! He rose from the table, where seven men sat. All now raised their heads to stare at her as he came to her, took her hand and touched it to his lips. Before them were papers and Ross's maps, and glasses of wine and brandy.

'I am sorry to have dragged you away from the fun. I believe you have been enjoying yourself,' he added in a quiet tone that belied disapproval. Then, louder again, 'I have need of you here, however, for I must return downstairs, before questions are asked about my absence.'

'I am sure everyone will think you are still entertaining the Lady Alicia,' Roxanna said in a low whisper, and bit her lower lip as his fingers clenched painfully over hers.

'That was unworthy of you, Roxanna. You shall explain yourself to me later on.'

It was of small comfort to remember the heavy chest she had pushed against the entrance to the passage. He would not take that way to her tonight or any other night, and she knew he would not risk openly walking the corridor to her room. She would meet fire with fire when need be, until he accepted that she was not some chattel he had acquired and could dispose of at will.

'I leave you in the capable hands of Lady Roxanna, gentlemen. Please partake of the food provided. My wife will continue to serve you with whatever liquid refreshment you require, but be warned . . . I want some of my brandy left for when I return.'

One of the men laughed heartily—he looked as if he had already consumed more than sufficient for one night, Roxanna thought, looking at his red cheeks—and slapped his friend on the back as he passed. Ross gave a good-humoured grin, even though the gesture had all but knocked him off his feet, and left through the secret passage.

No wonder it was so easy for him to come and go unseen, she thought. How many more dark tunnels did she not know of? Russell came quickly to her aid as she hesitated uncertainly. Had he been left to help her—or to watch her? As always, his manner was impeccable, and his expression told her nothing.

'You play the lady well.' Nicholas came to her side some time later, as she sat on the sofa. The men around the table obviously trusted her implicitly, for they had gone back to discussing their maps, ignoring her. No one gave her a second glance—except for the suspicious-eyed man staring down at her, who had closely watched her every move. 'Whatever you hear in this room tonight, forget it.'

'I am sure I do not know what you mean,' Roxanna returned, wishing he would go away and let her listen to the conversation. Someone had mentioned a Captain Wright, an English ship's captain who had been arrested and imprisoned in the notorious 'Temple' prison in Paris, accused of being a British spy. From the way the talk was flowing, she soon realised that there was a definite plan in action to oust Napoleon from power and return a Bourbon prince to the throne of France. And Ross was somehow involved in all this. But why did an Englishman involve himself so vigorously in the affairs of an enemy country? What did it matter to him who sat on the French throne? Did the answer lie below with the Countess and Lisette? Or the Comte de Villon, who had just re-entered the room . . . with the strange assortment of *émigrés* who ate and danced at this *bal masqué* tonight?

'You may have them all eating out of your hand, but I am not taken in for one moment. I haven't changed my opinion about you. The way you've treated Ross betrays the fact that you are interested only in climbing the social ladder. If he didn't have money, you would never have agreed to remain his wife.'

'Your assassination of my character is of no interest to me,' Roxanna replied coldly. How dared he presume to know what was happening in her marriage! 'I care not what you think of me.'

'If you betray him . . .' Nicholas said in a low, threatening tone. Across the room, she was aware of Russell watching them intently, a frown creasing his forehead. The last thing she wanted was for him to report to Ross that she had been encouraging the company of his closest friend.

'Please go away.' When Nicholas did not move, but continued to stare down at her balefully, she added hastily, 'Do you not know the law? I assure you my husband does. A wife cannot speak against her husband. He is perfectly safe.'

'If I thought you would even consider it . . .'

'You would what?' Roxanna's green eyes flashed with sudden spirit. 'Kill me? As you did Griffith? Not all women betray their husbands, sir, as your wife did you.'

She had the satisfaction of seeing him flush uncomfortably. He drew back from her, swallowing the last of the wine in the glass he held. Of all the men present, her was drinking the most.

'That was an accident. He was drunk, and I—I was mad with rage . . . If you know about my wife, then you know why . . .' He broke off with an oath as he realised how easily he had fallen into her trap. 'You are too clever by half!'

'And you are drinking too much, *mon ami*.' Claude de Villon stood beside them. 'And you have monopolised this charming young woman long enough. LeGrande wants to know how well your ship is armed. I suggest you go and tell him.'

Roxanna allowed a sigh of relief to escape her as Nicholas ungraciously turned away to the table. The Comte asked her permission to sit by her, and settled himself on the sofa, his eyes intent on her face. They were blue, like Lisette's, but a darker blue, and she was given the impression that behind the lazy smile, the gentlemanly courtesy, which he bestowed upon her was an alert brain, and that he was acutely aware of everything going on about him.

'Josephine herself would envy the gown you are wearing, madame. But you have doubtless been paid many compliments tonight.'

'Your sincerity, sir, I do not doubt . . . As for the others . . .' She lifted her slim shoulders with a dazzling smile, and he laughed. Nicholas turned to glare at her, the same warning lingering in his eyes.

'Do not think that because of my advanced years I am beyond paying compliments to a beautiful woman in the hope of her giving me something in return! Have you not been told that all Frenchmen are incurable romantics, and passionate in their emotions? But then, of course, you will have discovered that, even though you have been married to Ross only a short time.' Roxanna felt her cheeks begin to burn at the assumption . . . Never would she have had the courage to admit that it was true.

'Ross is a true Frenchman at heart, is he not? Although I fear the added fire of his Spanish ancestors adds some harshness to his nature. He will be jealous of the woman he weds. Very jealous—no? I have often thought—and said to him—that he should have lived two hundred years ago. He would have been a pirate, I suspect. A charming rogue—a devil on the high seas. A lover of beautiful women.' He laughed softly again. 'That one has craved excitement ever since he was a child and used to come and stay at the château with my family. He grew up with Lisette . . . But then you know this, of course?' Roxanna could only nod. Everyone took it for granted that she knew more than she did. 'Did he tell you that when he was seventeen he could best me with a sword? Me, the greatest swordsman in Provence! I had cause to see him in action only a few days ago. *Mon Dieu!* His blade was still an extension of his arm. If anything he was faster, more deadly, than I remembered . . .' He leaned forward to take one of Roxanna's hands in his, the smile fading. 'But you have grown pale. I have frightened you with such talk. I am an old fool. Of course you do not want to hear of the danger he faces because of us.'

Us! Us! Us! Who were these men, that Ross risked his life so recklessly in their cause, Roxanna thought in frustration.

'Lisette has spoken of you to me at great length,' the Comte said, as Russell moved away after offering them refreshments. He had taken a glass of brandy, and she accepted wine, hoping it would calm her increasing nervousness. 'I am glad you are her friend. With you and Ross to watch over her, I have no fears for her safety. Guard her well, madame; she is so precious to me.'

'I think you have risked much to come here tonight,' Roxanna said quietly, in the hope of drawing him out again.

'Ross was quite scathing in his condemnation of my foolhardiness in coming here. I shall stay only a few hours, and return at first light tomorrow. I would not like my presence here to be discovered—it would be dangerous for you all. But I am a father who longs to see more of his daughter.' He gave a deep sigh, which touched Roxanna's heart. 'I have seen so little of her these past years, since her poor mother, my wife, was taken from us by those accursed *sans-culottes*.'

The Comte slowly drank his brandy, and continued. 'Your husband is an exceptional man, madame. He risked his life to wrench us from the very jaws of hell. The day he came to the "Temple" . . . *Mon Dieu!* If you could have seen him . . . a filthy, stinking peasant . . . I almost throttled him before I discovered it was he. I did not want to live . . . I thought my daughter already dead, along with my dearest wife, but he told me that Lisette was safe. He had plucked her from Fontainebleau, where they had taken all the women and children that terrible May, with the same daring, the same courage, as he then came for me. I was to live, he said, to live to fight another day to free my country. Heaven only knows how many others he had performed the same feat for. I imagine that half the men and women downstairs owe him their lives. Forgive me—I do but sing his praises, for he is the truest friend a man could ever have. With you I hope—nay, I know—he will find the happiness he has denied himself all these years, because of his precarious work.'

Roxanna found her thoughts flying back to the day at the inn when she had first met her husband. 'He is a close friend?' she had asked the agitated Nicholas. 'The best any man in this world could have', had been the sincere reply. At that moment, she realised again that she did not know her husband at all.

'I see my wife has been taking good care of you, *cher ami*,' Ross drawled from behind them. Roxanna realised that the Comte was still holding her hand, and quickly withdrew it, much to the amusement of the older man.

'Did I not tell you he would be jealous?' He turned to Ross. 'I find her a fascinating little creature. Far too good for a wild rogue like you! If I were ten years younger . . .'

'You might well find yourself at the end of my blade,' came the softly veiled threat. 'Friend or no friend.'

The look which passed between them made Roxanna uneasy. The Comte rose, and kissed the tips of her fingers.

'I return her to you with gratitude for the pleasure her company has given me.'

'Forgive me, old friend. I am tired, and my temper is too quick this night for many reasons,' Ross said, resting a hand on Claude's arm. 'I have just had word from the village that not only has there been a stranger asking questions about the house today, but the volunteers are searching this area. I have just sent Mark up to the old house to ensure that there is nothing there to betray us.'

'What about my ship?' Nicholas asked, swinging around, his face bleak.

'Your papers are in order. You are a perfectly respectable ship's captain about to sail for Holland with a cargo of copper. Providing you are sober, of course.'

'I shall be. When have I ever let you down?' Nicholas demanded angrily, and several of the men exchanged concerned glances as he swayed unsteadily.

'Never, and I don't intend there shall be a first time.' Ross did not raise his voice in return, but Roxanna saw how cold his eyes were.

The other man saw it too, looked around him, and then forced a smile to his lips. 'Your pardon, gentlemen. I have wallowed in too much self-indulgence this night. I am forgetting that, without me, none of you will ever reach your destinations. I shall be in my room, if some-one can fetch me some coffee.'

'Shall I?' Roxanna asked, as Nicholas left the room and the atmosphere returned to normal. She, too, wanted to leave. To get back to the crowd downstairs and lose herself in the dancing and merrymaking. She did not want to be alone with Ross now, while her mind reeled with questions. She had to take stock of what she thought she knew, and try to put it all in some kind of perspective.

'No, Russell will attend to it. You and I are going below to dance. Do you not think I have neglected you enough? I shall return in a short while, gentlemen,' he said, taking her arm.

'Ross, a word before you go.' A tall, rather thin, man with a pointed chin upon which rested the sparsest amount of hair rose from his chair and placed a pair of rimless spectacles on his nose. Roxanna knew him to be English, for she had heard him discussing the possibility of an 'army of reserve' as it would be called, being raised in the coastal parishes. He gave Roxanna the impression that the French could be making an assault on English shores at any moment. He was someone of importance, she decided, for no one interrupted him as he spoke, or voiced objections to the proposal. He had discussed it with both Lord Wyndham and the Prime Minister, he had said, and her incredulity at what was going on about her grew . . . if that was possible after all she had overheard tonight. Wyndham, the Prime Minister's Secretary of State of War! And Pitt himself!

'Lord Stafford?' Ross inclined his head slightly towards the man. 'Can it not wait?' She had the impression that he disliked the man intensely.

'I am at a loss to understand why your brother is not with us tonight. During your absences he is surely master here . . . Is he not in your confidence?'

'No, sir, he is not.' There was an edge of annoyance in Ross's voice. 'I involve no one without good cause.' As the man's eyes became fixed on Roxanna, she was astounded to hear him add, 'Had it not been for my wife's good ministering when I was unfortunately the victim of—an accident—shortly after leaving you in London, I might not be here. I trusted her with my life then, as I do now. She is my concern, sir. Not yours or anyone else's in this room.'

'More so than your own brother? I find that strange. With so much at stake for us all . . .'

'If you—or any of you,' Ross said slowly, looking at each man at the table before him, 'have any doubts about me, I shall, of course, stand down in this venture.'

There came a splutter of indignant French from one of the men, and another followed suit. Ross laughed and answered them, his gaze mocking as it rested again on Lord Stafford.

'I shall hear your decision, sir, when I return.'

Ross helped Roxanna into the passage, eased himself past her, and, taking her hand, started off along the uneven floor at such a pace that she had at times to run to keep up with him. He carried no candle and seemed to have an uncanny sixth sense which headed him in the right direction. He knew the way without a light, for he had used the passages over many years, she suspected. But she often brushed her arms against the sides of the wall and scraped an elbow as she followed him down the circular steps. He took her hand again, leading her not to the right, which she knew was the direction in which her bedroom lay, but to the left. Was this the way she had come with Russell? She had noticed several more tunnels branching off away from the steps, but now it was too dark to see anything. She stumbled again, and cried out as she cannoned heavily into him.

She heard him swear, and was aware of him turning in the blackness, brushing against her, and caught her breath as she was pushed back against the wall and his mouth descended on hers. So startled was she at his action that she had no time to resist, to ward off the hands which caressed her beneath the flimsy muslin—to stiffen her lips beneath the fierce pressure of his mouth.

And then fire consumed her!

'Ross . . .' His name broke from her lips, and she heard him utter a short laugh. It chilled her, for there was no humour in it.

'So it's Ross, now, is it?' His hands continued to move searchingly over her body, exploring the curves of her breasts and thighs with a roughness which began to frighten her. He had made love to her only once, but he had been gentle and thoughtful with her, despite his determination that she would not resist him. When the last of her protests had died beneath his kisses, he had transported her to a world of pleasure and contentment she knew she longed to know again. But would she? Did he hold Alicia Brandon as he held her now, or was he gentle with her?

'You are hurting me!' She tried to twist free of him, but he held her immobile against the uneven wall with the weight of his body. She could feel the hardness of his legs pressing against hers, as he sought and found her mouth again, bruising it with a ruthless pressure.

As abruptly as he had seized hold of her, he let her go. His voice came to her, cold, yet mocking, as if he had been aware how close she had come to answering his kisses.

'Has that quelled your inclination to jealousy? Now you will have no need to look elsewhere for your pleasures until I come to you later.'

'You look elsewhere, sir. Why should I not do the same?' she cried bitterly, wishing to hurt him as he had done her.

'That is the second time tonight you have accused me of—of what, in God's name? You desire me to touch you—don't deny it,' he snapped, sensing even in the darkness the denial which sprang to her lips. 'Dammit, I begin to think you are everything Nicholas says you are! I've had many women in my life, but you are the first to lead me such a merry dance. My patience is at an end. I shall come to you when the *bal masqué* is over, and you can show me how grateful you are to have your father here at Talland with you. Tonight, once and for all, we shall settle things between us.'

Roxanna choked back a scream as she felt his hands reach for her again, and closed her eyes as he lifted her. Dear God! What did he intend now?

She slowly opened them a fraction as she was set down again and found she was standing in the library. Ross reassured himself that the panel had returned to place correctly, and turned to face her. She was horrified to see a smile twitch at the corners of his lips. Producing a handkerchief, he began to wipe it across her cheeks and shoulders, warning her to silence with a frown.

'Be still, you look like a chimney-sweep,' he said.

Roxanna looked down at her gown, and gave a cry of distress to see the smudges of dust clinging to it. 'I cannot go back like this!' she gasped.

'Nonsense. Hold still a moment longer.' She stood as stiff as a board as he proceeded to brush the marks from the muslin, conscious of his hands on her body as he did so. By the time he had finished, her cheeks were flaming; luckily they showed little beneath the mask she had quickly put back to hide her confusion.

She felt a hundred pairs of eyes on her as they returned to the Blue Room and he danced with her, but knew it was only her imagination. While there might be some speculation as to who he was partnering, no one knew her or cared, she surmised. Many couples had paired off and slipped away to find a quiet corner somewhere in the house. A good portion of the men had retired to the dining-room and the abundance of port and wine and brandy awaiting them there, leaving the women to cluster in groups, no doubt catching up on the latest gossip. Many eyes watched Roxanna and Ross together, and then transferred their interest to the woman in black who stood amid a throng of admiring males, totally oblivious to their praise as her gaze followed the man she had decided long ago would be her second husband.

For some while after their return, Ross monopolised

Roxanna until her temper was almost to boiling-point, for she felt that he was deliberately trying to humiliate her, to make her feel so uncomfortable that she did not look at another man or accept the offer of another dance. It was his way of bringing her to heel. So angry did he make her feel, that the many questions she wanted to ask went completely out of her mind, as she fought to combat his skilful rhetoric, of which he was a past master, with frigid comments of her own. She knew none touched him. He was as oblivious to her discomfort as he was to her scorn, to the anxiety raging inside her, her fears relating to his visit to her later on. He cared nought for any of these things in his ruthless determination to dominate her, to subdue her to his will.

'My lord, there are soldiers outside. Volunteers.' A nervous-looking footman came to his side as they stood beside the long tables still covered with an amazing amount of food.

The goose in aspic had gone, Roxanna saw, and most of the delicious little sugared cakes and sweets which was the speciality of the cook. The glazed ham, heavily coated with mustard, would deliver up only three more slices. Servants came and went, removing empty platters, bringing more crammed full with sliced turkey, sea trout baked with herbs, sea-fresh crabs and lobsters, their wicked-looking claws no longer able to inflict a painful nip. She had eaten little in the course of the evening, consuming continuous glasses of wine, however, in an effort to relax. She saw Ross frown slightly as she accepted a glass of champagne from a hovering servant. Did he suspect that she had not touched wine before?

'Are you thinking to drink yourself insensible in the hope of avoiding me later on?' he taunted, and she deliberately drained the glass and smiled into his narrowed eyes, undaunted by the blackness lurking there.

'My lord,' the footman said again, and Ross wheeled on him, irritated that he had spoken so thoughtlessly before a servant. Roxanna was fast becoming a thorn in his side. Unless he halted her rebellion now, he would risk losing her to the first man who came along and used charm where he had used coercion. He had been too long alone, he thought bitterly, and it was beginning to show itself. Now, when he needed all his wit and cunning, a clear head and untroubled thoughts, she filled his mind night and day, clouding his judgment, rousing him to unreasonable anger. In accepting that his treatment of her, although necessary, was at times a little hard, he found himself wondering if he had not also unknowingly acted in a like manner with his own brother. Was it his fault they had grown apart?

'Major Lewis is a frequent visitor to Talland, man. Bring him in and offer him a brandy, as is our custom. We have nothing to hide from His Majesty's revenue men.'

'It's not the Major, my lord. I don't know this one— and he doesn't look too friendly. Asking for you he is . . . demanding. His name is Maynard.'

'Demanding!' Ross put down the glass he was holding so violently that the red wine spilled over on to the spotless damask cloth. Roxanna found herself staring at it wide-eyed. It was like an omen! Blood! Death! She raised a hand to her forehead and found it was quite hot.

'Are you all right?' Ross demanded, aware of the movement, even though his eyes were fixed on the hall where a uniformed figure stood, tapping one highly-polished booted foot impatiently on the wooden floor.

'Yes. It's nothing. What is wrong?'

'We have unexpected visitors,' he returned drily. 'Be a good girl and go back upstairs. Use the stairs. It will be quicker for you than stumbling through the passage. Tell my friends to stay where they are. Bring Russell down here, and if you see Mark, warn him we may have trouble. Now, Roxanna! Unless you want to wait and see if I am about to meet an untimely end. I assure you I am not ready yet—I have too much to do. Go!'

She turned and thrust her way to the door. Picking up

her skirts, she headed in the direction of the stairs, ignoring the officer now pacing the floor. There was a hardness about the face which indicated that he was not only impatient but highly contemptuous of the occasion he had interrupted, she thought, as a laughing girl brushed past him and he turned quickly aside, his expression registering annoyance.

No sooner was she out of sight than she ran up the last dozen stairs. At the top of them, Rosie clutched at the carved banister rail, gazing at the man below with fearful eyes.

'Lord, Roxy, are we found out? They've come to arrest him, haven't they?' she wailed. Roxanna grabbed her and thrust her back into the shadows. So she, too, knew about the smuggling! It seemed as though the whole household was involved, one way or another.

'Pull yourself together, and listen to me. Go down to the kitchen and tell the other servants they are to act normally. Do you understand me? The *bal masqué* is to go on, regardless of what is happening.' What was happening? A King's Preventive Officer had come to Talland, and he was not the one Ross knew—a frequent visitor who drank his brandy and no doubt turned a blind eye to his activities. It was well known all over the countryside that customs officers and crews of revenue vessels could be bought for a share in the profits of such operations. But this man was a stranger! And a danger to Ross!

She shook the girl, who had begun to cry. 'Pull yourself together and do as I say. Go down the back stairs and stay there until you are in control of yourself again.'

As she headed towards the stairs again, a door opened in front of her and Mark stepped out, and after him Lisette, brushing down her skirts which were noticeably creased. Behind them, rumpled bedcovers told their own story.

'Spying again, Miss Dane?' Mark sneered, quickly closing the door. She could have hit him. How she restrained herself she never knew. Instead, she fixed him with a frosty look.

'Your brother is below with a Preventive Officer. No, not the man you know, Major Lewis. This one is new. Have you been up to the ruins? Are they clear of contraband?' she demanded, and he gaped at her show of knowledge.

'How do you come to be questioning me? You are not mistress here yet, Miss High and Mighty Dane, nor will you ever be.'

'Mark, don't. Listen to her. Ross may be in trouble. If he is, you must go down and help,' Lisette protested, her face clouding with anxiety. Tomorrow, Roxanna knew, she would have to speak to the Countess about them discreetly.

'Perhaps he would like to see his brother dragged off to be hung at the end of a rope,' she said stiffly. 'If you have any feeling—any love—for him at all, you will go down and stand at his side, where you belong.'

Mark's fists clenched tightly at her words. For a moment she thought he might strike her for daring to speak to him thus, but then he strode to the edge of the landing and peered into the hall below. Without a backward glance, he began to descend the stairs.

'Go after him. I have something to do,' Roxanna said, pushing Lisette in the same direction, and then she was gone in a rustle of green silk and muslin.

When she returned to the corridor some five minutes later, pausing to gain her breath before descending the stairs—for she had run all the way to Ross's room and back—Roxanna found him and his brother side by side in front of the library door. Hesitantly she went down, and was startled to hear Ross say in a polite tone,

'Will you not take a glass of wine with us, Captain, before you go? These windy nights are still inclined to chill a man to the bone, and it is a long ride back to Polperro.'

Polperro was where the Preventive Station was situated. It had aroused such hostility along the coast when it was established some three years before that no houses were made available to the men who waged war on a most lucrative trade and offered rewards of from £20 to £500 in the hope of gaining information from turncoats. For lighting a fire to warn off an incoming ship laden with contraband, the penalty was £100. Crippling, if not impossible, demands were made on people often without a penny in their pockets.

'I have no stomach for wine, sir. However, a little brandy would most certainly keep away the ague. If you have some to spare, that is?' Captain Maynard replied, and Roxanna felt her heart leap into her mouth. The brandy being liberally distributed at the party had come not a week ago from France. The Countess herself had remarked that it was only fitting for a Frenchwoman to drink French brandy on her birthday.

Mark stiffened just a fraction, she noticed, but Ross remained unruffled by the request and beckoned to a servant, who went away to return with a tray on which were three glasses, half full.

'My apologies for the short measure, Captain, but these are hard times,' Ross chuckled, as he handed one to his guest and then one to his brother. Roxanna was aware of the look passing between them. For this moment at least, they were one, fighting a common enemy.

The officer wasted little time in consuming the contents of his glass. He returned it to the tray, his mouth tightening noticeably. A few people had begun to linger near them, yet Ross gave them none of his attention. His manner was relaxed and casual, his smile guarded, but a stranger would think this normal.

'An excellent year, Lord Talland. Your source of supply has not dried up, then, with this war which plagues our lives?'

'On the contrary, you have just drunk from my last remaining cask. But this is a special occasion . . . the birthday of Elizabeth, Countess de Villon. A great friend of mine and of Major Lewis, your commanding officer. He was to have been here tonight to enjoy it with us, but I believe he took a tumble from his horse. Too much—or not enough?' Ross's smile deepened. 'Convey my wishes for a speedy recovery to him, and tell him, if you would be so kind, that I have kept him some for his next visit.'

'It will be my pleasure.' Maynard looked and sounded as if it would be far from a pleasure.

'Let us hope that when you come again—and please do not prevent your soldiers from patrolling this area whenever you deem it necessary, Captain—I shall not take offence that you consider me incapable of controlling matters in my own domain.' The Captain shifted uncomfortably from one foot to another, no longer showing impatience, but a certain amount of discomfort. 'Perhaps the war will soon be over and my cellars restocked. My servant will show you out. Good night, sir.'

'By God, that was close,' Mark exclaimed, as the door closed behind the man. 'You are a damned cool character, Ross. I was fair shaking in my shoes.'

'No need. I suspect he would have been dead before he could call his men—had he wished to,' Ross drawled, and pushed open the door behind him. Nicholas stepped out, thrusting his pistol back inside his coat with a tight smile.

'You always did have the ears of a cat,' he growled. 'I wouldn't have hurt him—just tapped him over the head with the butt and put him somewhere safe until you had seen Major Lewis. He suspected, you know.'

'He can prove nothing. The cellars are empty at the old place?' Ross asked, looking at his brother.

'Just in time. I barely got out before they started searching up there—without your permission, it seems.'

'The Captain will have to learn that he cannot trespass on Talland land just when he pleases. You will have to go to Polperro tomorrow. Take a keg of brandy to the Major, and tell him our problem. I want no one prowling about here for the next three weeks. Make that clear to him. By then, I shall have made other arrangements to get the Captain off our backs.'

'I suppose you will tell me what they are, eventually,' Mark said, and the old enmity had crept back into his voice.

'When it is settled, yes.'

'But the man knew, I saw it in his eyes,' Mark insisted.

'Of course he did, he's no fool!'

'What about our own consignment?' Mark demanded, ignoring Lisette's hand curling round his. Ross's eyes narrowed sharply as he saw it, but for some reason he said nothing, much to Roxanna's surprise. He was always taking great pains to keep the two of them well apart, so what deep thoughts occupied him now that he allowed this to pass without comment?

'Hidden behind the wall of the cellar, where it will never be found. Russell and I took care of it this afternoon, while you were gambling away your allowance at the pot-house.'

'Damn you!' Mark growled, and turned away, pulling Lisette after him. He came face to face with Roxanna, and his eyes fastened on the opal around her neck. The face he showed to his brother was suddenly ridden with hatred . . . 'Blast you, Ross! They belonged to our mother. What right . . .?'

'Right?' His brother's voice fell to a dangerously low level. Nicholas turned back into the library, a scowl on his face, as if the sight of them at each other's throats again disgusted him. 'They were given to me, to do with as I please. You were given the sapphires she wore on her wedding day, were you not?'

With a strangled oath, Mark rushed away from them. Roxanna felt as if Ross wanted to go after him. He stepped forward, and then, as if only now becoming aware of the people surrounding him, of her presence, silent, but disturbing . . . he stopped himself. The opals had belonged to his mother. She could not believe it!

'The others are still upstairs?' he asked instead, and she nodded. 'I must join them and finish our business.' His head jerked as a door banged loudly upstairs. She watched his face go blank with disbelief, then pale as

Mark returned among them. Without a word, he placed a necklace of five large sapphires about Lisette's neck.

'Mark . . . No, not this way. This was to have been given to me on our wedding day. Oh Ross, why can you not be friends? I love you both so much . . .' Her lips quivered and she broke off, near to tears.

Deliberately Mark slipped an arm about her shoulders to draw her closer. Ross said nothing, but a terrible anger burned in the depths of his eyes which made Roxanna feel afraid for the outcome of his brother's foolishness. Reckless and foolish—how alike they both were . . . Yet they hated each other. Was it hate? Or had they grown so far apart that neither could make the first move in healing the breach, the gaping chasm that separated them?

'These, too, are mine, to do with as I please. I give them to Lisette, who will some day be my wife, whatever you say. Not to some . . .'

'One more word, brother . . .' Ross threatened through clenched teeth. 'I have no objection to your giving them to Lisette. Why should I? So long as you understand that the gesture affords you no special privileges in return.'

Brother measured brother. Roxanna was sure her heart was beating so loudly, so unsteadily, that everyone must hear it. She was rudely pushed to one side.

Alicia Brandon sailed past her and possessively slid her arm through that of Ross. She swept his companions with a disdainful smile before gazing up at him and fluttering her dark lashes. 'Where have you been keeping yourself, you elusive man? I have been inundated with proposals, which I know you do not want me to accept now that you are coming back to London with me. Come and dance?'

Refuse her, Roxanna wanted to cry out. Ross looked neither at her nor at his brother as he left them, the woman clinging heavily to his arm.

She found Mark's eyes on her, heard his scathing comment as if in a dream as the room reeled about her.

Ross was going to London with Alicia! Abandoning her for the arms of another woman.

'Tomorrow he may well take your opals back, Miss Dane, to give to his other . . . interest. Did I not warn you that no woman can hold him for long? Alicia will find that out soon. No woman will ever have my brother's love. He has none to give!'

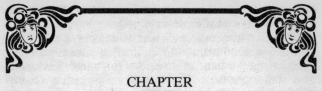

CHAPTER
NINE

As soon as it was possible, without arousing the Countess's suspicions at her desire to leave the celebrations, Roxanna asked to be excused, saying she was concerned for her father, who had seemed restless when she had last seen him. She had begun to lie so calmly, she thought, as permission was given and she slipped away, after saying good night to Lisette. Mark ignored her, smirking, as she told the lie again. He thought Ross was waiting for her upstairs, she thought. Had he not seen him escorting Alicia Brandon outside some half an hour before? Neither had returned. So much for his business . . . his friends . . .

The woman was like a clinging vine. She had not left his side since dragging him away in the hall, yet in a way Roxanna was glad she had appeared at that moment, for she felt it had averted another deadly fight between the two brothers.

A clock struck twelve somewhere behind her as she mounted the stairs, and she quickened her steps as, below, masks were torn off, cries of surprise, horror or jubilation as identities were revealed. On top of everything else, she could not have borne being stared at as she unmasked. Her identity would still remain a mystery, but not a very intriguing one, compared with what went on beneath Talland's slate roofs! Not until she reached her father's room did she dare remove her mask.

Her father slept peacefully, the books she had brought him piled on the table beside the bed. Carefully, so as not to disturb him, she removed the one beneath his

hands and smiled at the title. Another of Molière's plays
. . . how he would have loved to have been downstairs
tonight, amid people who had actually seen them performed in the theatre, and could discuss them with him.
She brushed a light kiss over his forehead. He stirred,
but did not waken. She slipped down into a near-by
chair, loath to leave him. He looked so peaceful—so
content. And she had no desire to return to her room too
early for fear Ross would fulfil his threat and come to
her. If he found it empty, he would think she was still
below, but perhaps Alicia would keep him fully occupied the whole night long. Her company seemed to
appeal to him, and he did not mind everyone seeing
them together. Masked or not, she was known to the
other guests, and so was he—for his stature and bearing,
if not for the impeccable cut of his clothes. She had heard
it whispered discreetly that he would soon marry the
woman who showed no shame in her pursuit of him. But
he had a wife, Roxanna thought miserably, as she stared
into the dying fire—then she rose to poke the embers
vigorously, scattering sparks over the hearth, as if to
thrust him out of her mind.

Her father stirred again and she was instantly still,
angry at her thoughtlessness. He was the last person she
wanted to learn of her unhappy plight. Nothing must
mar the brightness of the future she had given him.
Nothing!

Wearied by the dancing, and the strain of the evening
as a whole, she removed her shoes and stretched her toes
out towards the flames. She froze, her attitude one of
intense concentration as some while later she thought
she heard a sound from the other side of the wall . . . but
after a moment she relaxed, and shook her head rue-
fully. She was on edge, and little wonder after the events
of the evening. What would tomorrow bring? More
arguments between Ross and Mark . . . A confrontation
perhaps? A confrontation between herself and Ross,
when he discovered that access to her room was no
longer available to him? She was supposing he could

drag himself away from the 'black widow' to continue
with her lesson, for she was sure he intended it as such.

She closed her eyes, allowing her head to relax on the
cushion resting along the back of the chair. For one mad
moment when he had held her in the darkened passage,
she had felt a wild impulse to blurt out her love. It was
not the first time, but it must be the last, she told herself.
She must never give him the slightest cause to think she
cared for him. She could only dream of how it might
have been between them . . . remember the fierceness
of his kisses that stirred her senses so . . . the pleasurable
touch of his hands sliding over her skin . . .

She sat up with a start, rubbing her hands across
sleepy eyes. The fire was low again. How long had she
been here? An hour . . . two . . . ? She lifted the candle,
now almost burned down to the holder, and peered at
the clock on the mantel.

Two o'clock! Surely it would be safe to return to her
room now! She was beginning to get cold. After one last
look at her sleeping father she stole from the room, her
stockinged feet making no sound. So quiet was she that
the woman who came out of the dimness at her gave a
startled cry and fell back against the wall, a hand against
her heart.

'Oh! You startled me so . . .' Alicia's eyes rested on
the tell-tale green gown, and a cunning look crept into
her eyes, which Roxanna could not see, for she was
in the shadows. But she had also recognised the dress
the woman wore, and knew great confusion as Alicia
composed herself and came close.

'Why, it's Ross's mystery lady, isn't it? I do hope we
are not both about to go to him? That would be too
embarrassing . . . and he did tell me around two o'clock,
when everyone was safely abed.'

'I'm sorry . . .' For a moment Roxanna failed to
understand, then she stiffened, clutching her reticule
tightly to her. She was going to Ross's room. He had
asked her to come to him! She felt sick with horror—and
shame for the love she bore such a man. Mark was

right—every word he had spoken. 'Have no fear that you will be disturbed . . . I am about to retire—alone.'

'Have I offended you? How naughty of me. Tell me, have we met before? In London? I don't seem to know your face.'

'My name is Roxanna Dane. I am Lisette's companion.'

'Companion! You! Dressed like that . . . Oh, I see. Dear me, Ross is lowering his standards. But I suppose I must expect him to have a few little diversions in his life. I have neglected him these past months. Still, once we are married, I think—I know—he will not need to look elsewhere. Certainly not in the servants' quarters . . .' Alicia purred maliciously and moved away.

Roxanna leaned weakly back against the door of her room, feeling the tears rolling unchecked over her cheeks. That woman! That awful woman! Her support was suddenly removed as the door was opened and she fell backwards into the room. She was caught and steadied on her feet, then thrust to one side as Ross reached past her to turn the key in the lock.

'That will ensure that your gentleman friend does not disturb us,' he said coldly, and she retreated away from him, alarmed by the fierceness of his countenance. He had heard voices, and thought . . .! How dare he!

'I was . . . it was no man,' she snapped. 'I was with your lady friend,' she laid heavy emphasis on the word, and he scowled even more. 'Lady Alicia Brandon. She has just gone up to your room. As you arranged.'

'What?' He looked so incredulous she could hardly believe he was guilty, but then she reminded herself that he was so adept at deception. 'I did no such thing. I left her in the garden. It took me some while to do it, too, and went to my room. I left it at half-past twelve to come here. Russell has had to put Nicholas to bed, dead drunk, and I spent an unpleasant hour arguing with Stafford over you. So don't try my patience any longer.'

Roxanna saw that he was now in his shirt. His coat lay on her bed. The rumpled covers showed imprints of the

heels of his shoes where he had obviously rested them
while waiting for her. So she had not been mistaken. She
had heard him arrive . . . . Her eyes flew to the chest, and
found it had been pushed back away from the opening.
No mean feat from the passage! Had anger given him
strength?

'Don't ever try to keep me out again, Roxanna,' he
warned, stepping towards her. 'I overlook it this time,
but if you ever attempt it again . . .'

She did not struggle as he caught hold of her. She
knew it was useless to resist with her limited strength,
and in the end he would have his way. Better that he
make love to a cold, lifeless body and gain no pleasure
from it. Then, mayhap, he would leave her in peace. But
could she remain cold beneath his touch, and ignore his
kisses?

She closed her eyes in despair as he began to stroke
her breast, to slide the muslin away from her shoulders
and lay his lips against her bare skin. She shuddered,
knowing that no defences she could erect would hold
back her own desire for him . . . the longing in her heart
to belong to him and be a true wife.

Mistaking the tremor, Ross lifted his head and stared
down at her searchingly.

'Why do my kisses make you tremble? Do you dream
of another man when I hold you? From all I hear of you,
Roxanna, you were eager enough for Lord Carsewell's
arms about you!' The cruel words came at her without
warning.

She gasped as if he had struck her, sagging dazedly in
his grasp. 'You don't know what you are saying. You are
drunk.'

'If I were, I would not care that my touch offends you
so. I would take what is mine.' His voice grew menacing.
'I *will* take what belongs to me.'

'By force? Or will you send my father back to the
squalor and poverty he knew in London as revenge
against me?' Roxanna cried out, trembling in every
limb.

He held her at arm's length, and shook her until her hair came free of the pins holding it and cascaded down her back, past cheeks lost of all colour.

'My God! Is that what you think of me! That I would . . . I didn't realise how much you hated me. It would seem I am a man destined to have hatred thrust upon him, rather than love.'

'What do you know of love? You only take—you never give.' Roxanna was beside herself with fear and anger. She only knew he had stopped kissing her, and she had to prevent him from starting again.

He thrust her away from him with such force that she fell back across the bed and lay there, her breasts rising and falling tantalisingly beneath the sheer material of her gown. He had only to reach out and take her—she was his! He must shut his ears to her protests. She was his wife! He stepped back, an expression so cold, so fearful settling over his features that Roxanna felt as if the room had suddenly been invaded by a blast of icy wind. She dared not move and could hardly breathe.

'Damn you.' The fury which leapt across to tear at her heart made her wince. 'Why should I bother with an unwilling woman, when there is one in my room who is more than willing to accommodate me?' He stepped back towards the tunnel, his eyes still burning into her ashen face, and laughed harshly. 'There will be no need to replace the chest, Roxanna. I shall not come here again. I shall not touch you ever again!'

She watched him duck into the darkness, heard him swearing beneath his breath as the wooden panel closed behind him, and fell back on to the bed, her hands over her face . . . too shocked . . . too overcome with emotion even to cry . . .

When the tears came, they washed over her with the force of a tidal wave, draining her of the last of her strength. The first grey light of dawn stealing through a chink in the shutters found her huddled on the bed, still fully dressed.

*   *   *

In the days which followed the *bal masqué*, Roxanna was to learn the utter misery of the love she had denied herself, to watch the man she loved with another woman, to hear his laughter, to see his dark head bent close to hers as he hung on every word she spoke to him. For him, Roxanna no longer existed. She was Lisette's companion, and he treated her as such. Always polite, but formal and horribly distant, without even a faint glimmer of interest in the black eyes as he surveyed her. The day after he had come to her, she moved the chest back against the wall, but it was unnecessary. He kept his word and did not come to her again.

Luckily at least a dozen people remained at the house for over a week, mainly young friends of Lisette, who spent most of their time riding, gambling, drinking with Mark and generally creating havoc wherever they went, so that Roxanna, although preferring to remain always on the outskirts of their activities, despite Lisette's plea that she considered herself one of them, found she had little time to dwell on the unhappiness which weighed so heavily on her heart.

There were trips to Polperro and Looe, and supper-parties which usually ended with the young men drunk and the ladies a little too bold in their manner for Roxanna's liking. The Countess was shocked to discover that Mark had taken Lisette, with her companion and the others, to the local village pot-house, where a great deal of money had changed hands as wagers were laid on the cockfights which were the favourite pastime of the villagers.

Roxanna heard Ross arguing with his brother over his losses the next morning, and the latter stormed out of the Blue Room, almost knocking her over, when he heard that they were not to be settled. How long had Mark burdened him with his gambling debts, she wondered. With his allowance and his share of the contra-band sales, he had more than enough to live on in style and comfort. Ross paid for everything in the house and to do with Talland as a whole, she knew. Was this the

crux of the matter? Did Mark resent his older brother
holding the purse-strings?

Two days after the visit to the village, she found the
house strangely quiet when she rose, later than usual, for
none of them had gone to bed before the early hours.
Not until she sat at the breakfast table did she learn that
the guests had gone—except for one.

Alicia Brandon always took a seat on Ross's right—
the place where Lisette usually sat. She saw the girl
purse her lips in anger when the woman took her chair
that first day, forcing her to sit elsewhere. As the days
passed, her dislike seemed to grow. Only Mark enjoyed
her presence among them, and Roxanna knew that was
because it upset her. It was agony to sit at every meal,
aware of Ross a few feet away, constantly paying attention to the other woman. She found conversation
coming to her as it might to some mechanical doll.

It was then that Mark threw down a challenge Roxanna was sure Ross could not refuse to take up . . . and
was flabbergasted when he ignored what went on under
his very nose. He openly held hands with Lisette
whenever they were together—even in the presence of
Elizabeth de Villon. He partnered her on her morning
rides, while Roxanna trailed in a miserable silence some
way behind. He made it quite clear, from the looks
directed at her, that he would bear her company because
it was necessary, but he would not have her at their side,
joining in their conversations. She began to feel an
outcast—unwanted—unnoticed, and, in Ross's case,
even despised. And Ross said not a word to his brother!

For solace she turned to her father's company and
often sat with him as he worked in the library, trying to
read, but more often than not remembering—and hating
herself for being so weak as still to be in love! Even when
Ross treated her in such a contemptible fashion she
loved him, wanted him! She was a wanton! Had he cared
for her even a little, she might have thought he was
trying to make her jealous by paying so much attention
to Alicia. She was still his wife, after all. What did he

intend to do about that? The question haunted her. Would he send her away, divorce her, send her father packing?

Ross was so different with him. Many nights she knew they sat together in the library over a decanter of port and discussed the books. He was pleased with his work, her father told her one day, showing the first excitement she had seen in many, many long months. She prayed that Ross was not playing some cruel game with him, too!

The Countess, who in Roxanna's opinion had looked quite pale and drawn since before her birthday, was taken suddenly ill, and the doctor who attended her prescribed bed rest for at least two weeks—longer, if she did not show signs of improvement by then. Like her father, Roxanna thought, the old woman's heart was weakening under the strain of her past unhappiness. She would sit with her for hours and read to her, as did George Dane, and between them sprang up a friendship which gladdened Roxanna's heart. With her father becoming so involved not only with the cataloguing of Ross's books, he did not notice if she was not her usual bright self, for he had found an ally, an ardent reader like himself in the Countess, and the old world he had thought lost to him once more opened up to provide him with hour upon hour of pleasure.

After dinner, after the men had rejoined Lisette, Roxanna and Alicia, the latter idling away the time until they arrived by playing the piano—something else Lisette had been deprived of—Ross announced his intention of returning to London with the woman who sat at his side on the couch, toying with a glass of sherry.

'London?' Mark echoed, and Roxanna felt his spirits rise instantly. He would be alone with Lisette. With the Countess ill, and most of Roxanna's time now occupied with her, at the former's request, she would not be able to watch over her charge as she should. She had always known that the Countess was not as averse to the match between them as Ross was, and wondered if this was not her way of encouraging them without being seen actually to offer encouragement.

'I have convinced your brother that he should now have a little time to himself,' Alicia purred, laying a hand possessively on his arm. The smile he bestowed on her made Roxanna turn away. Mark's eyes were on her, full of unspoken triumph. 'He says a week only, but I shall prevail upon him to stay longer—a month at least.'

'Lisette will be coming with us,' Ross added, quashing his brother's hopes and plans in one fell swoop. 'She has not enjoyed the social life she should—as you well know. And you know why. You will stay here, of course, and manage Talland until I return. You can handle things?' he added, and Mark nodded tight-lipped, obviously not daring to speak. Roxanna watched Lisette's fingers slide into his, and envied them what they shared even so precariously.

'It will not be necessary for Miss Dane to accompany you, Lisette, as you will be with me. She will be of more use here with your grandmother.' His words made Roxanna stiffen in indignation and shame. Alicia's eyes rested amusedly on her taut features and there was satisfaction in that look. Was it she who had suggested this arrangement? How could he? Were his morals as lax as those of other men? His wife he kept a secret from everyone, while he openly went to London with his mistress! It took her breath away for a moment. His mistress! Was she, Roxanna, soon to be discarded and this creature put in her place? He could have it arranged discreetly and quietly, and there was nothing she could do about it. Nicholas would never confirm her story that a marriage had taken place, and the servants all considered her to be nothing more than a passing fancy for the master of the house.

A week passed with interminable slowness and the house was like a graveyard. The Countess took the opportunity, as there were so few people in residence, to get the servants to clean it from top to bottom—with the exception of her own room, which she refused to have touched by anyone but Roxanna.

She did not mind. She had grown fond of Elizabeth de Villon, and the work was no harder than the menial jobs she had been forced to do to earn enough to eat before she came to Talland. She became responsible for all the Countess's meals, and grew to know her likes and dislikes—and her weakness, which was two glasses of brandy before she went to sleep, every night. The doctor had forbidden spirits of any kind, and allowed only her one glass of sweet white wine a day. In this she obeyed him. But every night, before she bade her good night, Roxanna would take the decanter from a side-cabinet and pour her some brandy, wait until she had drunk it and then leave another at her fingertips. After the hell she had been through in France, she did not begrudge her one little drop.

'What is wrong, Roxanna?' 'Miss Dane' had long since ceased to be. It was Roxanna, or 'dear child' . . . Sometimes, when she was in a reminiscent mood, *mignonne*. Roxanna's vocabulary of French words was growing quickly, as on odd days the Countess would often speak nothing but her native tongue. 'Since when?—Since the *bal masqué* you have not been yourself. Something troubles you. Tell me.'

Roxanna forced a smile to her lips, took away the cup and saucer and rearranged the Countess's pillows. Even confined to bed, she was still a picture of elegance in a fur-trimmed robe, her hair dressed, her face rouged and powdered.

'Nothing is wrong, madame. I think perhaps I miss Lisette.'

'Only her? I think perhaps it is Ross?'

'No, of course not. Why should you think such a thing?' Roxanna quickly turned away, pretending to tidy the room.

'Don't play games with me, child. Come and sit down. I don't know what happened between you that night, only that, since then, he has been a different man.

Oh, he has always been quick of temper . . . The Spanish blood in him, I suppose. But to act the gallant, as he has done since that night, that is not the Ross I know.'

'Perhaps he is in love,' she suggested, inwardly wincing at the idea.

'With Lady Alicia? That—That . . .? In France we have a name for such a woman. If he is, he's a fool, and that is one thing Ross Talland is not! He's never allowed any woman to come so close as to pierce his armour. Yet suddenly he turns a blind eye to young Mark and his dangerous pastime of pursuing my granddaughter. In love, or so hurt inside, that he is seeking to forget the pain he carries with him. You would not know what I am talking about, would you?'

'No, madame. Perhaps he has lost someone he cared for . . . in France, perhaps?' Roxanna ventured to suggest. She sat in a chair beside the bed, forcing her voice to be calm and uninterested, and fought to keep her composure.

'He has—too many. But in the past. Of course there are Cadoudal . . . and Wright . . . He would help them if he could, but his hands are tied. I suffer with him for those two brave men. Have you heard the latest news from France? The *Morning Post* was full of it. Rosie managed to pick up a copy the other day when she went shopping for me. That arrogant, grotesque little Corsican has proclaimed himself Emperor of France, and Josephine his Empress. A fine pair they make! He was afraid the whole country would return to the hands of the rightful and only true rulers—the Bourbons—on his death. A Corsican adventurer Emperor! *Mon Dieu!* A thousand times I had wished Cadoudal had been successful in his attempts to kill that man . . . *Pauvre Goliath!* That is what we all called him.'

Roxanna suddenly found herself under intense scrutiny and began to grow uncomfortable. At length the Countess said slowly, meaningfully,

'You say nothing—why?'

'I—I know nothing of such things, madame,' she protested with a shrug.

'You were wearing opals belonging to Ross's mother that night . . . a gown I know could have come only from Paris . . . He is not the kind of man to give away his mother's cherished jewels. They were intended for his bride on her wedding day, as Mark should have given the sapphires in his possession to his wife on hers. Two grown men playing games—with each other, with the women in their lives—and he with death!'

'I do not understand you,' Roxanna said quickly, and knew she was not believed.

'*Pauvre, pauvre Roxanna!* Do you love him so much?'

'Perhaps he meant the opals as a thank-you gift for my help at the inn.' Her voice held no conviction, and she saw a flash of disappointment in the Countess's eyes.

'As you wish.'

'Shall I read to you, or would you like to rest for a while?' Roxanna suggested, relieved that the cross-examination was at an end.

'Neither. I shall lie here and remember the old days when I was young and attractive and men flocked to my side with endearments and promises of love. You should go down to the village more often, child, or get Rosie to take you into Polperro. You should have a young man to dance attendance on you. Have you no wish to be married, to raise a family?'

Once! Once she had wanted these things, but now they were forbidden to her. Roxanna lifted her shoulders again.

'In time, perhaps. I am only nineteen.'

'I was married with a year-old baby when I was that age,' came the reply. 'How my heart pounds when I think of those times. Go and fetch me a brandy.'

'Do you think you should?' Roxanna protested, and was silenced with a stern look.

'If I am going to go, then I shall do so in my own fashion. Ross said that to me once . . . ' Roxanna caught her breath, remembering the same words spoken to her

at the inn! 'I remember it was just after he had brought
me to Talland. He returned to France, ignoring the
dangers, to rescue my son Claude and little Lisette. She
was only seven, then . . . terrified by what she had seen.
It was months before she could sleep without hideous
nightmares. Thank you, my dear.' Roxanna sat down
again, wishing she would not keep mentioning Ross.
Was he to haunt her, even when he was absent from the
house?

'I tried to stop him, and that's when he said those
words to me with such a strange look on his face . . . He
was different when he came back . . . He had failed to
save the lives of my grandsons, you see, and he blamed
himself for not returning sooner. There was nothing he
could have done, of course. Like Lisette's mother, they
were some of the first to be guillotined because of their
association with the princes of Bourbon. He would come
and go from this house like a will-o'-the-wisp. Sometimes here, then gone, then here again, until none of us
knew when he would appear. Rather as it is now . . .'
She *knew*, Roxanna realised. Elizabeth smiled. 'I could
not again bear the pain of losing someone I loved, so that
is why I refuse to become involved with this . . . foolish,
dangerous, oh so heroic, thing he does now . . . But I am
not ignorant of what goes on, you understand?'

'You have known all this time?' Roxanna asked, and
Elizabeth's hand rested lightly on hers.

'Known what? That he makes frequent trips to France
. . . that he is engaged in some plan, together with the
British government, to kill Napoleon and put a Bourbon
prince on the throne? d'Enghien was obviously their
choice; that's why he was arrested and executed. He and
Ross were once close friends. The British care little who
it is, as long as Napoleon is removed. Now they will have
to look elsewhere. The Comte d'Artois must surely be
their next choice. If they have a choice, now that half the
conspirators are in gaol.' She gave a heavy sigh, finished
her brandy and handed Roxanna the glass. 'You should
have asked more questions of me than you have, do you

know that? Your silence has told me all I want to know. Ross has confided in you, of that I am sure. Why you say you mean nothing to each other is beyond me. He has trusted you with his life . . .'

'I love him,' Roxanna said simply, and the hand took hers with a gentle, comforting pressure. 'I beg you to keep this secret between us.'

'Because of Lady Alicia? He will not return with her. You will have him all to yourself, for a while at least . . . until he leaves again. The next time he will not be going to her. I pray it is not to another woman, far more deadly than Alicia . . .'

'Who? What other woman has he?' Roxanna asked, aghast.

'None. I speak of *Madame la Guillotine*. If any of those men have broken under Fouché's tortures, they will be waiting for *him* the next time . . .' The Countess's eyes closed and within minutes she was asleep.

Roxanna stayed with her for a full half-hour before seeking out her father in the library. He looked at her in surprise as she asked her questions, and took off his spectacles, polishing them absent-mindedly for several minutes as he always did when he was concentrating.

'Fouché? Why do you ask about Napoleon's Chief of Police?'

Roxanna gave a gasp and slid down into a chair. 'It was something the Countess said.'

'A brilliant man, by all accounts, but totally ruthless. It was he who insisted on the execution of the king and the queen in the Revolution. He has the qualities of a great statesman . . . if Napoleon will ever allow him to exercise them, which I doubt. Can you stay awhile?'

'No, I must go back in case the Countess wakes. She usually likes me to read to her in the afternoon.'

'Take this,' he handed her a leather-bound book embossed with gold. 'Have a glance through it if you can, later on. Fascinating reading . . . fascinating. I found it on one of the top shelves along with papers and diaries. It's the history of Talland, from the very first day

that Spanish sailor was washed up in the bay from a
wrecked Armada ship. That's why the cannon you found
bore the date it did. That was the old house, destroyed
by Cromwell in the civil war. Charles II restored the
family fortune when he came to the throne, and this
house was built.'

The Countess slept for the whole afternoon, and
Roxanna sat in the chair by her bed and read the book.
Fascinating reading, indeed! There had been a shipwreck off the bay. A Spanish man-of-war fleeing home
had been caught in bad weather and blown off course.
The only survivor, a man in his early twenties, had been
washed ashore, barely alive.

He had been found and nursed back to health by the
daughter of Lord Savage, whose lands at that time were
far in excess of the Talland she knew now. He had
married her, and they lived in the ancient castle that had
seen blood-feuds and wars since the day the first stone
was laid. Lord Savage and his men had risen in support
of Margaret of Anjou during the bloody Wars of the
Roses, and a party including Cornishmen from Talland
and Polperro had helped to storm the gates of London.

As the Spaniard had no memory—the injuries to his
head were the reason given—he had taken the name of
the place where he was found—Talland. And so the
House of Talland came into existence.

It was all here—all the questions and answers to the
background of Ross James Talland. The marriage of his
father to a wealthy young woman from London, who
had soon tired of the country and a husband older than
herself by some twenty years, who had left him to bring
two sons up alone. Ross, the elder, had been sent to
France to be educated, staying at the home of a close
family friend, the Comte de Villon. He had grown up
with Lisette as a companion, together with the two
grandsons of Elizabeth de Villon who were to be so
cruelly deprived of life by the guillotine.

It was more a diary than a book, for every page was

handwritten. At times the ink was so faded that she could scarcely make out the words. The carefully compiled story of the origin of the Talland family ended abruptly in the year 1801. After the year 1794 the writing was noticeably different—a bold hand, with a flourishing scrawl. Instinctively she knew it belonged to Ross. He had written everything exactly as it must have been in his mind when he returned from one of his trips to France. The joy at saving a friend, the utter despair at being too late. The loneliness with Mark being in London, his wildness and passion for gambling growing each month. The bitterness of a life he could share with no one.

The final passage he had written brought tears to her eyes . . . It was written by a man who had seen death and bloody carnage as a young man and grown hard because of it, absorbing the pain, withdrawing within himself so that nothing touched him or hurt him ever again. Nothing and no one, she thought, as she closed the book and hugged it against her breast. It was dated 19 September 1801. *'I have today settled the last of Mark's outstanding debts, thus saving him from the squalor and degradation of a debtor's prison. I have done so on condition that he return to Talland with me to take his rightful place here in these troubled times. But we are as strangers! I fear I have lost my brother. I am still alone!'*

Still alone! She, too, in her turn had denied him the friendship, the understanding that he seemed to be seeking. His arrogance and her pride would forever keep a wedge between them, unless one of them gave way . . .

In the bed, Elizabeth de Villon opened her eyes and looked for a moment at the pale-cheeked girl who sat with head downbent. She recognised at once the book she held. A faint smile touched her lips, as she closed her eyes again and went back to sleep.

With Mark out of the house most of the day—when he was not at the mine or at the ruins about other business, he spent hours at the pot-house, gambling and drinking, not returning home until first light many times—and Lisette in London, Roxanna found that the time dragged. Her long walks no longer held the attraction for her they once had, for she always found herself at the ruins where Ross had kissed her so ardently after his fight with his brother. Her interest in books waned, and she grew quite morose. She longed for Ross to return, even though she knew he would be cold and hateful to her. Nevertheless, to see him every day, to be near him—she asked no more.

She was with the Countess one morning when a carriage rolled to a halt in the drive outside. Roxanna could hardly contain her joy at the sight of the red-headed girl who alighted with the help of a tall man, whose dark features were relaxed and smiling as he turned towards the door. They were alone—Lady Alicia was not with them! For a fleeting moment, Ross's gaze swept the upper part of the house and came to rest on the slim figure at one of the windows. Roxanna sprang back, cheeks flaming, as her heart began to pound.

'He is back, then?' Elizabeth asked with a soft laugh.

'Yes, madame.'

'I suggest you breathe deeply to compose yourself, or he will guess your secret the moment he enters the room,' she added, and Roxanna quickly busied herself with something on the far side of the room, praying that her cheeks would not continue to flame when he appeared. How could she be so eager to see him after the way he had treated her? How shameless she was!

'Elizabeth!' He went direct to the woman in the bed, kissing her on both cheeks. 'How well you look. Is the doctor pleased with you? When will you be able to get up again?'

The pleasure in the deep voice stirred old memories in Roxanna, and her hands tightened over the nightgown she held. Hurriedly she pushed it away into a drawer. Ross looked round and saw her, and came to his feet again. 'Miss Dane, you are well, I hope?'

'Perfectly, sir.'

'She has been a perfect treasure to me while you were away. I have been spoilt, and loved every minute of it.'

'I am pleased to hear it. Lisette has gone to her room. You may go to her if you wish.'

It was a dismissal. So obvious that even the Countess frowned up at him, but he showed no sign of having seen her disapproval. As Roxanna closed the door behind her, she heard the woman say, 'It is arranged?'

She knew she should not linger, or eavesdrop on a private conversation, but her legs refused to function. She had to know if he was to leave again.

'No. The young Pitt is afraid the men may have talked, and Fouché will be expecting a rescue attempt.' Ross's tone indicated disappointment, and something more. Anger . . . or resentment that he was not to be allowed to go to the help of his friends. 'Dammit! I argued with them for hours. Wyndham was on my side, but of course he does not have the last word. Pitt is right. I would be walking into Fouché's open arms if I risked going now. We must wait—and hope.'

'That man would like to get his hands on the rest of you.'

'I would like to get my hands on Fouché—round his throat.' Ross gave a harsh laugh, and Roxanna shivered and hurried away. He was not going to France. He was safe for a while longer.

It was not enough to see him, to be near him at meal-times. She wanted more, and knew she could never have it now, for she had repulsed him once too often and he had turned from her to another woman . . . a woman who welcomed him, accepted him, in any way she could have him. Why had she been so proud, Roxanna wondered miserably? She would give anything to undo the things she had said and done, but it was impossible. They were as strangers. In fact she began to realise that he went out of his way to avoid her, for if he saw her coming into a room where they would be alone together, he quickly departed. Yet his attitude to her father did not change. It was the only consolation she could draw from those painful, lonely days. The endless, sleepless nights.

Lisette's descriptions of the delightful parties she had attended and the new friends she had made were repeated over and over again whenever the two girls were together. She never tired of telling how outrageous Alicia was in Ross's company, and how everyone now believed that she would soon wed him. She was totally unaware of the forlorn look in Roxanna's eyes as she gazed out of the window, waiting for a sight of the man she loved as he rode to the mine—as he did every day—oblivious to the excited chatter going on behind her.

Mark's visit to Polperro to see Major Lewis apparently had some effect, for although the scarlet-coated soldiers came close to Talland land, they did not venture on to it, and it was business as usual, Roxanna surmised, whenever there was a light in the church. Several strangers came to the house, however. Ross would receive them in his study and sometimes remain closeted alone with them for hours. He never introduced them to anyone else. When their business was concluded, he personally saw them off the premises and said not a word of what had passed between them. Often Roxanna saw the Countess watching him when she knew his thoughts were elsewhere, and realised that she was worried greatly by these visits. But, whatever took place, Ross continued to keep it locked inside him . . . as he had always done, Roxanna remembered, her mind going back to the book she had read. He had been alone so long that it had become impossible for him to share anything with anyone . . . *'I am still alone!'* Those words haunted her.

And then, with the return of Nicholas Pendennis from Brittany with a cargo of rum and brandy and oriental spices, not to mention a consignment of the finest French china concealed below decks, came the news that Roxanna knew would drag Ross once again from his home and thrust him into terrible danger . . .

She had been summoned to the smaller drawing-room, which was used mainly in the afternoon, and found there not only Ross and Nicholas but the Countess, propped up against a mound of cushions in a comfortable chair, and Lisette. It was then that Ross, looking grave, his voice quiet but somewhat uneven as he gazed at Elizabeth, looked away as he told them that Claude, her beloved son, the Comte de Villon, had once again been arrested and imprisoned in the 'Temple'.

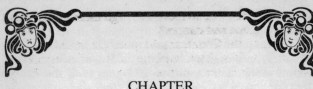

CHAPTER
TEN

'FORGIVE ME.' He looked into Elizabeth's tortured features, knowing her thoughts were dwelling on that terrible place where her grandsons had been confined before they died, and from where Claude had been spirited from under the very noses of his guards on that last occasion. 'There was no easy way to tell you.'

Lisette gave a cry, and tears flooded her eyes. Roxanna drew her into her arms, soothing her as best she could. The news had stunned her, too. She had sat with the Comte on the night of the *bal masqué*, and through him had learned much about Ross. She had liked him. And now he was a prisoner of the French and destined for *Madame la Guillotine* for his part in this scheme to remove Napoleon from power, which had already claimed the life of the Duc d'Enghien, executed within five short days of being kidnapped from his home in exile in Germany and taken forcibly to France to be tried for treason before a military court. All because Napoleon had needed a scapegoat. Yet even his death had not stopped the determination of those who remained to carry on.

George Cadoudal, the peasant from Breton whose secret work in France had made him the most wanted man on Fouché's list of conspirators, languished in gaol awaiting trial and certain death, as did the English Captain Wright, who had often used his ship to ferry conspirators to and from France. Now the Comte himself was added to the growing list. How many more must die to put a Bourbon back on the throne of France? Not Ross! Her heart grew cold with fear. Surely he would not—could not—be so foolish as to go there in the midst of all the chaos and danger?

'Tell me,' the Countess said quietly. She did not look at her granddaughter, sobbing in Roxanna's arms. It was if she had been turned to stone. 'Tell me everything.'

'The news was brought by one of our men to Nicholas as he was leaving Brittany. Claude was arrested four days ago. He went to meet a contact and found Fouché's men waiting for him. He had no chance to run, or to fight, even. They did not want to take him dead . . . someone talked.'

'They will torture him, won't they?' Lisette broke free of Roxanna's grasp and sprang to her feet. 'You can't let that happen, Ross! You can't allow my father to be hurt. He is your friend . . . He gave you a home when you were in France. You owe it to him.' Her tone rose to a hysterical pitch.

Ross's mouth tightened into a bleak line at the outburst, but it was the Countess who spoke, waving him to silence.

'Ross owes your father nothing. He more than paid us back for our hospitality all those years ago when he rescued us from certain death and brought us to live in safety here in England.'

'Well, well, what a cosy little gathering.' Mark entered the room. It was clear to see by the flush in his cheeks that he had been drinking. For a moment he did not see the tears on Lisette's cheeks, as he threw himself into a chair and helped himself to a glass of wine from the decanter beside him. 'Still here, Ross? I thought you might have tired of Talland again by now and gone back to London.'

'Be quiet, you young fool,' Nicholas snapped, and Mark stared at him through narrowed eyes.

'You captain his ship, Pendennis, but you do not have any standing with me, so hold your tongue.'

'Why, you . . .'

'That's enough, from both of you,' Ross ordered, and

stepped in front of Nicholas to bar the way as he turned menacingly on the figure lounging in the chair. 'Calm down. We cannot afford to lose our tempers—any of us. It's barely eleven in the morning,' he continued, looking at his brother. Was she the only one to see the open pain in his eyes, Roxanna wondered? He had glanced at her only briefly when she had entered, and had not looked at her since. He was including her in a private family conference. Why, when he did not consider her part of it? 'I would suppose you took your first drink with breakfast.'

'We are not unalike there, brother. I've known you drink the whole day through,' came the sneering reply.

'But I don't look like you at the end of the day, or at the beginning of it. God! You are a fool, and I have to leave things in your hands.'

'Alicia calls . . .' Mark chuckled, reaching for the decanter again.

In two long strides, Ross had reached him, and his outstretched hand knocked it from his grasp. It barely missed Nicholas as it fell to the floor. 'Touch your glass, and I'll ram it down your throat,' he threatened, and Mark became still. He had seen his brother's temper before, and knew that he was too drunk to use a sword against Ross at the moment. 'The Comte has been arrested in Paris.'

'What? Arrested?' His brother blinked at him dazedly, his mind refusing to function because of the amount of gin he had consumed at the mine. He always took a bottle of something along with him to keep out the cold and ease the boredom. 'In God's name, why? Lisette . . .' For the first time, he saw her tear-streaked face. Roxanna was brushed aside as he came to her and took her in his arms. 'Oh, my poor darling, I'm sorry! Why?' he asked again, looking at Ross.

'He was part of a band of insurgents planning to oust Napoleon from the throne and replace him with a Bourbon prince. Most of the conspirators are now in gaol, and some are dead. We gambled—and lost.' He gave a tight smile, and looked down at the decanter at Nicholas's feet. 'I'm sorry, Elizabeth, I have broken your favourite decanter.'

'You should have broken his neck,' the Countess snapped, glaring daggers at the man who held her granddaughter. 'The young puppy should have been taught a lesson long ago. And I was beginning to think he was becoming a man at last.'

'Ross, for pity's sake,' Lisette lifted her face from Mark's shoulder, and the misery in her eyes pierced Ross's heart like a knife. 'We can't—just leave my father there.'

'You don't know what you ask, foolish child,' Elizabeth said, moving for the first time in her chair as she turned and looked at her coldly. Roxanna marvelled at her self-control. It was the past coming back to haunt her all over again, yet she showed no sign of grief, of losing control. Thousands of French aristocrats had gone to the guillotine with the same pride in their hearts, and showing on their faces, oblivious to the rowdy, obscene calls of the *sans-culottes* crowding around the tumbrils which carried them through the streets to their place of execution. Some did not notice . . . others wept. Some were reduced to a shameful silence—for in the faces of these people they saw the pride of France—and they were destroying it little by little.

'There is more at stake here than your father's life. They will be expecting him. Would you condemn him to the tender mercies of that devil Fouché?' Elizabeth asked Lisette.

Ross looked at Nicholas, his face an expressionless mask, and said tonelessly, 'How soon can we leave?' No, Roxanna cried out . . . but the plea came from within her; no sound escaped her lips.

'As soon as we are unloaded. We could make it on the next tide, but we run the risk of engaging the revenue cutter in broad daylight.'

'We shall have to risk it. Besides, we can outrun her. If not, we outgun her. Nothing must stop us. Do you understand me? Make sure the crew do . . . anyone who wants to cry off can do so, and I'll not hold it against him. There's no time to wait for approval from London. We sail on the next tide, Nicholas.'

'What are you going to do?' Mark came to his feet, his face paling. 'You can't mean to . . . Are you mad? Why should you risk your life for . . .' He broke off, a frown furrowing his brows, and ran a hand through his wind-swept hair with an oath. 'You said "we" gambled and lost. You! You are part of this insanity?'

'It may well make you Master of Talland sooner than you expected,' Ross returned humourlessly. 'If you fail in this, you will not be failing me, but yourself. Talland is in your hands, Mark. Guard it well, for it is all I have left . . .' His gaze came to rest on Roxanna. She caught her breath at the strangeness of his eyes. Did they accuse her? But of what?

'Those trips . . . You were *not* in London, were you?' Mark challenged. He seemed to be coming out of his daze, and there was anger in his tone.

'Not all the time, but sometimes. There is a camp in Romsey where the British government are training re-cruits to fight against Napoleon when it comes to the big day. I spent a great deal of time there, teaching them how to use a sword and how to blend into the back-ground like a peasant.'

'You?' his brother exclaimed. 'You? The second-best-dressed man in London!'

'He has done it before, while you were gambling away your father's legacy to you,' Elizabeth said stiffly. 'While you were wining and dining your latest mistress, he was risking his life to bring people out of France. When the mine had to be shut down and there was the possibility of great hardship for everyone—everyone, do you hear, villagers and master alike—he and the Captain here began a little smuggling trade of their own. How do you think your gambling debts were paid in those difficult days, young man? And when you came home, saved the shame of a debtor's prison because he again paid your losses, how did you reward him? With anger, with hatred, even. You are not worthy of the name you bear. And now he is willing to sacrifice himself again to help a friend. Would *you*, Mark? Would *you* willingly place your neck beneath the blade of *Madame la Guillotine*? I think not.'

A hand clutched suddenly at her heart . . . Her breathing became laboured, and Roxanna ran to her side, pulling out the little bottle of salts of ammonia she always carried, and putting it beneath her nose.

'You must rest, Elizabeth,' Ross said, bending beside her chair. His hand brushed Roxanna's as she drew back. Brief as the contact was, her skin began to tingle.

'Yes . . . Yes, I am too old for all this. Lisette, take my arm. No, not you, Roxanna. Mark will help her.' Roxanna was aware of the question in her eyes as she said, 'I think you surely have something important to say, have you not? You can come up when . . . later . . .'

Ross frowned as Elizabeth was helped from the room, leaving Roxanna standing by the empty chair, still clutching the bottle of salts.

'You have things to do, Nicholas,' he said, starting towards the door. 'As I have—and damned little time in which to settle my affairs.'

His words chilled her. She could not—would not—let him go like this.

'Wait—please!' she cried. It was Nicholas who spun about on her, his face working furiously. Only after a full minute did Ross follow suit. The coldness in his face made her hesitate, but for a moment only. 'I must speak with you.'

'Can't you leave well alone, woman?' Nicholas thundered. 'If you were mine . . .'

'She is not, and I shall rectify any mistakes I have made in my life without your help, my friend,' Ross interrupted. 'You will not interfere. I hope that is understood between us. Go and see to the ship.'

He waited until the door had closed behind the man

before speaking again. 'You are concerned about your position here, with the possibility that I might not return and provide for you and your father?' His words robbed her of speech. How could he be so cruel—so heartless—as to imply that her only thought was of money? She swayed, and clutched at the chair beside her for support. Ross's eyes surveyed her bleakly, without compassion for the agony of her expression. All women are great actresses when they want something, Nicholas had once told him. Looking at Roxanna now, he would have thought her look indicated that she cared for him. But he knew otherwise. She had rejected him in no uncertain terms, and he had shut the door on that part of his life that had brought him such pain.

He should have known better. First his mother had gone away, forsaking husband and family for the glitter of the society she had been forced to abandon. Every woman he had ever contemplated becoming emotionally involved with had been lacking in some quality or other. Only this one had penetrated his defences, laid wide his armour and conquered his heart. And she had thrown what he offered her back in his face, accusing him of one heinous crime after another. She was not worth the time he had spent with her. Yet, when he looked into those green eyes, his only defence against her was attack. Attack and destroy—as she had destroyed him.

'I shall, of course, arrange for Mark to see to that kind of thing. Had there been a child, you would have inherited Talland and held it for my son, but as there is no heir . . .'

'I shall leave as soon as another companion has been found for Lisette,' Roxanna said, fighting to hold back the tears. The words of love she had sought to say died unuttered on her lips. He wanted nothing from her. He had Alicia. Then let him go alone . . . as alone as he had always been in his life. He wanted no one and needed no one. Love was just a word without meaning.

'That must wait until—I return. Then you may do as

you please, and I shall be well rid of you. You will be well taken care of, I assure you. Consider it payment for services rendered.' He saw her flinch and the blood surge into her cheeks.

'To maintain my silence, don't you mean? When you have disposed of me and married Alicia, you will need to see my silence is well paid for.'

It was his turn to stiffen, and she saw a flush steal into the dark cheeks and was glad she had the power to hurt him as he did her. No, no! her heart cried. This is not how it should be!

'There is an easier way to ensure it—if it was my prime concern, which at this moment it is not. I have far more important matters at hand. We shall discuss this at a later date . . . perhaps. In any case you will not lose by remaining here a few weeks longer. Elizabeth needs you. I would not like to think of her alone—and Lisette has great need of your friendship at present. Now, if you will excuse me, I have things to attend to. Be so good as to ask Mark to come to my study.'

The door had opened and closed behind him before Roxanna came out of her trance and realised he had gone. Stay for the Countess! Stay for Lisette, but not for him! Yet he was the reason she would stay. Wild horses could not drag her from Talland until she knew he was safe—or dead!

Roxanna and Lisette ate a small meal with the Countess in her room, but all three trays were returned to the kitchen with the plates still practically full. They had picked at the food, uninterested in what lay before them as their thoughts dwelled on what had happened.

Elizabeth de Villon remembered the prison where her son Claude had languished for many months before Ross rescued him. Of her own imprisonment, and the dread that one day, when the doors opened, she would be dragged to a tumbril and driven through the howling crowds to her death. Her chest pained her, and she could hardly breathe, yet she did not think to ask for brandy.

Lisette thought of the father who had danced with her at the *bal masqué* . . . the jovial, gentle man who had bounced her on his knee as a child, played piggy-back with her while Ross sat on the lawn of the château and roared with laughter at their antics . . .

Roxanna remembered the one and only night of love she had spent with her husband . . . Those moments when he had teased her, taunted her, mocked her. None of them mattered as they had then. She could feel no anger any more, only pain and bitterness that she had been too proud to reveal her feelings to him. What did it matter if he did not love her? She had enough for two! If she told him she suspected that she carried his child from that night? No, that was not the way to attempt to hold him.

Mark rejoined them an hour later. He came into the room a different man, Roxanna thought, watching as he went to Lisette and took her in his arms, burying his face against her shoulder. He was trembling, she saw. What had taken place between the two brothers to affect him so? Was it too much to hope that they had resolved their differences in the face of the crisis looming over them?

'A little brandy, I think, Roxanna,' Elizabeth murmured, and she fetched it from the cabinet and poured Mark a glass. He swallowed it quickly, but shook his head when she offered another.

'If I touch another drink until he comes back, may I rot in hell!' he said in a fierce tone. He drew Lisette to the small sofa at the bottom of the bed and they sat down together. He still had not let go of her hand, Roxanna noticed, and inwardly winced as she remembered how tightly Ross had clung to her at their first meeting. He was badly shaken, and having trouble gathering his thoughts.

'He has told you what it entails?' the Countess asked when no one seemed capable of breaking the strained silence. He nodded. 'Roxanna has a book that you might like to read while Ross is away,' she added, and he threw her a puzzled look.

'Read? While he is out there? God in heaven—how did we drift so far apart? He blames himself, but it was my fault, too. I must share the guilt . . .'

'That you must. Roxanna will give you the book anyway. Read it. I think you will understand your brother all the better for it—as she did.'

'Understand Ross—her? Of course she understands him! She's his wife, isn't she?' He looked across to where Roxanna stood, the blood draining from her face. 'It's true, isn't it? You were his wife when you came here?'

'Yes.' She had no reason to deny it now. The Countess gave a strange, almost knowing, little smile and patted the side of the bed. Roxanna went to her, and was drawn down to kiss the lined cheeks. Straightening, she looked at Mark—and at Lisette, who did not seem capable as yet of absorbing this fresh shock. 'He told you?'

'He had to, so that you will be provided for if anything happens to him. The papers drawn up at your marriage kept me from inheriting Talland.' He frowned to himself, a bitter smile deepening his mouth. 'That was as it should be. I was not worthy of it—or him. I have much to learn, not only about my own brother, but you, too, it seems. I shall care for you, Roxanna—you need have no fears on that score. For your father, too. After all, you are part of the family . . .'

'You speak as if he is not coming back,' she cried.

'From the way he spoke . . .' Mark paused as he saw the distress registering on her face, then continued in a quieter voice, 'He gave me the impression he might not. He is not the Ross I have known. Arrogant—sure of himself—I can't explain it. While I was with him, I felt as if he had lost a great fight within himself. My brother has never accepted defeat in his life! Not like me—I've wallowed in it for years, and in my own self-pity. But Ross! He was so—empty—so . . .'

'Alone,' Roxanna finished dully. 'He has always been alone. I have hurt him as deeply as you . . . I must see him before he goes.' She wheeled towards the door, a determined look on her pale features.

'No! He's gone!' She turned back as if in a dream, her lips moving soundlessly. Mark came forward to take her arm as she swayed unsteadily. 'I thought you knew . . . that he had told you he was leaving directly, when you spoke together downstairs.' Wordlessly, she shook her head. Gone! Without one word of farewell! She would not let him go, not like this! He had to know she loved him.

'How—How long ago? I have to catch him. I must, don't you see? Please! Please help me . . .'

His fingers tightened over her wrist, and he flung open the door and pushed her through. 'We shall go through the tunnel—it will be quicker. The tide is almost right, so we must make haste.'

Roxanna picked up her skirts and ran after him. They raced through the tunnel that led from the library, past the stairs leading up to Ross's room, the way she knew, and took a narrow sloping passage that grew damper and more slippery underfoot as they progressed.

'We are close to the caves on the beach,' Mark said, as she slipped and slid to her knees, badly grazing them. She scrambled up again, urging him to go on. 'We bring the cargoes this way from the ruins. It leaves Talland in our wagons, and no one is the wiser. Sometimes it's taken overland, but that's getting risky these days with the new Captain about. He dare not come on to Talland land, but by God he stays pretty close. If Ross gets past the revenue cutter in daylight, it will be a miracle . . .'

So this was how it was all made so easy, Roxanna thought, as the tunnel began to widen. They emerged into faint light from the glow of a fading wall torch. Before them was a large room filled with crates and kegs and boxes. He gave her a one-sided grin, somewhat guarded, as if he still felt awkward about their new relationship, as she herself did.

'Nicholas Pendennis brought this from Brittany.' They wound their way through the boxes until they heard voices ahead. They were in the cellars of the ruined castle which had once belonged to the Savage family, Roxanna realised, and then grew stiff with apprehension as she recognised the two men who were talking.

'My God, I never thought I'd see the day you'd take to a bottle like your brother!' It was the voice of Nicholas. Beside her she heard Mark stifle an oath at the remark. 'Didn't I tell you she wasn't worth it? No woman is worth the pain of being torn apart as I was—as you are now.'

What was he saying? Roxanna strained her ears. Pain! Ross? But he cared nothing for her.

'I would have sold my soul to the devil for that one, do you know that? Yes, I've told you many times before, haven't I? You must be sick of hearing it. You go on. I'm going to finish this bottle.' How tired he sounded.

'Be quick about it! The cutter carries sixty guns. I don't want to be on the receiving end of them and have my ship blown out of the water.'

Silence. Roxanna edged past Mark, and came out into another cellar, where water dripped from the walls and green slime was inches thick on the stones.

'Ross.' She thought at first he had not heard her, for he did not move. Slowly, very slowly, he came to his feet from before the rickety wooden table where he had been sitting. She saw a half-empty bottle behind him as he turned and faced her.

'What the hell are you doing here?' And then he saw his brother. 'I should have known. Still trying to have your revenge, Mark?'

'Don't talk like a fool. Can't you see the girl is half out of her mind with worry, or are you blind as well as indifferent to her?'

'You told her what we discussed?' The jibe was ignored, but only just.

'It is her right—as your wife. I'll leave you two alone for a few minutes. Perhaps you can settle what is between you before it's too late.'

Neither of them was aware of him leaving, as they had eyes only for each other. Roxanna saw his gaze wander over her dishevelled appearance, the dirt on her dress, her dusty shoes, and return to the strange brightness in her eyes.

'He—He told me . . . about the provisions you have made for me.' She found herself stammering under his scrutiny. 'Ross—you have to come back!'

'Why? Do you want more?' His bitterness lay between them like an open wound. 'Ask him, not me! Talland belongs to him now.'

Mark was right! He spoke as if he would not return. Did his life mean so little to him? Roxanna took a hesitant step forward, stretching out a hand towards him. He did not move. No expression crossed his strained features, yet in the depths of those eyes she glimpsed something—a momentary gleam that gave her hope.

'I love you! Don't you understand that?' she cried tremulously.

He cursed her vehemently in language which at any other time would have made her turn and run from his presence. She stood her ground, steeling herself against the fury in every word flung at her.

'Don't spit that lie at me! God, you know how to twist the knife, don't you?'

She came closer, her hand still thrust out towards him. She touched his arm, and he flinched as though she had burnt him. Naked pain rose in his eyes.

'Get away from me! You have what you want.'

'I want you—my husband.' She ignored his harsh laugh, allowed her body to relax against his and heard his sharp intake of breath. Still he did not move, or touch her, and how those eyes gleamed with disbelief and contempt! She lifted her arms and placed them round his neck, her fingers toying with the black hair at the nape of his neck, above the thick jerkin he wore.

'Very well, I can see it is no use. You do not believe me. You prefer to be alone, don't you, Ross? You have always been alone . . . I shall go—but first kiss me farewell, as is fitting and proper when a husband and wife are to be separated.'

'I shall not touch you again. I told you. Damn you . . .'
She felt a tremor run through his body. He was not as
immune to her as he would have her believe. She felt a
sudden wild triumph surge through her, urging her on
to a final gesture which could win—or lose—him for
ever.

'Then I must kiss you. You did not mind, the first time
we met, do you remember? You will no doubt remind
me how inexperienced I am, and how much in need of
your expert guidance. Would I were Alicia Brandon,
perhaps I would have had it.'

His fingers bit into the thin material of her dress as she
leaned on tip-toe and laid her mouth against his. Dear
God, had she been mistaken? She roused no response
. . . His hand fastened in her thick curls, tugging back
her head—she glimpsed his glittering eyes, the hunger
in them as he took her mouth roughly, possessively,
as if he hated her! Why, oh why did he not believe
her?

'Why now?' He held at her at arm's length, and shook
her when she did not answer directly. She fought for
breath, still clinging to him as much for support as
anything else. He looked so terrifying with his brows
drawn together, those eyes devouring her very soul.
There was a battle raging inside him. She could feel it in
the roughness of his grasp.

'Mark said you spoke as if you did not think you would
succeed in rescuing the Comte . . . that you were risking
your life—in vain—and knowing it.'

'My life is my own. You wanted no part of it, if you
remember?' he answered harshly. His fingers slid over
the satin smoothness of her shoulders.

'I have too much pride,' Roxanna's voice was barely a
whisper. 'I thought you to be using me . . . I could not
bear it, when I love you so. Oh Ross, don't go! I have
loved you since that first day when you touched my hair,
kissed me, laughed at my inexperience . . .'

'You gave me little chance to teach you.' The wildness
was dying out of his face. He turned his head and laid his

lips against her hand as it lay on his shoulder, and felt her quiver. Not from fear as before when he had touched her—but something else. Was it possible . . .?

'Come back, then. Teach me to be the wife you want. I shall try, I really shall. You do not have to care for me . . . I know you never will.'

His mouth descended once more on hers, robbing her of speech. Time stood still as he transported her away from the damp, dingy cave to a world of beauty and light and great happiness. Her lips opened beneath his, and answered him kiss for kiss as the fire of her love swept over her, washing away all guilt, all suspicion, all fear of him.

'Ross, come! The ship is ready.' From somewhere behind them came Nicholas's voice. Ross heard him, yet gave no sign. To leave her now . . .! He could feel her whole body trembling against his as his hands caressed her and roused her as he knew only he had ever done or ever would. She loved him! It was as if he had struggled up out of a black abyss into blinding light. What fools they both were to have wasted so much precious time! Time—he had so little left. He felt it inside him, but he would not say so to her.

'Ross!' Nicholas's voice was urgent now. 'Remember the cutter.'

With a deliberately controlled movement Ross drew back from her, and nodded to Mark standing silently behind her. He took hold of her from behind, and held her fast as she realised that Ross still meant to leave her and tried to retain her hold on him.

'No, Ross. No!' Tears streamed over her cheeks. He wiped one away, and touched the wet finger to his lips with a faint smile. The magic of the moment was past. He had withdrawn from her again and the promise of what might have been, his mind returning to what lay ahead for him in France.

'Care for my wife, brother. As diligently as you care for the woman you love,' he said, his voice noticeably unsteady. 'Remember what I said. They may try to take

Lisette. If they have her, they can break her father in one minute.'

'I shall, never fear.' Mark's voice was almost as unsteady as that of his brother.

'Strangely enough, I do not. Will you give me your hand? Finish our enmity here and now?' Mark clasped the hand thrust out towards him. Ross hesitated, one brief moment longer, staring at the ashen face of his wife, then was gone.

'Come back! You must!' Roxanna screamed after him. The cry rang round the cellar.

'The devil looks after his own, little cat.' At the mouth of the entrance, he ducked his head to go through, then looked back at the two figures watching him. 'I shall come back, for I intend to spend the rest of my life making up for this hell we have been living in because of my foolishness. Nay—our foolishness. As you say, you have too much pride. No woman has angered me before as you do.'

Roxanna sagged in Mark's arms, her senses reeling, and slowly became aware of him shaking her slightly.

'Come, we can watch the ship sail from the headland,' he urged.

They stood in the shelter of one of the ruined walls of the old castle, two solitary figures bathed in the glow of late afternoon sunshine. Roxanna did not feel its warmth upon her cheek, nor the comfort of Mark's arm about her. She was cold, terribly cold.

'Why could you never live in peace together, as brothers should?' She accepted that what had been between them was now gone. She saw it in the shadowed eyes as he looked at her.

'I always resented that our father's will left me only a small amount of money, and an allowance that did not allow me to live as I wished.' He made no attempt to keep the truth from her now. He was done with hatred and anger. The knowledge that he might lose his brother had stunned him, and forced him to come to terms with what he was fast becoming—a gambler, a drunkard, a wastrel. And all these years Ross had supported him and carried him when he failed in his duties, at the same time risking life and limb to help others.

'Ross was his favourite, you see. He didn't ask for it, it just happened. As children, we were very close for a while, as we should have been. Then gradually I found myself beginning to resent the way he did everything so well. Our father was a fighting man, and Ross has inherited his love of fighting. Always he would seek the excitement of a hunt on the wildest horse he could find in the stables. And sword-play? He excelled at it, and shone in our father's eyes. With his fists he could beat anyone, too. We began to drift apart. I gambled; he turned his attention to Talland, in those days before Father died. I felt shut out, I suppose, and unwanted.'

'As Ross has felt all these years,' Roxanna whispered, and he nodded.

Mark looked down at her, and wiped the last of her tears from her cheeks as gently as if she was Lisette. She did not know this man, this considerate brother who had always mocked her so cruelly, who made her despair of Ross ever loving her.

'He will come back. Don't you know why? I do—at long last—and I beg your forgiveness for the terrible pain I have inflicted on you these past weeks.' He smiled as Roxanna looked at him, dry-eyed now, but the beautiful colour of her eyes was marred by the sadness in their depths and the hopelessness which lay in her heart. 'He loves you, Roxanna. The devil has a heart, after all, and it belongs to you.'

Nicholas Pendennis returned to Talland a week later. He came alone. The news he brought from France chilled Roxanna, and heightened her fears that she would never again see the man she loved. George Cadoudal had been tried and found guilty. Captain Wright had appeared at his trial but had refused to speak, proclaiming himself a prisoner of war—not a spy. The Comte de Villon still languished in the 'Temple' prison, and nothing had been seen or heard of Ross since he landed. If he had reached Paris safely, no one knew. He had not been at the rendezvous point when his ship returned for him. After waiting a full day in the hidden cove that was their usual meeting-place, Nicholas had returned without him, as had been arranged. He would return again in six days.

Six days! He could blend into the background like a peasant, the Countess told her continually, hoping to reassure her, but words failed to ease the agony of her loneliness and despair. It was deepened by the knowledge that she carried Ross's child. A child he might never see!

She went every day to the ruins, and would spend hours there looking out towards the sea. Mark often came to escort her home, after posting men along the headland to watch in her place. The King had accepted Pitt's idea to raise an army of defence, and men from the village were now under Mark's command. He had changed beyond belief. She knew he had not touched a drink since Ross left Talland. If Ross did not return, he told her as they walked home one day, and she bore him a son, he would inherit Talland, as Ross would have wanted. Nothing she said would change his mind, and she at last accepted it. She did not want Talland for herself or her child. She wanted Ross!

It was there on the horizon—faint, but there! A sail billowing in the strong wind. Roxanna caught at her straw hat as a gust threatened to whip it away from her, and tightened the ribbons beneath her chin. Nicholas was coming back—Ross was coming back. Mark came running down from the church. He too, had seen it. As it drew nearer and became clearer, men who had been training with him began to cluster at the cliff edge, their excitement as great as hers. No secret had ever been kept as this one had, but at last it had leaked out. Everyone in the village knew why their master had risked his life, and had prayed night and day for his safe

return. Roxanna had discovered that, for all his blackness of temper, he was loved by those he had always
sought to protect.

'Wait! Roxanna, wait! Remember the child!' She
ignored Mark's warning shout as joy gave wings to her
feet. She wheeled about into the ruins, and slithered and
slid over the uneven ground to the cellars below. She
heard him in pursuit, but did not stop until forced to do
so by lack of breath. Mark came up behind her,
breathing heavily, and caught her arm to hold her fast as
she stood on the edge of the sand. The ship was so close
that she could see figures on the deck. He was not
there . . .

'Patience!' Mark murmured gently. She had lost her
bonnet in the wildness of her flight, and her hair had
come unpinned and hung in disorder down her back.
The new dress she had put on for the first time today was
covered along the hem with sand and dirt. 'Calm yourself! You are in no condition to run like that.'

'I can't see him! Oh, God.' Her heart almost stopped
beating with the thought which seized her. 'What if he is
not on it?'

It seemed hours, but was less than half an hour before
the ship anchored and a boat was put over the side. How
many figures climbed into it? Two or three? She shaded
her eyes against the sun. Roxanna leaned weakly against
the rocks as Mark gave a glad cry and ran towards it as it
reached the beach. In his excitement, he did not realise
that she was not following behind. She could not move!
She should be down at the water's edge with him,
flinging her arms about Ross's neck as he was doing now
. . . But her legs refused to carry her from the spot where
she stood, transfixed with joy and love—and
apprehension, in this moment of truth for them both.

Mark had said Ross loved her. But what if he was only
being kind that day, trying to soothe her fears? As Ross
had done, perhaps, believing he might never see her
again. He was back—but would he want her now?

She straightened, steeling herself to face him again as

Nicholas came towards her with a sailor, carrying the figure of the Comte. She caught her breath as she saw his face, bruised and heavily swollen. One arm hung limply by his side, and his left leg trailed behind him, weaving an erratc line in the sand to where she stood. He was barely conscious, and in great pains from the wounds he had sustained.

'It—It was bad?' she asked in as calm a voice as she could maintain, and Nicholas nodded grimly.

'Ask no questions of any of us now. We must get this man up to the house.' They hurried on past her with their burden.

'Who are those men?' She heard the startled note in Ross's voice as he raised his head before following his friends, and saw the look-outs on the cliff, who stretched in a thin line for two miles in either direction.

She heard Mark reply, with pride in his voice, 'My army of reserves. Your personal escort. You see, brother, I have managed quite well without you.' There was no enmity in the remark, and Ross laughed softly.

'That you have. Perhaps I should have stayed away?'

'No. There are those of us who have need of you.' Mark touched Roxanna lightly on the shoulder, before he started after the others. 'And he needs *you*,' he murmured softly as he passed. 'As never before. Cadoudal and Wright are dead. The conspiracy is over. Go to him!'

Ross had come to a halt just inside the cave entrance. Her eyes wandered in horror over his appearance. His shirt hung on him in ribbons. Blood had soaked the torn sleeve of one arm and dried unattended, as had that on one cheek. His face was streaked with dirt. He had worn a sword when he left, she remembered. He did not have it now, but there was a pistol pushed into the belt of his breeches. He looked thinner, and so tired! She went to him and put her arms round him. He held her for a long moment in a fierce hug that threatened to crush her ribs. She felt his lips against her hair as he buried his face in the tawny gold mane.

'I dared not hope you would still be here.' His voice was little more than a hoarse whisper. 'Now, holding you, I know the nightmare is over.'

Touching the dark face with her fingertips, she gently kissed the cut which seared one cheek. She held back the tears which threatened to burst upon her. This was a time to show strength, not weakness. She would not be like all the other simpering women he had known.

'You will look like a pirate when that heals. The Comte said you should have been one. A charming rogue. A devil on the high seas! A lover of beautiful women.'

'Only one woman, and I have no wish to leave her ever again.' Still he did not look at her, and, drawing back, she saw a certain wariness lurking in the depths of his black eyes. Uncertainty?

'Did you not think I would be here?' she reproved softly.

'To think of the things you said . . . to dwell on what could be?' He shook his head. 'To think of you in these past weeks would have been far too disturbing, and I needed a clear mind. When—When the horror of it has passed, I would like to tell you. But not yet. Perhaps not for a long while.'

'We have all the time in the world,' Roxanna said, taking his hand. 'Come, those wounds need attention.' He had made no mention of love, but what did that matter? She had him back—safe!

Mark looked back from the entrance to the tunnel leading into the house, and gave a mock frown as he saw his brother leaning heavily on Roxanna's shoulder.

'It is you who should be helping your wife, brother. She carries your child!' he chuckled softly.

A startled oath escaped Ross's lips. He held her fast, waving his brother to go on. No uncertainty in his eyes now, but a gleam which made her legs grow weak again. He was pleased! She could see it, and feel it in his touch.

'Is it true? Why did you not tell me?'

'I—I did not want to hold you against your will. You are back—alive—and that is all that matters to me. If you wish me to go away, I shall,' Roxanna whispered, and his hands slid about her back, drawing her to him. 'No! No, you must not! Not out of—of pity. If it is Alicia you really want . . .'

'Are you mad?' he thundered, and his voice reverberated around the cellar. 'She has hounded me for almost a year. In truth, I used her the night of the ball to make you jealous. And afterwards, I wanted to hurt you for sending me away. But I love you! You are all I have ever wanted in a woman, but I . . .' His mouth tightened in pain, deepening the lines of stress already etched into the bronzed skin. 'I did not know how to tell you what was in my heart. I have been alone too long.'

He gathered her against him, laying his cheeks against hers. She quivered in his embrace, feeling his touch awaken the fire she had thought never to know again. He loved her! All this time, so much misunderstanding and mistrust between them, keeping them apart, denying them the love they bore each other.

'Most of my life I seem to have been fighting for one thing or another. First Fouché and those bloody hungry peasants in the Revolution, who sought to destroy the world of culture and beauty I knew in France. Butchered innocent men, women and children without quarter because of the names they bore. Then, when it became necessary to close—or pretend to close—one of the mines, I fought to keep my people alive. And myself, for that matter, even fighting my own brother to do so. He thought smuggling a game! I needed him, but he wanted no part of Talland.'

'I know,' Roxanna whispered. 'He told me about the will. And I read—read the entries you made in the Talland chronicle. It told me so much about you.'

'Then you know how sick I grew of him being idle and useless about the place, playing the gentleman. I told him to work or get out. He left, and went to London. A year later I paid his debts and brought him home, but we were as strangers. I put him to work in the mine, gave him responsibility for our shipments, and he hated me for it. At every turn he thwarted me. And then, you! I loved you from that first day. I was afraid, when I realised how swiftly you had stolen my heart. Afraid that if I gave myself completely, you might one day look at me as Nicholas's wife looked at him. You did not know him then. He was a good, kind man. He adored—no, worshipped—his wife and gave her all he could afford. But he is as rough in his ways as I am, despite all my fine education'. He laid a hand against her lips as she opened her mouth to protest. The tenseness was slowly beginning to leave his expression. 'I am. I know it. I saw how he was when Griffith stole his wife away with sweet words and promises of a better life. He has never trusted a woman again. And my mother—she deserted my father, left Mark and me when we were only babes. It broke my father. Two strong men destroyed by the treachery of women! I feared that happening to me, and so . . . I became the *bête noire*, the black beast you know so well. I took. I gave nothing. I was afraid to!'

'You know nothing of me, if you think I—I would even look at another man,' Roxanna protested with mock indignation.

'You are right . . . Too little. It is time I rectified that.'

'I am your wife, and I love you, more than I know how to tell you. When you were gone, it was as if part of me was dead. Even the child within me brought me no joy,' she said, colouring slightly at the confession.

'And now?' His tone was questioning, and she smiled.

'There will not be a day when I do not tell you how much I love you. Our son will be the proof of my love. I shall never leave you.'

'Do you think I would let you?' he said, and swung her up into his arms, crushing her against him with possessive ardour. His lips on hers were tender and clinging, reminding them of what they had shared only briefly, but would now be reality for the remainder of their lives.

'Your arm,' Roxanna murmured faintly, as her fingers encountered the dried blood on his sleeve. But he silenced her, and she was content to lie in his hold and show him with her lips how deeply and passionately she loved him.

'I can walk,' she protested, as he at last became aware of their surroundings again, and of his brother's voice calling ahead of them in the darkness. 'Oh, Ross, put me down! Your arm . . .'

'Damn my arm! I'll not have our son coming into the world before his time. Besides, it's been a long while since I've held you so close and you haven't thrown something at me.'

As once before, he moved along the unlighted tunnel with unerring accuracy. Roxanna lifted her head from his shoulder with a gasp, as he began to mount the stone steps leading to . . .

'Where are you taking me?' she asked, a shiver of excitement, of anticipation running through her.

'Where else, little cat, but to my room, where you will minister to me like the true and faithful wife you are? And afterwards . . .' He chuckled, and kissed the scarlet cheek close to his face. Tiredness had fled from him as he felt the softness of her against him. The pain in his arms and the memory of the carnage he had left behind him in France were vanished into the deepest recesses of his mind with the knowledge that she was—and always would be—his. 'I shall show you what I have never been able to put into words . . .'

Discover the secret of

Gypsy

CAROLE
MORTIMER

Gypsy – the story of a
woman they called
Gypsy, a woman with
raven hair and a fiery,
passionate nature.

Four brothers try to
tame the Gypsy. Read
their story – and hers –
from 8th November 1985,
at just £2.25.

Gypsy. A longer, more
involving romance from
Mills and Boon.

Mills & Boon

The Rose of Romance